Quiver

Quiver

Peter Leonard

faber and faber

This is a work of fiction. All of the characters, organizations, and events portrayed in this novel are either products of the author's imagination or are used fictitiously.

First published in the UK in 2008
by Faber and Faber Limited
3 Queen Square London WC1N 3AU

First published in the US in 2008 by Thomas Dunne Books,
an imprint of St. Martin's Press

Printed in England by Mackays of Chatham plc

A CIP record for this book
is available from the British Library

978–0–571–24111–8

2 4 6 8 10 9 7 5 3 1

For Elmore

Quiver

One

Kate was standing at the island counter, eyes swollen from crying, makeup smeared across one of her cheeks, staring at the
food: platters of cold cuts and bowls of potato salad, plates of
cookies, assorted cheeses and fresh fruit. Owen's obituary, half a
page in the *Detroit Free Press*, was folded open next to the sink. A
line under his photograph said, "Owen McCall, age 49, October
11, 2006."

Everybody had paid their respects and taken off, and now she
felt exhausted, drained. She poured a glass of chardonnay and lit
a cigarette. She was numb, her mind a blur, still trying to come to
grips with what had happened.

Luke entered the kitchen, walked past her, detached, expres-
sionless, the same zombie trance he'd been in since the accident.
He opened the refrigerator and grabbed a Gatorade, purple liquid in a plastic bottle called Riptide Rush.

Kate said, "Come here." She took a couple steps and wrapped

her arms around him. "I know you're hurting. I am, too." She could feel Luke, rigid in her embrace.

"I'm sorry," he said.

She could see tears in his eyes before he looked down, staring at the floor.

"You can't blame yourself. It was an accident."

Luke pushed away from her. "I don't want to talk about it." He moved across the kitchen into the breakfast room and disappeared.

It was dark when she went upstairs, leaning against the banister, right hand on the smooth polished oak as she scaled the winding staircase. A light in the foyer was on, but she was too tired to go down and turn it off.

At the top of the stairs, she went left to Luke's room. The door was closed, she knocked and opened it and saw him on his bed staring up at the ceiling. She said good night.

He didn't move, didn't look at her. Leon, their chocolate lab, was lying next to Luke. He got up, shook his tail and yelped.

Luke said, "Chill, Leon."

The dog sat down.

Kate closed the door and went to her room, walked through into the bathroom and stared at herself in the mirror hanging over the sink. She looked tired. She pulled her hair back behind her ears and turned the faucet on. Cupped water in her hands and washed her face. She glanced over, saw Owen's blue terry cloth robe hanging on the back of the door, went over and lifted it off the hook and hugged it. Now she sat on the side of the tub and wept, letting go.

Kate walked into the bedroom, pulled the spread down and stretched out on the king-size bed—Owen's side—and smelled his pillow, with its hint of Old Spice.

There were family photographs on the night table in gold and silver frames. She picked up a sepia-tone picture of Owen with short hair, age seven, wearing a white shirt and a bow tie, a smile on his little face, proud because he'd just made his First Communion. She put it back and picked up another, this one shot on their wedding day, Kate thinking it was one of the few pictures in sixteen years that showed Owen with his eyes open. She held it and remembered the day they met. Ran into him coming around a corner at Farmer Jack's, the store at Lahser and Maple. Their carts hitting head-on with impact and it was so unexpected, it was funny.

He said, "You okay?"

"I think so," Kate said, "except for the whiplash."

He held her in his gaze, maybe wondering if she was serious. "I'm Owen," he said. "And you?"

"Kate," she said, offering her hand.

He took it in his, looked her in the eye and said, "Kate, you doing anything tonight?"

"What do you mean?"

"Can I take you out to dinner? Make up for your injury."

"Is this how you get dates?" Kate said. "Run into someone with your grocery cart?"

He grinned. He had a grocery list in his hand, a five-by-seven-inch lined yellow sheet and his cart was filled with cans of soup and tuna fish. He obviously wasn't much of a cook.

Kate said, "I don't even know you."

Owen said, "We just met, didn't we?"

Kate said, "You could be a rapist."

"I could even be a Republican." He grinned.

"That was going to be my next question."

They went to a little place called Oliverio's that night—a dark, loud Italian restaurant with white tablecloths and waiters in black suits—had veal chops with cognac cream sauce, drank Brunello and told their life stories to each other.

Owen was a stock car driver.

"I knew I wanted to race from the time I was about eight years old," he said. "I'd go with my dad to his Chevy dealership in Dearborn and help the mechanics. All I wanted to do was work on cars. And when I turned sixteen, all I wanted to do was race them. My dad, on the other hand, wanted me at the store. His plan was to teach me the business, sell me the dealership and retire."

Owen looked down at his plate and cut into his veal chop and took a bite.

"This is good isn't it? I started racing for real right after high school. Teamed up with a friend, big easygoing guy named Charley Degener. He was a few years older and had been an over-the-wall tire changer for a single car team, but his real specialty was horsepower."

He picked up his wineglass and took a gulp, drank it like a soft drink.

"In the early days it was just me and Charley. He built the motors. I did the cars. We started on the dirt tracks, but our goal from day one was Winston Cup. We weren't going to settle for anything less. We pulled the racecar behind a converted bread truck. You looked close, you could see the faint outline of Wonder Bread on the side. It was loaded with tools, parts and tires. Charley and I even slept in it on occasion. The deal was, we had to make enough on the track to come back the next week."

Kate said, "Did you win?"

"You want to know about my checkered past, huh?" He grinned big.

He was corny but appealing, had a nice easy way about him—big hands and shoulders and a good face, handsome in a rugged way.

"First year we made ten races, including one pole, three top fives, and five top tens. But to answer your question, no checkered flags."

"How about since then?"

"We've done okay."

He was the master of understatement, Kate discovered when she got to know him better. He never boasted or lost his cool, played everything low-key.

"When you see it on TV, it looks like they're really moving," Kate said. "How fast do you go?"

"Two hundred and change, flat-footing it down the straights."

"I went a hundred and ten one time in my father's Audi and it felt like warp speed."

"Once you get used to it, it's like driving on the freeway—you almost feel like you're in slow motion—only there are twenty-five cars trying to blow your doors off."

Kate cut a piece of veal, dipped it in the sauce, and took a bite.

"You look as far ahead as you can and rely on peripheral vision," Owen said. He took a big gulp of wine. "And always be aware of where everyone is. That's basically it. After awhile, you do it without thinking."

"If it's that easy," Kate said, "maybe I should sign up. I'm looking for a new career."

"My dad took pity on us, I guess, and donated fifteen grand a year in sponsorship money. The rub was, I had to spend time at the dealership, learn the business. That was the tradeoff."

"It looks dangerous," Kate said. "My dad took me to a NASCAR race at Michigan International Speedway and there were three crashes."

"I had her buried down one of the straights at Martinsville, passed a slower car on the right, nicked the wall, spun off and flipped three times. It felt like it happened in slo-mo. I remember being airborne, seeing sky. I came down, blew out all the glass. Amazing thing was, the car was totaled—every panel damaged—and I walked away without a scratch. Watched a forklift pick the car up and put it on a flatbed and decided right then to break up with this girl I was living with. All of a sudden it hit me, I didn't love her and we were talking about getting married."

The waiter came and cleared their plates and came back, and they ordered espresso and Sambuca.

Kate said, "Do you like tiramisu? We could split one."

"Sounds good," Owen said. "But I want to hear about you."

Kate told him how she'd grown up in Birmingham, an only child in a neighborhood full of big Irish families. The Youngs had seven, the Ivorys, eight, the O'Clairs, ten and the Callaghans, eighteen.

"Eighteen," Owen said. "Must've been something in the water."

"Rhythm method gone wild," Kate said. "I went to Marian, an all-girls Catholic high school and played tennis, number one singles. I was ranked second in the state, eighteen and under, and I got a scholarship to Michigan, a full ride."

"You look like a tennis player," Owen said. "How tall are you?"

"Five seven."

"Yeah, that's perfect."

Dessert was served. Owen picked up his Sambuca and Kate picked up hers and they clinked glasses. He said, "Salut."

Kate sipped the warm licorice liqueur, put her glass down and took a bite of tiramisu. "You have to try this."

Owen reached his spoon over, scooped some up, and put it in his mouth. He nodded and said, "That is something, isn't it?"

Kate said, "I played two years and only lost four matches. I was All–Big Ten and honorable mention, All-American, and then I blew out my right knee, my ACL. It was the beginning of my junior year and that was it for collegiate tennis."

Owen opened a bag of sugar and poured some into his espresso and stirred it with a spoon.

Kate said, "I partied after that—drinking and smoking—something I'd never done much of before, and at the end of my junior year, decided I'd had enough of college, and sixteen credits shy of graduating, I joined the Peace Corps."

Owen stirred his coffee and took a sip and placed it back on the saucer. "You were so close. Why didn't you finish?"

"My knee healed, but I knew I'd never be able to play the way I had. I was bored, tired of going to parties and sitting around smoking weed. I wanted to travel, do something interesting. I knew a girl who'd joined the Peace Corps, lived in India for two years. She said it was the most incredible experience of her life, trekking through Nepal and going to base camp on Mount Everest, eighteen thousand feet above sea level. I looked around and thought, what did I have to lose?"

Owen said, "When I hear Peace Corps, I think of a bunch of happy, clean-cut kids sitting around in a circle, singing folk songs. Is that what it was like?"

Kate took a sip of Sambuca and said, "Imagine leaving here and flying to Miami and then to Guatemala City, the largest town in Central America—a million and a half people—and taking a two-hour ride on a chicken bus to San Pedro."

Owen said, "Where in the hell's that?"

"Eastern Guatemala," Kate said.

"What do they speak?"

"*Cakchiquel*," Kate said, "a local Mayan dialect, and also Spanish. The point I'm trying to make, I arrived in this little town and didn't know a soul and I had to find a place to live."

"Peace Corps didn't help you?"

"No," Kate said. "And people stared at me everywhere I went. Women would come up to me and run their fingers through my hair because they'd never seen a blond before."

"Or blue eyes, I'll bet," Owen said. "Why'd you pick eastern Guatemala?

"That's where they needed help. I signed on to teach English— second grade. Had fifty little Mayan girls who called me Seño

Kate, short for Señorita. I'd walk in the classroom and they'd surround me, hang on my arms and waist and not let go, giggling. I'd have to pry them off."

"You liked it though, I can tell."

"I loved it," Kate said. "The kids wanted to learn. I'd tell them stories and we'd sing songs and play games. It was fun."

"Wish I'd had a teacher like you," Owen said. He reached over the table and touched her hand. "You're better-looking than Sister Mary Andrews who I had in second grade. Nicer, too." Owen sipped his Sambuca.

Kate said, "Do you eat the coffee beans?"

"I don't," Owen said, "but you can."

"When I got to San Pedro, I went around to the shops, asking if they knew anyone who was renting. There weren't a lot of options in this town at the end of the bus route. It wasn't a tourist destination. People didn't go there for its deluxe accommodations or four-star dining." She could see he was interested, sipping the liqueur, giving her his full attention. "I spent the first night in the school where I'd be teaching, slept on a bench in the principal's office, and the next day, I found a little house with a patio in back."

"How much was the rent?"

"A hundred eighty quetzales a month," Kate said. "Twenty-eight bucks for a four-room house with running water. Not bad, eh?"

"What did they pay you?" Owen said.

"Nothing," Kate said. "It's volunteer. I got $150 a month for expenses. And they give you six thousand when you leave, when your tour is over."

"Were you afraid, living alone in a strange country?"

"My windows had bars on them and the doors were steel and the patio was surrounded by a cinder-block wall that was seven feet high, topped with chicken wire."

"Sounds like you were a prisoner."

"Most of the houses in the village were like that," Kate said. She took a bite of tiramisu, savoring it. "It was my first house and I loved it. I painted the walls bright colors and bought furniture and plants at the market. I'd never lived alone before. It was exciting, but also weird because it's a male-dominated, third-world culture where women have to ask permission to leave the house. You think they thought I was a little odd?"

She told him about having water only two or three hours every other day and getting up at five-thirty in the morning to fill plastic buckets. And about the water, during the rainy season, coming out like mud. She'd have to boil and strain it to get anything.

She told him about learning how to kill a chicken, snapping its neck and plucking the feathers and cooking it Mayan style.

She told him about her neighbor, a little old lady who sold moonshine from her kitchen, and about the drunks who would fall asleep on the grass in front of her house, Kate finally getting the nerve to tell them to find somewhere else to sleep, and they never bothered her again.

And she told him about her Guatemalan girlfriends, Marina and Luzia, bathing in the *temescale*, a sauna made of adobe and mud, behind her house and talking like girls everywhere, about boys, who they liked and their plans for the future.

"One time, Luzia asked me if I thought Guatemalan boys were handsome and would I ever have a Guatemalan boyfriend? I said no, but it had nothing to do with their looks, it was because our cultures were so different. I said I could never go out with someone I had to ask permission to leave the house.

"Marina said, but if you really loved him, and he wanted you to ask, wouldn't you do it? I said, in our culture, if my boyfriend or husband loved me, he would trust me. I said I didn't need a man to take care of me. I told them I had a boyfriend named Jack back in Michigan and I couldn't imagine asking him for permission to do anything. He'd think I was crazy.

"Luzia said she liked asking permission. Marina did too. They both said they'd feel strange not asking. While we talked, we were eating roasted cow udder."

Owen said, "Hang on a minute—roasted cow udder? What'd it taste like?"

"Chicken." She liked the way he grinned and liked it when he reached over and touched her hand.

And then she told him about Marina, who, in a town full of thick-bodied Mayan women, had the trim shapely figure of a *Ladino*. "She was the most beautiful girl in town."

Owen grinned at her and said, "She'd have to go a long way to beat you."

Kate said, "You want to hear this?"

Owen said, "I'm sorry, I'll stop giving you compliments."

"Marina was married," Kate said, "but her husband Benigno had been in New Jersey for a year cutting grass and shoveling snow, trying to save enough money to build their own house and start a family. Marina lived with her mother, a *muchacha*, a maid, in a small house with a tin roof that leaked.

"She came over early one morning carrying an old beat-up suitcase and said she had to leave San Pedro right away. She was crying and very upset. I asked her what happened and she wouldn't tell me at first and then started speaking in rapid-fire Cakchiquel and then slower in Spanish, saying that Captain Emiliano Garza, head of the National Police and a respected member of the community, had forced himself on her. She was going to New Jersey to be with Benigno. I said, 'How are you going to get there?' She said, '*Mojado*.'"

Owen said, "What's that?"

"It means wet, the literal translation, but it really meant illegally. How else was she going to get there without a passport and visa?

"I said to her, 'Who is going to take care of Ysabel?' Her

mother. She said she didn't know, but had to leave right away because Captain Garza was coming back that night. Of all the girls in town he had chosen Marina and she should feel honored.

"I was there at her house when the captain came calling. He was a short compact man, a *Ladino* in a crisp blue uniform and well-shined black boots that brought him up to about five six, a little bull with a neatly trimmed black mustache and dark serious eyes. I could see him studying me from across the room, taking his time, a man used to being in control. I was thinking he looked like a doorman at a nice hotel. I pictured him in a different uniform, one with epaulets and gold buttons.

"He wasn't expecting anyone else to be there with Marina and I could see he wasn't sure what to do. He asked Marina who I was and she said, 'A friend.'

"I said to him, 'If you touch her again I'm going to contact the American consulate and take whatever measures are necessary to have you prosecuted. That's who I am.'

"He smiled at Marina in a shy formal way and said, 'Do you agree with this?'

"Marina looked down at the floor and said, 'Yes.' Captain Garza said he understood. That was it. He walked out and got in his Jeep and drove away. Marina cried and we hugged."

"That took nerve," Owen said, "standing up to a cop in a foreign country. Was that the end of it?"

"Not exactly," Kate said. "I'll tell you another time." It wasn't the kind of story you told someone on the first date. Kate looked around. They were the only two people in the restaurant. She hadn't noticed before.

Owen paid the bill and drove her home. He walked her up to the front door and kissed her on the cheek and said, "Can I call you?"

Kate said, "You better."

Two

Owen said, "What happened in Guatemala, you didn't want to talk about? You can tell me now. You can tell me anything."

They were at 220 Merrill, sitting at a table in the bar, Kate drinking a glass of chardonnay and Owen a Heineken from the bottle. It was crowded, as always on a Friday night. Kate felt close to him, trusted him after only a few dates. She said, "I went to my friend Marina's and met Captain Garza. Remember that?"

Owen said, "The little guy in the uniform, right?"

Kate nodded.

"That night," she said, "I was in bed, sound asleep, when they came in the room. I remember opening my eyes as they lifted me off the bed, wondering what was going on. Was I dreaming or was it really happening? There were two of them. But it was dark. I couldn't see their faces. They cuffed my hands behind my back and wrapped tape around my mouth and eyes. It was hot, the air thick and wet and it was difficult to breathe through my nose."

Kate picked up her wineglass by the stem and took a sip.

"They took me out to a Jeep and strapped a seat belt around me in back and drove out of town toward the jungle."

Owen said, "Who'd you think they were?"

"Garza's men," Kate said.

Owen said, "The one who hit on your friend."

"He didn't hit on her," Kate said. "He raped her. I thought he was paying me back for standing up to him, offending his Latin sense of honor. It was the only thing that made sense. I thought they were doing it to scare me. I didn't think they were going to hurt me. I worked for the US government. They weren't that crazy, I told myself, but I was wrong.

"We drove for a while—fifteen, twenty minutes, maybe—and the Jeep slowed down and stopped and they pulled me out and took me into the jungle and one of them whispered: '*Tu vas a morir.*'"

Owen said, "What's that mean?"

"You're going to die," Kate said.

"Jesus," Owen said.

"I could feel the slash of wet branches across the front of my T-shirt and shorts and the mosquitoes were relentless, feasting on my neck and face. I remember the sounds: birds cawing and the low hum of locusts and the loud high-pitched clack of the tree frogs. I remember the smoke from their cigarettes mixing with the dense earthy smell of the jungle, trying to breathe that heavy humid air through my nose.

"We walked for some time—ten minutes, at least—and then stopped and they passed a bottle back and forth. I could hear the liquid splashing to the neck and back. They were drunk. I could hear the sound of their boots, feet unsteady, taking steps to keep their balance. They were speaking Spanish, talking about who'd go first with me, and then flipping a coin to settle it.

"They cut my T-shirt off with a knife. I could feel the blade pulling the fabric before slicing through it. Then they were mauling me. They pulled my shorts down and cut off my panties. One of them let go of me and I heard the jiggle of a belt buckle and the sound of a zipper unzipping. The other one started humping me from behind and I turned and brought my knee up into him and he grunted and let go.

"Then I was tackled, taken down hard and they were trying to spread my legs apart. I tried to fight them and they beat the hell out of me."

Owen picked up his beer and took a long drink. He said, "Jesus Christ, this is unbelievable."

Kate sipped her wine. "You want to hear the rest of it?"

Owen said, "I want to go to Guatemala, get those bastards."

Kate said, "I woke up trying to breathe through the one nostril that wasn't swollen shut. I started to panic, thinking I was going to suffocate. I knew I had to get the tape off my mouth fast. I could hear them close by, snoring. I rolled on my back and stretched my arms and brought the handcuffs over my hips to the back of my knees and then slid my legs through. I ripped the tape off my mouth, taking in gulps of air. I found the seam and pulled the tape from my eyes. It was early, the sun was just starting to rise. I was naked and put on what was left of my T-shirt, the back slit open, and found my shorts and sandals.

"Then I studied the men who were sleeping fifteen feet away, two *Ladinos* in blue *policia* uniforms. I moved to the closest one who was thin, slightly built like a lightweight fighter, and slid the gun out of his holster. It was a Beretta. I released the safety, and racked a round into the chamber. The second cop wasn't wearing a gun but had a knife in a sheath on his belt. He was a bigger man with a fat stomach—on his back snoring.

"I aimed the gun at the skinny cop and kicked him in the ribs with the wooden toe of my sandal. He opened his eyes and looked at me and grinned. I told him to give me the key to the handcuffs or I'd blow his head off.

"He said, '*Cálmese. Yo la tengo.*' He patted the outside of his pocket and slid his hand in his blue uniform pants and brought out the key, holding it up, showing it to me. 'See, I have it right here.' He grinned again and said they were having fun with me, that's all—like what's the problem? I wanted to walk over and put the gun in his mouth, see how much fun he thought that was.

"I pulled the hammer back on the Beretta and he tossed the key in the grass in front of me. I went down on one knee, searching for it and then seeing it partially concealed. When I looked up again, the fat cop was on his feet, the knife in his hand, charging me—up so fast I couldn't believe it.

"I raised the Beretta and fired twice. I remember how loud it was and birds squawking into the sky. I hit him both times, center chest, but he kept coming, the momentum of his body driving him into me, knocking me over. He landed next to me, and as I sat up, the skinny cop grabbed the barrel of the Beretta, trying to take it out of my hand, and I pulled the trigger. The round hit him in his left shoulder and he let go of the gun and fell back. The second time, I aimed higher and shot him in the forehead. He went down, fell on his back and didn't move."

Owen drank his beer, never taking his eyes off her.

"I unlocked the handcuffs and followed the trail through the jungle back to the Jeep that said *Policia* on the side in white letters.

"I drove back to the outskirts of San Pedro and ditched it in heavy ground cover and walked into town. I knew I was on my own. The Peace Corps couldn't help me now. No one could. I went home and got money and my passport. I had seven hundred US dollars and another hundred in quetzals. I took a final look at my house that I loved, knowing I'd never see it again and went to Marina's. We took a bus to Guatemala City and from there, flew back to Michigan."

He said, "Jesus."

They stared at each other.

Owen said, "They rape you?"

Kate said, "Does it matter?"

He reached over and held her hand.

"I think they were too drunk," Kate said. "Angry 'cause they couldn't get it up, I guess and beat the hell out of me."

"I think you got even," Owen said.

"I don't look at it that way," Kate said. "It was them or me."

Owen said, "Where'd you learn to shoot, or are you a natural?"

"My dad liked guns. He used to take me to the Metamora Gun Club and teach me how to shoot. He had a Walther PPK and a .45 Colt and a Smith & Wesson .357 Magnum."

Owen finished his beer and looked across the table at her.

He said, "What'd the Peace Corps do?"

"Asked me why I left."

"What'd you tell them?"

"Guatemala was weird and crazy. I couldn't handle it."

"They find the cops?"

"Marina's mother sent the newspaper from San Pedro, describing the execution of two *policia*, kidnapped and taken into the jungle and shot."

"That's how they spun it, huh? Incredible."

Kate said, "Now what do you think of me?"

"I like you even more," Owen said.

Kate and Owen got married five months later. Her only regret was giving up her name—Morgan—for McCall. She liked Morgan better, but McCall wasn't bad. Kate's dad asked why they were getting married so fast, what's the damn hurry?

Kate gave birth to Luke four months later, answering his question.

Three

"Conned the parole board, didn't you? Well, you ain't going to con me. Found religion, my ass." T.J. Hughes grinned, his thin weathered face partially hidden in the shadow of his Stetson, lower lip protruding behind a knot of chaw. T.J. arcing a brown stream of tobacco juice into a waste can next to his desk. "Been one way your whole life, found the Lord in the last two months. That sound about right?" He turned his head, spit again. "What were you doing, sucking the chaplain's cock? That get you parole consideration?"

"I think God worked a miracle for me," Jack said. He tried to gesture with his hands, forgetting they were still cuffed to the bellychain.

"He did, huh?" T.J. grinned and spit.

"He said, 'Jack, I need your help. I need you to turn your life around and make something of yourself.'" These were the chaplain's preachy lines Jack had memorized and now delivered with his own inspired conviction.

"He come down from on high, appear in your cell, or'd you just hear his voice?"

"All I know is," Jack said, "with the help of Almighty God, I can do it."

"Well, dude, you got six months to keep your nose clean, and I don't think you can."

"Thanks for your support," Jack said. "I appreciate your faith in me, Mr. Hughes."

"You getting smart with me, boy?"

Jack furrowed his brow, gave him a look of Christian innocence. Who, me?

"God, I hope not. That would be a mistake, I guarantee it."

He talked tough sitting behind a desk in an office building. Jack wondering how this wrinkled prune of an ex-cowboy—who must've been close to fifty—would handle the outlaw bikers in Central Unit. He'd like to see that. "No, sir. What I was trying to say—with the Lord's help, I have been able to banish that evil part of me."

"Let me tell you the way it's going to be," T.J. said, "so there's no misunderstanding."

He pushed the brim of his hat up, and for the first time Jack could see his dark, beady little eyes.

"I'm going to be checking up on you when you least expect it. I'll want to see your pay stubs. You don't have 'em, you're going back to Judy."

He pinched the bridge of his nose with his thumb and index finger.

"I'm going to be asking for u-rine samples. You give me a hot UA, you're going back to Judy. You know your warden's a lady, right? Judy L. Frigo. Got a degree in ball busting, I understand.

What tickles me, a little girl's in charge of keeping all you hard-asses in line. That's a good one."

T.J. was a wiry 170-pounder in lizard-skin boots, tight Levis and a western shirt with pearl buttons and piping around the pockets.

"Eighty-two percent of you assholes revoke," T.J. said. "What's called recidivism, the return to crime after a criminal conviction. You going to beat the odds, Jack? It's a real crapshoot out there."

"The portents of doom aren't going to deter me," Jack said. "If that's what you're asking."

T.J. got up, hooking his thumbs on the inside edges of his belt buckle, a heavy brass number with a star embossed on it. "Portents of doom, huh? Where'd you come up with that one? That's some big words for a convict."

Jack was a spectacle when he'd arrived an hour earlier to the parole supervision of Mr. T.J. Hughes—legs chained, making short hopping moves, getting used to how far he could step, hands cuffed to a belly chain, people staring at him as he got out of the van and was escorted into the Regional Reentry Center in Tucson after serving thirty-eight months for armed robbery at the Arizona State Penitentiary in Florence.

Under oath, in a court of law, he told the judge he didn't know the names of his two accomplices. He said, "Your Honor, ever see the movie *Reservoir Dogs*?"

The judge said, "This better be relevant."

Jack's court-appointed attorney, Joe Mitchell, said "Your Honor, in the film, five strangers are hired by a crime broker to rob a bank. They meet for the first time and don't know anything about each other. No names are used. Each one is given a color. Mr. Blue. Mr. Green. Mr. Brown. Like that."

"Life imitates art, is that what you're telling me, Counselor?"

Joe Mitchell said, "That's right, Your Honor." Assuming the judge got it.

"I saw the movie," the judge said, "thought it was preposterous."

Jack got the maximum for a class-two felony—five years. His unexpected parole, the result of befriending the prison chaplain who stopped by his cell one day and said, "Will you come and visit me? I'd like to talk to you about joining our Bible study program, part of my Prisoners of Christ ministry."

Jack grinned 'cause it sounded funny and was about to say, "You got the wrong guy." But paused, looking at the future, seeing eighteen more months of mind-numbing sameness, and started to panic—when a lightbulb went on in his head. Wait a minute. Maybe this was his way out.

The chaplain was a tall thin hawk-faced man named Ulrich Jonen. His prison ministry program was called New Beginnings.

"What's done is done," Uli said. "You cannot change your past transgressions, but you can start anew and you can do it today. God enables us to have a second chance, and more, if necessary. We're all human beings and human beings make mistakes."

Jack could relate. Jesus, nobody's perfect.

Jack told the chaplain what he wanted to hear and even let the chaplain hug him on occasion, Uli displaying some homo tendencies, but it never got out of hand.

After two months of studying scripture, Uli referred Jack to the parole board as a man, he felt, really wanted to make a change. "I see goodness in Jack Curran." Uli urged the "board" to at least meet him. "What's the harm in that? If you don't believe as I do, he's a changed man, he stays and maxes out his sentence."

The parole board interviewed Jack and agreed with the chaplain, giving him early conditional release—what they called discretionary parole, with a list of rules he had to follow.

As he was leaving the penitentiary, Uli said, "Jack, have faith, son. The next few weeks are going to be a critical time. There's going to be a lot of chaos in your world. My advice: 'Press on. Nothing in this life can take the place of persistence.' Know who authored those words?"

Jack said, "You?"

"Mr. Ray Kroc, who started a little fast-food franchise called McDonald's."

T.J. unlocked the cuffs and chains in his office and said, "I got the authority to detain you, arrest you and send you back if I have cause. Boy, I get even an inkling you're violating parole, you're going to be in a whole heap lot of trouble."

Jack rubbed his wrists. There were red marks from the handcuffs. He looked across the desk at T.J. and said, "I could use a little time to find my footing."

"Is that right? Well, you got ten working days to get a permanent job, and I expect you to work labor to meet expenses."

"How am I going to find a job if I'm working all day?"

"Talk to your buddy, Jesus, now that you're on a first-name basis—ask him. They're going to charge you $105 a week for rent at the house. And another $200 for an alcohol- and drug-counseling program."

Jack reminded T.J. he'd been arrested for armed robbery, not booze or drugs.

T.J. said, "I'm just looking out for you, buddy," and grinned. "But on the plus side, you don't have any restitution fees or back child-support payments."

What pissed Jack off, what seemed like pure bureaucratic lunacy, he had to have a phone location where he could be reached at all times. No cell phones. That eliminated a lot of better paying jobs right off the bat. They really stacked the deck against you.

There were framed photographs of T.J. on the wall from

another time: T.J. the rodeo honcho, roping a calf in one, riding a bull in another one.

"You were in the rodeo, huh? What was it like to be on the back of a two-thousand-pound Brahma bull?"

"It beat the hell out of keeping track of losers like you," he said, holding Jack in his gaze.

It took Jack a while to get used to life on the outside. The world seemed big at first, after spending eighteen hours a day in a six-by-ten-foot cell with no windows. It was also tough being around people, thinking everyone who came toward him wanted to kill him, walking with his back toward the shelves in a grocery store, seeing suburban moms and old folks and realizing he was overreacting, the survival instincts he learned in prison difficult to let go. He didn't need his "prison face" now. He didn't have to look mad and bad.

The clothes he was wearing on February 28, 2002, the day he went in, no longer fit, so he bought gray khaki pants and a shirt from the prison store, first deducting it from his hundred dollars of release money, leaving him fifty-two dollars till he could find a job. He thought he looked like a janitor in his new khaki outfit, but it was stylish compared to the red jumpsuit he'd worn for three and a half years.

Jack had read that most cons who were released were scared 'cause they didn't want to make a mistake but were too dumb or too unprepared to make it outside and got arrested and sent back after a couple weeks. T.J. said it was due to "gate fever," a malady that caused fear, anxiety and grouchiness in the hapless convict.

A lot of guys Jack met inside actually liked the "life." Three squares a day, no worries about getting a job and paying bills, no responsibilities at all. And they liked their prison friends better than their friends back home.

Jack lived on baked beans and canned spaghetti the first couple weeks in the halfway house, spicing up both with salt, pepper and Tabasco in the small kitchen, while he tried to find a job, interviewing at construction sites and trying to preserve his capital—now down to eight dollars and seventy-three cents.

Nobody was hiring ex-cons on parole and he was close to desperate, thinking he'd have to revert to crime to make ends meet, when he saw a want ad and got a job at a place in South Tucson, building modular homes. The company was Eldorado Estates. A sign in the warehouse said: "Making the American Dream a Reality." Jack wondering who in their right mind thought living in a trailer was attaining the American dream.

Hank Bain, one of the owners, told Jack the job paid ten dollars an hour, but when he found out Jack was on parole, offered him seven, Hank saying, "You don't like it, come over here, I've got a little spot on my ass you can kiss."

Jack cleared $205 a week after taxes and, after paying for his room at the halfway house, had a hundred dollars for food and entertainment. A line on the bottom of his paycheck said: "Eldorado Estates, built on family values of trust and loyalty." Jack liked that. Everything was a lie.

Hank's son Donny was the crew chief, a skinny effeminate heroin addict who was trying to kick the habit and trying to get by on weed. Donny'd twist one on the way to lunch and offer it to Jack, Jack saying, "I'm on parole, man, I give 'em a hot urinalysis, they're going to send me right back."

Donny said, "Fuck 'em, they can't do that."

Jack said, "They can do anything they want."

And did, T.J. stopping by at the factory checking up on him while he installed windows in prefab walls, rousting him in his room in the middle of the night, waking him up and making him piss in a plastic bottle. Standing behind him while he did it. Jack saying it's hard "to go" when someone's watching you.

"Come on, wake up, sleepyhead," T.J.'d say. "Let's find out what kind of fun you've been having."

But Jack beat the odds, got through parole without screwing up and six months later was on a bus back to Detroit with a fresh outlook and the intent of staying out of prison. T.J. said he had to have a forwarding address and Jack gave him his sister Jodie's.

From the Greyhound station downtown, he took a cab to Sterling Heights, hoping Jodie would be there. He knocked on her front door, his only sister, he hadn't seen in four years. She opened it, looking at him through the screen and said, "Oh . . . my . . . God." Stretching it out like it was one word. "I do not believe it. What'd you do, escape?"

Jack said, "I found Jesus."

"Yeah, right."

Jack said, "The parole board believes I am a changed man."

She grinned. "Well, they obviously don't know you very well."

He and Jodie had always gotten along, had always been close, closer after the death of their parents twelve years earlier when a fire broke out in their East Detroit home.

Jack said, "Can I stay with you for a few days?"

"I don't know that I'd be comfortable living in the same house with a criminal." She smiled now to show him she was kidding and opened the door.

Jack stepped over the threshold and she put her arms around him, hugged him and held on. She kissed his cheek and said, "Jackie, it's so good to see you. You can stay as long as you like. You're welcome anytime, you know that."

She was a thirty-two-year-old divorcée with short spiked hair, dyed red and long fingernails that were light blue with flecks of color on them.

"When'd you change your hair?" Last time he saw Jodie, she was blond.

"Couple weeks ago. It's an Emo style."

"Emo, huh?"

"Stands for emotional punk movement."

"I can see it," Jack said.

"Listen, I'm in the business—I have to look the look. Did you know coloring your hair dates back to the ancient Romans?"

"I guess it's okay then," Jack said.

They went in the kitchen and Jodie made them each a vodka and tonic.

She said, "I'll bet you'd like a home-cooked meal after all that time being incarcerated. I could whip us up some tuna noodle hot dish."

It was a joke between them. Hot dish was a casserole their mother from Minnesota used to make. She'd start with a can of Campbell's cream of mushroom soup and put in tuna and noodles or ham and lima beans, whatever she had handy.

They had another drink and Jodie made hamburgers on a gas grill and they ate on TV tables in the living room, watching *Jeopardy*.

At one point Jack said, "You still selling cosmetics?" Jodie had worked for Revlon and made good money, selling to high-end stores in malls around Detroit.

She smiled and said, "No, I'm a nail technologist."

Jack said, "Why are you doing that? You had a good job." He regretted it as soon as he said it.

"You ought to talk." She gave him a dirty look. "What did you say your current occupation was?"

He tried to smooth things over by asking a couple questions. "What do you like about your job?"

Jodie perked up a little. "You really want to know?"

Jack said, "You bet I do." Trying to put a little enthusiasm behind it.

"Well, for one thing, it gives me a chance to be creative. I design decorative, colorful little things for fingernails and toenails.

My favorites are gorgeous flowers made out of pink and green rhinestones and beautiful butterflies and ladybugs made out of crystal-clear teardrop rhinestones and pink round rhinestones."

Jodie was grinning. She couldn't help herself; she was so excited.

"I also do patriotic designs like American flags. They were very popular after 9/11. One of my customers met her boyfriend 'cause he loved the sunshine design I did on her toes. How about that? And I do New York manicures and French manicures and warm paraffin manicures. Once I did a pink ribbon for a breast cancer survivor. I do guys too, give them manicures and paint their toenails. I think it's great there are men who are masculine enough to express themselves in such a fun way."

Jack had stopped listening after "teardrop rhinestones."

Jodie's goal was to open her own shop one day. She was going to call it Ultimate Nails. "I think that says it all," Jodie said, "don't you?"

He thought, that's what happens, you try to be nice to someone, they bore the hell out you.

The next day he drove Jodie to work and went out for a few hours, looking for a job. He was almost out of money and Jodie'd made it clear right up front, she wasn't in a position to help him out financially.

In his brief job search, he tried a couple used car lots on Gratiot, asking if they needed an experienced salesman. They didn't. He tried a construction site, a landscaping company, and a painting contractor, saying he'd do anything they needed done and struck out each time. He tried two strip joints on Eight Mile, asking if they were looking for a bouncer. They weren't.

He stopped at a neighborhood saloon and sat at the dark bar that was crowded with afternoon drinkers. He sipped a beer and considered his options. Say he did get hired somewhere: now that he didn't have the motivation to make probation, how long could he work some menial, chickenshit job? The answer was not very, if at all. He didn't see himself showing up for work every day, doing something he didn't want to do. He couldn't see himself starting over, like he'd ever started in the first place. He was the way he was and wasn't going to change. Not at age thirty-eight.

For the first time since leaving Arizona, he thought seriously about getting a gun and hitting party stores, small markets and retail shops that one person could manage. He'd just be more careful this time around, the fear of incarceration fading after six months on the outside.

Four

She remembered the day it happened, waking up to a creaking noise, the sound of someone coming up the stairs. She was in her bedroom at the lodge, varnished log walls and a cathedral ceiling with interlocking oak beams. The clock on the bedside table said 5:07 a.m. There was a log smoldering in the fireplace, giving off the faint smell of wood smoke. She got up, crossed the room and opened the top drawer of her dresser, took out the Smith & Wesson .357 Airweight and went into the hall. She saw a man in mossy oak camouflage come up the stairs and head for Luke's room. She snuck up behind him and aimed the pistol at his back.

He heard her and turned.

"Hey, Rambo," Kate said, "better take this. Del Keane said he saw a bear last week." She handed the automatic to Owen, and he slipped it in his pants pocket.

"Del doesn't need a gun. Bear probably smelled him and ran away. What're you doing up?"

"I've got to see my men off," Kate said.

Luke came out of his room, rubbing sleep from his eyes. They went downstairs and Kate made coffee, carrying steaming mugs into the room. A backlog burned in the big fieldstone fireplace. Owen was kneeling on the oriental rug, putting gear in his backpack. He closed the top and laid it next to his compound bow that had a built-in quiver of arrows. She handed Owen his coffee, pulled her robe closed, and stood over by the fireplace to get warm.

Luke came in the room now, a skinny teenager dressed in Skyline Apparition 3-D camo, an iPod dangling from his neck like white plastic bling.

Owen said, "What're you listening to?"

Luke pulled the earplug out and said, "White Stripes."

Kate said, "I don't know that bucks are partial to Motor City garage bands."

Owen said, "Maybe he's on to something. Rock instead of doe scent, the new deer lure."

Luke picked up his dad's bow and tried to pull the string with its seventy pounds of draw, face straining. He couldn't do it.

"Lock your arms," Owen said. "Use your shoulders."

Luke took a breath and tried again, and this time, drew it about three quarters.

"You're close, almost there," Owen said. "Couple of months . . ."

Kate put her arms around Owen. "Be careful. You don't know who's out there drunk with a bow or a rifle. Man has enough bourbon, I'd look like a whitetail."

"A cute one, too," Owen said. "I'll tell you that."

Now Kate hugged Luke and kissed his cheek. She could see sparse, blondish fuzz on his chin and upper lip. He squirmed and tried to pull away from her, a look of pain on his face.

He said, "Mom . . ."

She let him go. His voice had changed in the past few weeks.

It was deeper now and she wasn't used to it. "I'll bet you don't mind if Lauren kisses you."

Luke said, "We broke up."

Kate said, "Why didn't you say something?"

"I don't know," Luke said. He seemed embarrassed, eyes looking down at the rug.

"Give him a break," Owen said and winked.

Luke walked out of the room. Owen grinned now and said, "I'll get all the details, tell you about it later, okay?"

Owen picked up his gear and Kate put her arm around him and walked him to the door. Luke was outside in the dark with Leon. Luke threw a stick and Leon charged after it and brought it back, looking up at Luke, ready to go again.

Owen bent down and kissed Kate. She held his big stubbly face in her hands and said, "Be careful."

"What're you worried about?"

"Keep an eye on Luke, will you?"

"You don't do this," Owen said. "What's the matter?"

Kate didn't explain it, the feeling she had, because she couldn't.

Owen opened the door and said, "Leon, get in here."

The dog came running, banged into Owen, hit the rug, a Persian, slid across it, regained his balance and moved toward Kate, slobbering and pressing himself against her.

Owen had been hunting since he was a kid, loved the woods and streams and wanted to pass the thrill on to Luke. For Owen, there was nothing like it, getting away from the shop, the track, the bullshit. He also loved it because it was the only place on earth you didn't hear cell phones.

Kate didn't care much for hunting, but she didn't impose her point of view too strenuously. What bothered her were all the bonehead stories about hunters getting hurt or killed. She'd just read one in the Traverse City *Record Eagle* about a man who was shot while he was going number two. The article said he answered a call to nature and was nearly done with his business, wiping himself with a white Kleenex, when another member of his hunting party shot the man in his backside, thinking he was a whitetail deer.

"That didn't really happen," Owen said.

"Want to bet?" Kate said. "I've got the article right here."

Another story told about a hunter who was gored by a deer and had to go to the hospital. The man had no hard feelings, though, and said he'd be ready with a load of double aught next time him and the deer's paths crossed.

Kate said, "If that isn't proof of the stupidity of hunting, nothing is."

Owen said, "Most hunting accidents—fifty percent—involve falling out of a tree stand, either climbing up or down." He looked at her and grinned.

Kate shook her head. "Oh my God." Leon moved in close and bumped her. "Listen, if you guys aren't home by dinner, I'm going to Big Buck Night at the casino."

Owen said, "What's that all about?"

"Roman Brady, a soap star from *Days of Our Lives*, is going to be there."

"He's the big-buck stud, huh?"

Kate said, "Ever seen him?"

"Not that I recall."

"You're not missing a whole lot," Kate said, "but the ladies love him because he's on TV."

Owen said, "So you're not going?"

"I'm just warning you," Kate said. "That's what hunting widows do—get their picture taken with Roman and play blackjack."

She stood at the window, listening to Leon's wet irregular breathing, watching Owen and Luke cross the yard, two contrasting shapes in the dim light of a half moon—like Lenny and George in *Of Mice and Men*, a book Kate had just read again. They moved toward the tree line, disappearing into the thick foliage like they'd entered another dimension.

That was the last time she saw Owen alive.

Five

Luke kept rewinding the scene in his head. Kept seeing himself wigging, hands shaking, trying to draw the bow, but no strength to do it. He couldn't think of any experience in his life that was like it. It was more than that he'd freaked out, it consumed him. He couldn't breathe. Couldn't move. Had no strength to pull the bowstring. His dad had described the symptoms, but Luke didn't believe it would ever happen to him. But it did, and in his soul, he knew if he hadn't lost his nerve trying to shoot the first buck, his dad would still be alive.

The whole thing was a blur after that, like a video in fast motion. Instead of going back to the lodge to get his mother, he ran toward farm buildings he'd seen from high ground in the woods. The farmer, a big man in a red flannel coat and a cap that said CAT DIESEL on the front, called EMS.

His mom arrived at the hospital and he felt worse than he ever had in his life. She hugged him, but he couldn't look at her. Didn't know what to do or say and that's the way it had been since he walked out the back door of the lodge with his dad to go hunting.

Owen McCall died on the operating table. The broadhead had severed an artery before piercing his lung. He'd lost too much blood. The surgeon telling Luke he didn't think they could've saved his dad even if they'd beamed him into the operating theater right after the accident. Luke wondering if the doctor was talking like a Trekkie to impress him.

He had to meet with a sheriff's deputy, too. Luke, his mom and the deputy, whom his mother seemed to know, met in the surgical waiting room. The deputy took his Smokey the Bear hat off and placed it on the end table next to him. He had a sweat crease where the hat gripped his head.

Luke told them what happened in straightforward sequence, leaving out the part about getting buck fever. What difference did it make now? The deputy wrote everything he said on a notepad in a leather case. He could feel his mom's eyes locked on him during the interview, boring into him like lasers. He never looked at her the whole time. When he finished, the deputy, whose name was Bill Wink, closed the notebook that had an embossed western sheriff's badge on the front and fixed his gaze on Luke's mom.

"I've been hunting most of my life and I've never heard of anything like it."

"What're you saying?" his mom said.

"Mrs. McCall, I'm saying it was a bizarre accident." Now he looked at Luke and said, "I know you're hurting, and I feel for you, son."

Luke watched him put his hat back on, finding just the right position, the brim an inch or so above his eyes, the hat the same dark brown color as his shirt. The pants were light brown and had a dark brown stripe that ran down the legs. Luke couldn't imagine wearing a uniform like that, but Bill Wink looked good in it, with his Marine haircut and muscular arms and his black leather gun belt, the handle of an automatic, a Glock—it looked like—ready to draw.

Out in the hall, Luke heard Deputy Sheriff Wink talking to his mother in hushed tones.

"The DA said it was an accidental death during the act of hunting. It is not a criminal case. It does not rise to the level of criminal negligence. The boy was licensed to hunt."

Luke couldn't believe they'd actually considered something else. What'd they think; he tried to kill his own father?

Then there was the visitation at Lynch and Sons, a place where Luke had been a dozen times for funerals of grandparents, uncles and aunts and now his own father. It seemed like hundreds of people came up and talked to him, and he couldn't remember one thing anyone said. People young and old shaking his hand and hugging him. All he wanted to do when it was over was be by himself.

He had a clearer recollection of being at the gravesite, watching the casket being lowered into the ground. His mother would look over at him, but he couldn't make eye contact with her. He felt too guilty.

After the funeral, he went in the basement and smashed his bow, the Darton Apache, on a structural steel post in the furnace room, breaking it in two pieces and then four, knowing it could never be repaired and vowing he'd never pick up another one again as long as he lived.

He didn't believe in God after that, 'cause it didn't make sense. How could this happen? Why'd God let it? He hurt inside and started drinking to feel better. Found a bottle of schnapps in the liquor cabinet and poured it in a white plastic flask he bought at Rite Aid. He drank before school, the hot licorice liquid burning his throat, but it numbed him, eased the pain, and now he was buzzed most of the time.

Then one morning in homeroom, Jordan Falby, a lineman on the football team, grinned and said, "Hey, McCall, been deer hunting lately?"

Luke, outweighed by sixty pounds, got up from his desk and swung the edge of *Algebra II* into Falby's cheekbone and blood spurted and Falby yelled and brought his hand up to his face and Luke swung at him again and then kids were grabbing him, holding him back as Miss Hyvonen, their teacher, came in the room and freaked.

Luke was suspended indefinitely pending an inquiry, the assistant principal, Helen Parks, a plump nervous woman with red hair, said.

Luke had to call his mother and had to wait till she came and picked him up. When they were in her Land Rover pulling out of the school parking lot, she looked at him and said, "What's going on?"

What'd she think was going on? She open her eyes this morning and forget what happened?

"What did Jordan Falby say that set you off?"

Luke told her.

His mom said, "I probably would've done the same thing."

Luke couldn't imagine his mother hurting a fly.

She said, "I'm not worried about that. I'm worried about you. I want you to see someone."

Luke had been thinking about killing himself for a few weeks. The pain he felt wouldn't go away. It was there in his head before he opened his eyes in the morning and stayed with him till he fell asleep at night, if he could.

He considered sleeping pills. Take a handful, nod off and it was all over. Or he could shoot himself. Load one of his dad's shotguns, put the barrel in his mouth, and *boom*. It might be effective, but he didn't want his mom finding him on the basement floor with his head blown off. That wasn't right. Carbon monoxide was another possibility. Drive in the garage, close the door and let the car run. After giving it a lot of thought, sleeping pills seemed like the best option. But where would he get them? Did you need a prescription?

His mom said, "When were you going to tell me you quit tennis?"

Her voice brought him back. "Didn't I?"

She glanced at him and looked angry. She turned away, staring through the windshield.

First light. Luke could see now, walking behind his dad along a ridge that sloped down through big Michigan timber and thick cover. They stepped over a fallen birch tree and maneuvered through tangles of alder and fern, boots sloshing on wet leaves. They'd walked a couple miles, at least. His ears were cold and he could see his breath, wide awake now after a slow start.

His dad stopped and took out binoculars and glassed a stand of oak trees in the distance, a place where whitetail liked to hang out and eat. He lowered the binoculars and looked at Luke. "What happened with Lauren?"

"She said she wanted to be friends. We both kind of decided."

"You're probably better off. Having a girlfriend's a lot of work."

"She'd get mad if I didn't call her every day, and sometimes, even if I did."

"Girls are different, in case you haven't figured that out yet."

"Yeah, they seem a little odd at times."

His dad smiled.

"Just wait. You haven't seen anything." He handed the binoculars to Luke. "Have a look?"

Luke gripped them, brought them up to his eyes, and panned

stands of oak trees and birch and aspen and cedar, the leaves still green, and followed another ridge up to a stand of maple. No deer, but the light was coming and he could make out the shapes and contours of things. A black squirrel darted across the trail and disappeared.

They kept moving through thick cover, feet unsteady on the slick terrain, approaching an area where the leaves were matted down.

Owen said, "Looks like they just got up from a nap."

Luke said, "Check this out." Pointing to tracks that went up-hill to a stand of oak trees on a ridgetop in the distance.

The canopy was high and thick, and it was dark as they followed the deer tracks upslope toward the trees. His dad stopped and pointed at deer poop, slick and green and still steaming.

"They're close. Remember what you used to call it?"

Luke didn't know what he was talking about.

"Gucks. You'd say, 'Daddy, I got to go gucks.'" Owen looked at him and grinned. "It's the perfect word, isn't it?"

"How about Grandma? I'd tell her I had a stomachache, she'd say, go sit on the toilet and do some popsie doodles, or popsies."

"Like we were living in a Disney movie," Owen said.

Luke liked that.

"The pros, like Del Keane, put their hand in it, tell you what Mr. Deer had for breakfast. Want to try it?"

Luke made a sour face.

They followed the tracks over a berm to a ridgetop that was littered with acorn husks, a sign that deer had been there. From the high ground, they could see the tracks continue downslope through a funnel of trees to a cornfield in the distance.

Owen said, "Give me about twenty minutes, then head down. I'll push them at you."

"How do you know they're in there?"

"It's got everything they need: food, water, and shelter. Make your way to the edge of the tree line and be ready. You're only going to get one shot. And that's if you're lucky."

Luke sat on a tree stump, the Darton Apache resting across the tops of his thighs, thinking how cool and exciting it was being out here. He scanned the woods with the twelve-power Zeiss binoculars, the sun rising fast now behind him. He caught glimpses of his dad in the distance, a dark shape, disappearing and reappearing through the trees. He panned right, saw something move, adjusted the sight, focused on a deer tail swinging back and forth. He panned left, saw a leg and followed it to the thick body of a high-racked ten-pointer. The deer lifted its head, rumen drooling from its mouth, sensors on full alert. The buck snorted and stomped its hooves and took off, Luke trying to follow it with the binoculars. Losing it in the thick woods.

He turned and picked up his dad again moving along the perimeter of the cornfield about a hundred yards away, the stalks at least a foot taller than him.

Owen pulled two brittle cornstalks apart and entered the field. He moved along a row that was so straight he could see down a hundred yards, the result of GPS, now available on farm equipment—taking any guesswork out of planting crops in straight lines.

The ground was pitted and irregular, puddles of water covered with a thin layer of ice that broke easily under his weight and made a sound like glass cracking. His boots were wet and soon heavy with mud, making it harder to walk. He carried a Browning Mirage in his right hand, the bow weighing a little more than four pounds with its quiver loaded with carbon arrows.

Wind whipped through the cornfield, rattling the stalks that sounded to Owen like the percussive beat of a jazz tune, and bringing with it the intermittent reek of cow dung and skunk and the heavy smell of wet hay.

He watched a hawk swoop in from a scattered cloud formation and dive like a fighter jet into the field and then soar back up with something squirming in its talons.

Owen adjusted his Detroit Tigers cap, pulling the brim down to keep the sun out of his eyes. Although his body was heating up under layers of thermal insulation and camo, it was cold. He could see his breath. He went about fifty yards and listened. The wind blew and the stalks clattered. It was tough to hear anything else.

He cut left through the field now, going against the grain, pulling stalks apart and knocking them down. It was the only way to cover a big area fast. He came to a stretch of field where the stalks were mowed down like a semi had driven through. He followed the path and heard them before he saw them: five deer, two big bucks and three does, stopping to eat corn destined for the farmer's silo and eventually to sell as livestock feed.

He knew the wind would bring his scent right to them, but they wouldn't know what direction it was coming from. He came up behind them and started yelling and they scattered, the bucks going one way, the does, another—Owen chasing the bucks, pushing them toward Luke and the cover of high ground—Owen catching glimpses of the bucks jumping, antlers clearing the seven-foot-high corn as they ran.

Luke moved down the ridge toward the cornfield. He stopped, brought the binoculars to his eyes and glassed a wild turkey and then another one—a whole family walking in a line through the woods. He let the turkeys pass and made his way to the edge of the tree line. Leaned against a big maple and waited. His nose was running and he wiped it on the sleeve of his camo shirt.

From this position, he could look straight down a row into the cornfield. He leaned his bow against the tree, slipped off his backpack, opened it, took out a plastic bottle of Gatorade, a cool blue flavor called Frost and unscrewed the top, taking a long drink. He saw something move out of the corner of his eye. A rabbit hopped out of the field and ran into the woods.

Luke was thinking about Lauren, wondering if they'd get back together. He didn't tell his dad he missed her and thought about her all the time. Maybe she was going out with someone else. The possibility of that bothered him. He remembered seeing Mike Keenan talking to her in the cafeteria, but decided not to dwell on it any further.

He heard something that distracted him—something big and fast coming toward him, crashing through the field. He thought he heard his dad's voice now, but couldn't make out what he was saying, like the wind was blowing it away. He picked up his bow, nocked a Zwickey broadhead.

He saw a buck in the row, coming right at him. The deer cut left and he lost it. He ran right, saw the buck appear again and disappear, zigzagging toward him. He was running along the edge of the cornfield. Luke heard the deer and saw it taking down stalks as it charged toward him. He tried to draw the bowstring, but his hands were shaking and he couldn't breathe. He felt like the strength had been sucked out of him. The deer was close now. Twenty yards. Ten. And then it went left and ran by him, darting into the woods.

Luke felt helpless at the moment. And stupid. He took a breath and tried to relax. He couldn't believe it. Maybe the best chance he'd ever have to shoot a whitetail, and he couldn't do it. His dad had mentioned it, a condition called buck fever that afflicted hunters and now he knew what it felt like.

His hands were steadier now and he sucked in air. Regained his strength and pulled the bowstring about halfway to see if he could do it. And there, coming down the row right at him, was another buck, a bigger one, and he remembered his dad saying, "Deer are color-blind, but they're good at picking up movement. So when you get in your stance, be as economical as you can. Don't move any more than you have to. Pull straight back."

And that's what Luke did. Stood balanced, in full draw now, centered the buck in the crosshairs of his sight. He saw his dad closing in behind the deer, just a glimpse before he released the arrow and followed its trajectory, hitting the animal in the meaty part of his upper body above the shoulder. The whitetail stopped running, stumbling now, staggered a few yards and fell over. Luke ran toward the deer, pumped, excited. As he got closer, he could see it was still alive, trying to get up, but couldn't, laying on a bed of trampled cornstalks, black eyes watching him. He looked for his dad, who had been close behind the deer, but didn't see him.

Owen could see the buck struggling to get up as Luke approached, not knowing it was bleeding to death, the broadhead having gone through its heart, blood pumping out, a dark purple-red. The deer had about five minutes before everything would shut down.

Owen wasn't in much better shape, sitting in the dirt, propped up by cornstalks, the ground cold and wet under him, a corncob digging into his back. It was strange: he didn't feel the arrow that had gone through the buck and somehow had hit him, the carbon shaft buried in his chest up to the white fletching. His shirt was soaked with blood and more blood bubbled out of his mouth as he tried to breathe. He knew he was in trouble.

Luke saw him now and ran over, falling to his knees, too stunned to comprehend what he was seeing. He dropped his bow, slipped off his backpack. "God, what'd I do?"

He had tears coming down his face.

Owen said, "Luke, listen to me. It isn't your fault. Just get help. Tell 'em they've got to bring a helicopter in."

Luke got up and took off, running.

Owen looked at the whitetail that would've dressed out at about two hundred pounds, the animal still trying to find its legs, movements becoming less pronounced, and then no movement at all.

How odd was this? After racing cars for twenty years going two hundred miles an hour in the tight confines of the racetrack, he'd only been in three accidents and wasn't hurt too bad in any of them. Although Kate would most likely have disagreed, taking care of him for three months while his injuries healed after Talladega in '94. She said it was the grumpiest she'd ever seen him. He said, "What do you expect, I'm missing a third of the Cup season."

Owen remembered it like it was yesterday. He was on lap 256 when Dale Senior came up behind him and must've taken the air out of his spoiler. Dale may have nudged him a little, too, but didn't bang him intentionally. In any case, Owen spun into the wall at about 205, rolled four times, smashed into the catch fence and landed upside down near the entrance to pit road. He was airlifted to the hospital. Broke his right ankle and his left wrist and was in a coma for two days. When he opened his eyes, Kate was sitting on the edge of the bed next to him, a look on her face like the day Luke was born.

He said, "You like watching people sleep, is that it?"

She said, "I must, 'cause that's all I've done for two days."

He thought he was in his bedroom at home till he looked around and said, "Where in hell am I?"

"Citizens Baptist Hospital, Talladega, Alabama," Kate said. "Remember hitting the wall and then rolling four times?"

He didn't. Not then. But it came back to him within a week. It also helped to see it on videotape replay, confirming what he suspected. Big E's black Monte Carlo coming up fast behind him, Dale trying to make up for penalties for driving too fast on pit road and having too many crewmembers over the wall on a pit stop.

Owen was leading at that stage of the race, but didn't get into another racecar for three months, and did it over Kate's protests.

"Are you out of your mind? You're lucky to be alive. Here's what's left of your car, in case you forgot."

She handed him a picture that showed wheels and tires, pieces of sheet metal and a roll cage—the thing that saved his life.

"And here's what's left of you," she said, indicating his casted limbs and hospitalized condition.

Owen remembered saying, "I'm a racecar driver—this is what I do."

His third wreck involved an altercation with a young aggressive driver named Teddy Hicks. Owen was going into turn three at Martinsville Speedway, lap 127, when Teddy's Ford banged his rear fender and sent him spinning. Owen did two 360s, spun off the track, but got it under control and kept going. He'd been in second place and finished eighth. Hicks was black-flagged and disqualified for rough driving.

After the race, Owen confronted Teddy in the pits. "I don't know what you're doing out there, but if you can give me a reasonable explanation, I'm willing to bypass this whole deal and move on," Owen said, giving him the benefit of the doubt.

"What I was doing was taking you out of the race, old man." Teddy grinned.

Owen stepped in now, threw a big left hand with some weight behind it, caught Teddy full on the side of his face, wiping the grin off and sending him down on the asphalt drive. Owen figured that was the end of it and started walking away. He didn't see Teddy pick up an impact wrench, but he felt it break his collarbone that took a year to heal. Owen didn't press charges, but Teddy lost his Cup ride, got booted off the circuit. No one would touch him after the assault. He heard Teddy was driving on the dirt tracks for a while and then disappeared from racing.

Owen was tired. He closed his eyes now and hoped when he opened them he'd see Kate sitting on the edge of his bed.

Six

Celeste put the bottle of Cold Duck under her arm, holding the handles of the plastic bag in one hand, opening the car door with her other hand and getting in.

Teddy said, "Get my candy bar?"

Celeste said, "What do you think?"

"I knew," Teddy said, "I wouldn't be asking."

Celeste opened the bag, reached in, grabbed a Nestlé Crunch, handing it to him.

He slid the sleeve off the candy bar and peeled back the tin foil, broke off a piece and put it in his mouth. Now he put the Z28 in gear, hit the gas and pulled out of the parking lot, tires squealing.

Teddy said, "What the hell took so long?"

"I had some trouble," Celeste said. "Man forgot his manners."

"Teach him a lesson, did you?"

"Let's just say he's going to have one whopper of a headache when he wakes up."

Teddy finished the candy bar, rolled the tin foil into a ball and threw it in the backseat. "Want to tell me what happened?"

Celeste heard a siren and said, "Think you could go a little faster?" They were on 94 passing City Airport outside Detroit.

"What's the matter?" Teddy said. "You got to go tee tee?"

He didn't catch on real fast.

Teddy said, "Give me a beer."

Celeste opened a minicooler on the floor next to her feet, took out an ice-cold can of MGD dripping water, and handed it to Teddy. She wiped her cold wet hand on her jeans. He popped the top, took a long drink and put it between his legs.

"Anyway," Celeste said, "I was standing in line waiting to pay for a bottle of Cold Duck, this rude dick with ears steps in front of me with a couple six-packs like I wasn't there."

"What'd he look like?"

Celeste said, "Just a normal-looking redneck in Levi's and a wifebeater, could've been your twin brother."

"Didn't look anything like me," Teddy said. "I seen him get out of a red Dodge 4×4, go in the store."

She liked messing with him, pushing him to a point where he'd start to get angry and then ease up. A Wayne County sheriff's deputy blew past them going the other way, Ford 500, lights flashing.

Teddy looked over at her. "You do something back there?"

His little brain was starting to catch on. "That's what I was getting to, if you'd let me continue."

Teddy fixed his attention on the rearview mirror, watching the cop car.

"I said to him—"

"Who?" Teddy said.

"Redneck in the party store," Celeste said. "You got the attention span of a fucking gnat."

"If you weren't taking all day to tell this exciting story, maybe I'd be able to follow you."

"I said to the redneck . . ." She looked at Teddy. "Still with me, or should I go slower?"

Teddy gave her a dirty look.

"I said to him, 'What am I, invisible? You don't see me standing here?'

"Know what he said? Nothing. Ignored me."

Teddy brought the beer can up to his mouth, finished it, squeezed the can almost flat and threw the empty over his shoulder into the backseat and glanced at Celeste. "Another one bites the dust."

She opened the cooler, took out a can of MGD, gave it to Teddy, reached over and wiped her wet hand on his T-shirt.

He said, "Hey, you're getting me all wet."

"I was standing behind him. Gripped the Cold Duck bottle with two hands, swung it like a baseball bat, hit him on the side of his head, and believe me I got all of it. Would've been an off-the-wall double. The bottle exploded and he went down, crashing to the floor and didn't move. The skinny geek manager behind the counter whose name was Jerry asked if I could find everything okay? And was there anything else I needed."

Teddy drank some beer and played air guitar to "Lookout Mountain" by the Drive-By Truckers, looking over at her occasionally, grinning.

"I said, 'Jer-Bear, I need two packs of Marlboro Lights, some Juicy Fruit, a couple of Nestlé's Crunches, a twelve of MGD and a bottle of Cold Duck.' And while he was getting everything together, I thought, what the hell. He put it all on the counter, looked up at me and I said, 'There is one more thing—I'll take your money, too, all of it, including the big bills under the tray.' I had the .38 Ruger pointed at him. He cleaned out the register and asked me if I wanted a bag. 'No, dumbshit,' I said, 'I'm going to walk out of here, let everyone see the money I just robbed.' Know what he said then? 'Paper or plastic?' You believe it?"

Teddy's eyes were glued to her now. "What kind of dumbfuck stunt was that? You don't go in, rob a place by yourself—you don't know who's in the back watching you on a video monitor, come out with a shotgun."

"It just happened. Police would've come one way or the other. I figured I'd take advantage of the situation. What's the problem? You're going to get half of what's in the bag and it was a piece of cake."

"You don't do that," Teddy said. "We got rules."

The car was drifting over the center line now, heading for an approaching SUV.

Celeste said, "We got rules on the highway, too—you keep your car in the lane, don't run into somebody head-on like you're about to do."

Teddy looked up, swerved right, went too far, and overcorrected, the Z28 sliding off-road on gravel. Celeste thinking they were going into the ditch, but Teddy surprised her, got it under control, and they were back on the highway, cruising like nothing happened. He'd said he was a racecar driver—and maybe he was.

"Don't say nothing," Teddy said. "Don't say a fucking word."

They rode in silence, Celeste staring straight down the road listening to the Truckers doing "Hell No, I Ain't Happy":

There's a lot of bad wood underneath the veneer
She's an overnight sensation after twenty-five years

Teddy trying to sing along, getting a word right here and there like he knew it—in a voice that didn't understand tone or style.

After a time, Celeste said, "Want me to drive, let you enjoy your buzz?"

Teddy looked over and grinned. "Tell me why I shouldn't haul off and pop you?"

" 'Cause if you do, I'll leave you." She pulled the Ruger out and aimed it at him. "Or maybe I'll shoot you."

"Go ahead," Teddy said. He looked at her with a lunatic grin and started turning the wheel back and forth, the Z28 doing slalom turns in the lane, going wider, tires making contact with gravel.

Celeste said, "What're you doing?"

"What're you doing?" Teddy said.

"Fucking with you," Celeste said.

"Me too," Teddy said.

Celeste put the gun back in her shoulder bag.

Teddy stopped turning the wheel, put the car back on course.

He had the hair-trigger temper of an adolescent, like somebody put him to sleep when he was fourteen and woke him up yesterday. Give him shit, he'd give it back to you harder.

"Before I get any more pissed off," Teddy said, "tell me how much you got?"

Celeste took the money out of the plastic bag, a pile of bills in her lap and started counting. When she was finished, she looked at Teddy and said, "Guess."

"It's never easy with you, is it?"

"Want it to be easy, get yourself somebody has no imagination, does what they're told." She reached over, slid her hand slowly, gently, along his inner thigh, fingertips gliding over his jeans. She reached between his legs, felt the bulge of his manhood, fondling him, teasing him, holding him and tightening her grip, Teddy squirming, looking down at her hand with red nails painted a color called Passion Punch.

Teddy saying, "Easy."

A look of concern on his face now, not sure what she was going to do, but wanting more.

Celeste said, "Ou okay?" in her baby-talk voice. "I'm not hurting widdo Ted, am I? Should we get him out, have some fun? Or should I count the money? Decisions, decisions."

In spite of their differences—and there were a couple thousand of them—they'd been together three years. Teddy had a few hang-ups, which wasn't surprising for a guy who grew up an only child on a farm in Perks, a little town in southern Illinois.

Celeste said, "Where exactly is Perks at?"

Teddy said, "South of Carbondale, east of Cape Girardo." He laughed, Jesus, bent over like it was the funniest thing he'd ever heard in his life.

Celeste said, "Okay, I give up."

"Cape Girardo's on the other side."

Celeste said, "Other side of what?"

"Mississippi, dummy. What do you think?"

Celeste got it now: you'd have to cross the river to get there, and you'd probably get wet. She guessed that's what he was saying. She gave him a fake laugh. In his hick farm-boy way, Teddy was being funny. She wanted to say, "Don't quit your day job to be a comedian just yet," his day job involving smoking weed, drinking Jack, and robbing liquor stores.

Celeste asked him what they grew on the farm.

Teddy said, "Corn and soybeans. We also raised sheep—Hampshires and Suffolks."

Celeste said, "You know what you call a guy with two thousand girlfriends?"

Teddy looked at her and said, "Huh?"

Celeste said, "A shepherd."

Teddy grinned.

"Ever have your way with one?"

Teddy grinned bigger. "Matter of fact, I lost my virginity to a 120-pound Hampshire ewe named Winky."

Celeste was surprised he was so open about it. She'd've thought he'd want to sweep that one under the rug. "What was it like? You know, making it with an animal?"

"Winky was better than some of the farm girls I've done. And I didn't have to take her out or sweet-talk her."

"What do you need me for?"

Teddy got a big grin on his face and said, "I can't tell you." Then he started laughing and couldn't stop.

Celeste searched her mind now, trying to remember what she saw in this hick clown to stay with him for going on three years. He was nice-looking. He thought he looked like Billy Ray Cyrus. They did have a mullet in common. Teddy's looked like it had 10W-30 motor oil on it half the time, Teddy not being a guy who liked to shower. He didn't mind being clean; it was the process he didn't care for—getting wet and cold and shaving and getting soap in his eyes. Not showering much wasn't a deal breaker, 'cause Celeste liked the gamey smell of unwashed man. It turned her on.

She met Teddy at a Hank Williams, Junior, concert at Pine Knob. Started talking in the beer line; Teddy behind her, checking out her behind. It sounded like the title of a country-western love song.

He said, "Hey there, good-looking, got an extra dube you could part with?"

Celeste had rolled a couple of bad boys and this nice-looking guy—with an honest-to-god mullet—sounded like he could really use one. She said, "Buy me a beer, I'll fix you up."

Teddy handed her a twenty-ounce Miller High Life and they sat on the grass together, smoked weed and listened to Hank Jr. do "I Really Like Girls."

Teddy said, "What's your name?"

"Celeste."

"Celeste what?"

"Celeste Byrnes."

"Nice to meet you. I'm Teddy. I'd like to get out of here, take you back to my place, but first I got to hear 'Country Boy Can Survive.'"

Celeste said, "I'm with someone." She was out with this show-off ad guy named Ronnie Rockman; a friend had fixed her up. Ronnie had been speed-rapping her about his accomplishments since he'd picked her up. He'd just won a Clio, an Effie and a One Show, the equivalent of an advertising hat trick, not bad for a week's work, huh?

Celeste had no idea what he was talking about but gave him a fake smile when he looked over at her, beaming. Then he told her about his car, the BMW M5 they were riding in, Ronnie quoting its horsepower rating—394 SAE at 6100 rpm and zero-to-sixty in 5.3 seconds. He said he could afford to drive any car but chose the M5. Know why?

Celeste's brain hurt this guy was so boring.

"'Cause, for the money," Ronnie said, "it's got everything: handling, performance, comfort—you name it."

It wasn't a conversation; it was a monologue.

Teddy said, "You having a good time with him?"

Celeste said, "Not really. Who're you with?"

"I'm flying solo."

"You went to a concert by yourself?"

"Far as I know, that's not a crime, yet."

Celeste took out her cell phone and called Ronnie, who was sitting in row two in his pressed jeans and peach-colored Polo shirt. She said, "Ronnie, this is Celeste . . ."

"What the hell happened to you?"

"I'm leaving," Celeste said. "Just wanted to let you know." She hung up as he started to say something. Fuck Ronnie and his BMW M5.

Teddy's full name was Theodore Monroe Hicks. Celeste got a kick out of that after she found out where he was from—a hick named Hicks. What was that called? She thought it was irony, but had quit after her junior year at Walled Lake High to go to beauty school, so she didn't trust herself to be right.

They got in Teddy's Ford Ranger pickup with the rebel license plate on the front and went to Teddy's rented house, a dump in Clawson, and spent the weekend in bed, Teddy making her watch *Predator*, his favorite movie, stopping at a scene with a big muscle-bound dude firing a machine gun in a dense jungle setting at an alien you couldn't see.

Teddy said, "Know who that is?"

There was an element of pride in his delivery, like they were related or something.

Celeste said, "Someone from the WWF? An ex–football player?"

Teddy grinned now. "That's Jesse-damn-Ventura, governor of Minnesota's who that is."

Celeste felt bad for the citizens of Minnesota now. They had it tough enough with forty-below winters and summers that lasted about three weeks. And now they had an action hero actor guiding their fortunes.

What did she see in Teddy? The question popping back in her head. Celeste believed it came down to some kind of chemistry thing, some weirdo attraction. It certainly wasn't his intellect. One time she asked him if he believed in love at first sight.

He looked at her and said, "No, 'cause blind people can fall in love, too."

Sometimes he surprised her.

Celeste counted the money, stacking the bills on her lap. When she finished, she locked her gaze on Teddy and said, "How much you think? Guess right, it's all yours."

"What if I guess wrong?"

"It's all mine," Celeste said.

"What do you think," Teddy said, "I'm dumb or something?"

Celeste was thinking, "Boy, as a rock." but she said, "I'm just messing with you. Come on, give it a shot."

Teddy stared at the money, taking his time like his life depended on it. He said, "$1,243," and grinned. Then the grin disappeared and he said, "No, I want to change it. I guess $1,427."

"You were closer the first time," Celeste said.

Teddy was mad now. "That's not fair."

"What's not fair? You guessed wrong."

"You're cheating."

"Why don't you count it yourself?"

"Maybe I will," he said and turned into a strip-mall parking lot, downshifting, the high-performance engine rumbling, coming to a stop in a parking space in front of a Rite Aid drug store. "Give it to me," Teddy said. "Let's see who's right and who's not."

Celeste was confused. Who's right? He was the only one who guessed, and he was wrong both times. She handed him the money and he started counting, stopped and started again.

"Want some help? I know it's a lot of numbers."

Teddy gave her a dirty look.

Celeste cracked the window, lit a joint and blew the smoke out.

Teddy looked over like he wanted a hit.

Celeste said, "When you're through. I don't want to cloud your razor-sharp mind."

Teddy finished counting and locked his gaze on Celeste. "One thousand, three hundred fifty-eight, didn't I say that?"

Celeste said, "Quick, what's that divided by two?"

Teddy said, "Huh?"

Celeste said, "Six seventy-nine each. And you didn't even have to get out the car."

Teddy grinned, getting it now. He put his hand up, reached over and said, "High five."

"This is the address he gave his parole officer," Teddy said, pulling up to a tan ranch house with a robin's-egg-blue garage door in Sterling Heights.

Celeste glanced over at him. "And you believe it?"

It was in a subdivision that didn't have any trees. Just single-story houses and concrete streets.

Celeste said, "Let me clue you in on something. If Jack's got the money you say he's got, he ain't staying in Sterling Heights with his sis."

Teddy turned in the seat, facing her. "What the hell do you know?"

He hated people telling him he was wrong. Girls most of all. Celeste said, "Think about it. Would you stay here if you were rich and just out of prison?"

"We'll see," Teddy said.

God, he was hardheaded. He got out of the car, walked up to the front door and rang the bell, turned, looked at her and waved.

Celeste saw a car coming toward her, a silver two-door Chevy. It passed her and turned in the driveway, a chick with bright red hair behind the wheel. Teddy saw it too and moved around the front of the house toward the garage.

Seven

Dick May said, "I apologize it's taken so long."

Kate said, "It's not your fault. How many times have I postponed it?" She could see the trust documents on the desk in front of him.

"Did you and Owen ever talk finances, assets, net worth?"

"I was never too concerned," Kate said.

"I can understand."

Dick May was Owen's attorney and good friend. He'd retired from a big Detroit firm and Owen was his only client: kept him busier than he wanted, but it was fun and lucrative—a nice combination for a former Princeton grad who'd just turned seventy but still had the energy and enthusiasm of a guy twenty years younger. Owen and May played tennis and golf and shot skeet, Owen giving him a handmade Benelli twelve-gauge for his seventieth birthday.

Kate sat in a comfortable armchair across the desk from May

in his quaint Bloomfield Hills office, which had a fireplace and a wet bar.

"Owen left you everything—his controlling interest in the company, the house in Bloomfield, apartment in New York, place in Aspen and the equities, cash, and cars. No surprise, I'm sure. We're talking, conservatively, twenty million."

Twenty million—and Kate was thinking about the house she rented in Guatemala, thinking it was the happiest she'd ever been in her life and she had less than a thousand dollars to her name. Money made it easier but not necessarily better. Not many people subscribed to that point of view, but for Kate, it was true.

May said, "You're free to run the company if you want."

"You think I'm going to go in there and tell those motorsport pros how to do their job?"

"You wouldn't be the first if you changed your mind."

"Not likely," Kate said.

"I didn't think so, but you never know." May took off the reading glasses and furrowed his brow. "There is one thing I have to explain," his tone serious now. "Owen wanted Luke to have the lodge in Cathead Bay."

"Dick, if you think that's a problem," Kate said, "let me ease your mind."

"It doesn't go into effect till he's twenty-four."

Kate didn't care. She just wondered if Luke would ever go back.

That was it. The reading of the will took about five minutes, Counselor May offering his time if Kate needed further explanation about anything.

She didn't.

Kate drove home and met her friend Maureen Kelso. They stood at the island counter in the kitchen, smoking and drinking wine. She put out a wedge of Saint Albray that smelled like a locker room but tasted like the best Camembert she'd ever had. "Try this," Kate said. She sliced off a piece and put it on a stone-ground wheat cracker and took a bite.

"I'm not eating for a while," Maureen said. "I feel like a fat pig. I had a pair of jeans on the other day, bent over and split the seat. Imagine what that does for your ego."

"I think you look good," Kate said. "Don't get so skinny you look sick like Lindsay Lohan and Nicole Richie." She took another bite of cheese and sipped her wine.

"Oh, okay," Maureen said. "Are you kidding? I could lose twenty pounds, you wouldn't notice. I'm back on South Beach, my last diet. If this doesn't work, it's lipo. Plastic surgeon said he'd take two quarts of cellulite out of my thighs and stomach. Said he could use some of it to give my ass more definition. What do you think?"

Kate said, "I'd try exercise first."

Maureen took a cigarette out of her purse and lit it with an orange plastic lighter.

"I did. Had a personal trainer, even. Little muscular guy named Avis."

"Was he Greek?"

"I think Albanian. All he talked about was abs, delts, glutes and obliques. First couple of days I thought he was teaching me the language, pick up Albanian while you're getting in shape."

"You have a crush on him?"

"Who?"

"The trainer."

"He was too little. Like a toy man. I need a guy with meat on his bones."

Kate took a bottle of wine out of the refrigerator, cut the top off with a foil cutter, and opened it with a screwpull opener. "Since you're not in training at the moment, try this." Kate reached over the island counter and poured Maureen a glass.

She took a drag and turned and blew smoke toward the breakfast room. "The neighbor hit on you again?"

"It's been six months, he thinks that's long enough," Kate said. "I'm fair game now. He came over yesterday and said somebody looks like she could use a hug." Kate poured more wine in her glass.

Maureen said, "What's his name?"

Kate said, "Anders."

"Let me guess, he's Swedish."

"You don't miss much," Kate said, "do you?"

"Is he the real thing?"

"You mean, was he born there? I don't think so."

"I mean, does he eat raw fish for breakfast? Real Swedes eat it like they're going to the chair. I dated this scene-maker named Sven Lundeen, couldn't get enough, had breath like Shamu. He was a hottie, too. Had blond highlights in his slicked-back hair. Always wore a white shirt unbuttoned to his navel and tight jeans." Maureen sipped her wine and took a drag, blowing smoke out. "What'd the hugger say?"

"He put his arms around me and said, 'I bet you could use a hug.'"

"How well do you know him?"

"We've been neighbors for ten years. I see him over the fence or through the pine trees. We'd wave to each other, but that's about it. Anders and Sukie came over for dinner one time a bunch of neighbors got together."

"Sukie? What's her real name?"

"I think Susan."

"What's she like?"

"Kind of ditzy," Kate said. "A secretary who married her boss."

"So he came over and hugged you. Then what?"

"He had his body pressed against mine and I could feel something hard sticking into me."

"Jesus," Maureen said. "What'd you do?"

"I said, 'What're you doing?' And he said, 'I can't pretend anymore. I'm crazy about you.'" Kate remembered the dreamy look in his eyes.

"Were you nervous?"

"I said, 'Anders, why don't you take your little buddy home, give it to Sukie.'"

"I'll bet she doesn't want it either."

"He said, 'I can't stop thinking about you.' I said, 'What are you doing? We're neighbors,' hoping that would bring him to his senses, snap him back to reality."

"How about your husband died seven months ago," Maureen said. "Did you remind him of that?"

"I looked him in the eye and said, 'You'll be all right. Try to keep busy. Go clean the garage, take the empties back.'"

Maureen grinned. "What'd he say?"

"Nothing. He walked out and I haven't seen him since." Kate finished her wine and poured a little more. "Another neighbor asked me to call him and said he had something important to tell me. I dialed the number, he answered, recognized my voice and started saying things."

"What do you mean?"

"Describing what he'd like to do to me like he was reading a porno script."

"How dirty was it?"

"Dirty," Kate said.

"What'd you say?"

"I laughed. He was so serious, and it was so dumb. I said, 'Frank, am I giving off some kind of desperate vibe, or what?' He's an engineer at GM. He drives a Buick and has outlines of all his tools on a pegboard in the garage so he doesn't put something in the wrong place. I thought, wow, where'd that come from?"

"What kind of neighborhood do you live in? All these perverts coming out of the woodwork." Maureen finished her wine.

"He and Owen were friends, played tennis in a league together for years."

Maureen lit another cigarette. "So how're you doing? You doing all right?"

"I'm okay." Kate looked away, glanced out the kitchen window at the pool still covered for a couple more weeks.

Maureen said, "You're not very convincing."

"I'm fine—most of the time, but then I'll see something of Owen's, or a picture of him. The other day, his Corvette pulled up in the driveway and for a couple seconds I forgot and thought he was home. He left it at the shop and one of the young guys was returning it." Kate felt her eyes well up. "Night's the worst, I reach for him in bed." She lost it now, tears coming down her face like she had no control, and Maureen came around the island counter and hugged her and she was crying too.

"Should've happened to those two schmucks I married—not Owen."

Now they were laughing, Kate picturing Maureen's first husband, Carlo, a short balding director who shot *Five-Step Restroom Cleaning*, thought he was the next Spielberg.

"All right, I'm going to stop asking questions. I came over to cheer you up and look what I've done."

"I'm glad you're here," Kate said. She lit a cigarette. "People have been calling, offering ways to help me cope, handle what I've been through."

Maureen said, "Like who?"

"A group called Afghans for Widows invited me to stop over," Kate said. "They express their grief by knitting."

"What's that all about?"

Kate said, "They knit afghans to help relieve their stress and loneliness."

"Come on."

"And a woman from the Community House asked me if I wanted to join her poetry workshop. Said poetry is a common way of expressing grief."

Maureen lit a cigarette.

"Every workshop starts with a reading—it might be 'Grieve Not' by William Wordsworth, or 'Grief' by Elizabeth Barrett Browning." Kate sipped her wine. "And then all the grieving poets write a poem. The woman said a few lines of poetry can express deep emotional feelings."

"Are you putting me on?"

"It's okay. People are trying to help," Kate said. "I packed up all Owen's clothes in boxes and had the Purple Heart come and pick everything up."

Maureen said, "Why?"

"It's time . . ." Kate said. "I think about him every day and I probably always will, but . . . it's time to move on."

Maureen poured more wine in her glass. "How's Lukey?"

"He's not getting any better," Kate said. "I'm worried about him. His counselor called and said his teachers are concerned about him. He's in class but he's not there. Doesn't do his homework. His grades have dropped."

Maureen said, "Do you talk to him about it?"

"He doesn't talk. He comes home and goes to his room. He doesn't see his friends. Doesn't do anything."

"Isn't he seeing someone?"

"Yeah," Kate said. "A psychiatrist recommended by the school."

"What about you?"

"I don't need help, I've got all the neighborhood men."

Maureen grinned. "What did the dirty-talker say?"

Kate took a sip of wine, trying to remember and then she did and started to laugh.

Eight

Amber told DeJuan about this dude was looking for someone to pop his wife. DeJuan said, "Why you telling me?"

Amber said, "'Cause he's offering ten grand and I thought maybe you'd be interested."

She was behind the bar, mixing a drink, looking fine in her black low-cut outfit. DeJuan said, "I strike you as somebody going to kill some motherfucker for money?"

Amber said, "Why you think I'm telling you?"

"That the way you see me, huh?" He picked up his drink, Courvoisier and Coke and finished it.

Amber said, "Want another one?"

He nodded. The music was so loud he could hardly hear her. Place was packed with scene-makers on a Thursday night. Two-deep at the bar. He was in one of the swivel bar chairs, watching an early-season Tigers game on the flat screen. Amber put a fresh drink in front of him. He said, "How you know this dude is looking for someone?"

"We used to go out," Amber said. "Let me put it another way. He used to take me to his place in Bermuda. Fly down in the Gulfstream, Marty doing lines like the governor just pardoned him."

DeJuan said, "You tell him about me?"

Amber said, "That's what I've been saying."

"Where's he at?"

"See that guy with the long silver hair?"

DeJuan saw him down the bar. Weird-looking, kind of freakish dude, bald on top with long hair hanging off the back of his head, mid-fifties, drinking what looked like vodka on the rocks—the right glass, with a slice of lemon. He was all over this young thing, blond in a tank top, seemed to be ignoring him.

Amber said, "Go talk to him if you're interested."

She moved down the bar to get a drink for someone. DeJuan looked up at the TV, saw Maggs hit a tater to left against the Twins, watched him run the bases and win the game, Ordoñez making it look easy. DeJuan looked down the bar again, saw the dude with the hair finish his drink, get up and move through the crowd. DeJuan put his drink on the bar top and followed him outside, standing behind him on the street, waiting for the light to change. It was dark, the marquee of the Birmingham Theater casting light on the scene. And the people were out, little bitches in their skimpy, skin-tight outfits, the man checking them out, not missing a thing.

He crossed the street. It was easy to follow him with that hair—compensating for being bald on top, that silver pelt he had, saying, look motherfucker, I got all the hair I need. Check it out.

DeJuan followed him, trying to catch up. The man walking fast, almost running. He stopped in front of a restaurant, sign said 220, went down the stairs into a place called Edison's, high-priced Birmingham nightclub look like somebody's basement—pipes and shit exposed in the ceiling—like it was under construction. Place was dark and crowded and filled with smoke. DeJuan felt his eyes burn. He didn't care for cigarettes. Never had one in his life, never would.

The man stopped at the bar, ordered a vodka, took his drink into the men's. DeJuan followed him in, only two guys in there and watched him take out a coke vial, do a one on one.

He saw DeJuan looking at him and said, "You a cop?"

DeJuan said, "I look like a cop?"

"Want a bump?"

DeJuan said, "Amber say you're looking for a contractor."

Man said, "What're you talking about?"

DeJuan said, "Looking for somebody to fulfill a contract is what I understand."

He put the little black spoon up to his nose and snorted it up his left nostril, then his right.

"Got somebody around, you don't want around no more."

He pinched his nose and snorted hard and screwed the top back on the vial and put it in his shirt pocket. "Now's not the time. Maybe we can meet somewhere, discuss a business arrangement."

DeJuan liked that, the man talking about it in his serious business voice now. He wrote his phone number on a piece of paper, handed it to him. "My private line. Call when you're ready to talk."

DeJuan went through the door back into the smoky nightclub, Thornetta Davis doing "I Ain't Superstitious," belting out the lyrics as DeJuan passed in front her, checking out the country club dudes dancing with their ladies, if you could call it that, stiff moves and no rhythm like they dancing to some other song.

DeJuan was robbing a 7-Eleven the next morning when his cell phone rang. It was the dude with the hair.

He said, "Hey, this is Marty, can you meet me in the parking lot of Bed Bath & Beyond on Sixteen Mile in thirty minutes?"

At first, DeJuan had no idea who this dude Marty was, thinking it was a wrong number, but then he recognized his voice.

DeJuan said, "I'm kind of busy at the moment, can you give me an hour?" It was a shocker. DeJuan would've bet his diamond pinky ring he'd never hear from the dude again. He glanced down at the 7-Eleven manager lying on the floor in his green vest, hands and feet wrapped in duct tape—angry sawed-off little dude. Before DeJuan taped his mouth, manager Mr. Richard Ferguson said 7-Eleven would prosecute him to the full extent of the law and did he want to reconsider and turn himself in?

"Yeah," DeJuan said, "Straight up, I want to turn myself in. You're such a bad ass, I'm worried." Did he want to turn his self in? The fuck was wrong with his head?

DeJuan had come in the back door. Walked up, there was a dude named Russ—Russ smoking out behind the store when DeJuan approached, placed the barrel of his SigSauer Nine against Russ's cheek, said, "Break over, motherfucker, get back to work."

He dropped his cigarette and DeJuan walked him through the stockroom into an office. There was a desk with a phone and a bank of TV monitors that showed different parts of the store. There was a guy behind the counter working the register.

DeJuan said, "Who's that?"

Russ said, "The manager, Mr. Ferguson."

"Tell Mr. Ferguson, get his ass in here, you got an emergency needs his immediate fucking attention."

Russ grinned. "He's not going to like this."

After DeJuan secured Mr. Ferguson, he had Russ show him how to turn off the video cameras. Then he tied Russ up, put him in the stockroom.

He was cleaning out the register—look like about $1,700—when a customer come in, old lady, had something in her hand, coming toward him. He closed the register and turned toward the woman. "How you doing? Beautiful day, isn't it?"

The woman held up a carton of cottage cheese and said, "I want my money back." She pulled the top off and pointed to a green circle of mold. "Know what that is?"

DeJuan didn't like her attitude, old bag coming in getting in his face, fucking with him 'cause she think the customer always right. He picked up the cottage cheese, read the small type on the back, found what he was looking for. "Look here," DeJuan said. "See, it expire."

Old lady look like she going to throw the shit in his face, said, "I want to see the manager."

"He tied up right now."

"I want my money back or I'm never shopping in this store again."

DeJuan said, "You promise?"

"What's your name? I'm going to write a letter."

"Richard Ferguson. Now, why don't you take your moldy cottage cheese and your moldy old ass, get the fuck out of here."

There was a silver Benz, big one, S600 out by itself in the parking lot that was getting busy at one in the afternoon. DeJuan drove by, saw Marty behind the wheel, spun around and parked next to him. DeJuan put his window down and so did Marty, Marty saying, "Get in, let's talk."

DeJuan got out, walked around the back end of the Benz and got in the front passenger seat, sat back against the plush leather. Man, it was cold, like a meat locker in there, but Marty look like he was sweating in his Ryder Cup at Oakland Hills golf shirt, DeJuan trying to figure out what color it was—teal or coral some bullshit exotic name like that.

DeJuan looked through the windshield at Bed Bath & Beyond

in the distance and said, "What's up? Need help picking out sheets and towels?"

"I want you to kill my wife." He said it like he meant it. Had a serious look on his face.

DeJuan said, "Love is a bitch, isn't it?"

"I'll pay you ten grand, but you've got to make it look like an accident."

"Accident? Nobody said nothing about no accident." DeJuan pulled the SigSauer, aimed it at Marty, said, "Boom! Was just going to pop her like that, drop her like that." DeJuan thinking it sounded like lyrics to a rap song.

Marty put his hands up like he was going to catch the bullet, said, "Hey, what're you doing?"

"Be cool, Marty, not going to shoot you. Only illustrating a point, is all."

Marty put his hands down now and let out a breath. Looked relieved.

DeJuan slid the Sig back in the waistband of his Sean John denims. He said, "Make it look like an accident, a lot more difficult. Going to cost you more."

Marty said, "How much more?"

"What do you care? You rich."

DeJuan found out—following the man—Marty was a Mormon. He wasn't just your average Mormon either; man was bishop of the temple on Woodward Avenue, looked like a mausoleum, all decked out in white marble.

It occurred to him somewhere in the back of his mind—Mormons were the dudes had all the wives. Part of it sounded good, DeJuan picturing a harem, man. Ladies dressed up, having cocktails, waiting for him to come home. He walk in, check 'em out, pick the one he want to get naughty with. I'll take Shirela over there with the big knock-knocks, feel like some African trim tonight. Or maybe take Shirela and LaRita, get a doublay on a singlay going.

But part of it sounded bad. DeJuan thinking about all the ladies in the harem on the rag at the same time, PMS hanging over his head like a cloud of doom. No, on second thought, he didn't want no harem, stick to his current arrangement, pay for what you want, never have a problem.

Marty live on a street called Martell and man they had some cribs in that 'hood. Houses look like small hotels, department stores. He found Marty's, a modern, single-story place built up on a hill, tennis court out front. DeJuan pulled up in the drive- way. Could see the whole house now and it was big, kept going across a long stretch of yard. Man had a four-car garage with coach lights over the individual doors, had an oriental garden with a pond, little pagoda building look like a Chinese restaurant sitting out there.

He knew nobody was home. Marty was at his company in downtown Birmingham, had a whole floor in a big building called Martin Smith Securities. Named after the man's grandfa- ther. DeJuan checked it out on the Internet, had a whole story about the grandfather going through the Depression with noth- ing and starting the business with a three-hundred-dollar loan.

Shelly, Marty's wife, was getting her weekly massage, must've had a lot of stress in her life living in this 7,500-square-foot shack, only had help four days a week. Marty telling him her rou- tine: lunch and bridge and tennis and shopping, home between three and four, and telling him it had to be today 'cause the maids didn't come on Thursday. Or he'd have to wait another week.

DeJuan pulled up in the driveway behind the house, pushed a button in the car Marty told him to push, and the garage door farthest from the house started to go up. He drove Marty's silver Benz in, pressed the button and watched the door go down.

Marty said if DeJuan took his own car people might notice. De-Juan could see his point. Probably weren't many gold metalflake Malibu lowriders in the neighborhood.

He opened the door to the house, went through the kitchen, reminded him of the kitchen at Brownie's, where he was a busser, worked his way up to greeter, which was sort of like acting, put-ting on a fake smile and fake enthusiasm as he greeted people coming in the door—same kind of stove. Remembered the name Viking and the little Viking dude on it. Problem was, everybody was fat and everybody wanted a view of the lake. He'd take these four whales to their table, they'd say, "What about that one over there," pointing to a table wasn't bussed yet. Or they'd say, "Don't you have anything closer to the lake?" DeJuan wanted to say, "Get a carryout, go sit in the water have your meal. That be close enough?"

He liked to watch the looks on they faces as the food came, like junkies, man, couldn't wait to stuff those perch sandwiches in their mouths.

Why they have a kitchen that big? And Shelly, Marty say, don't cook. He went through the dining room and living room. Was a Japanese sword hanging on the wall, looked like the Hat-tori Hanzo sword the Bride used in *Kill Bill*. DeJuan picked it up, slid the blade out the case. The metal glimmered. He felt the edge, see if it was sharp. Sharp? Could've shaved with it. He gripped the handle with two hands and slashed the air the way he'd seen ninjas do in movies. "Hey, motherfucker, want some of this?" He moved now, attacking three imaginary dudes, thrusting and slashing the sword, the blade making a swishing noise as it cut through the air.

DeJuan carried the sword around the living room looking at things. On one side of the room was a wall of glass that looked out on the backyard, and a sliding door that opened to a walkway that led to the pond and the pagoda. Furniture looked oriental, too. Black lacquered tables with oriental figures, Japanese bitches in kimonos and ninjas with swords. More Jap warriors in pictures on the wall, DeJuan trying to figure out what the connection was with this Mormon dude and all this Japanese shit.

He moved through the living room into an office, had a desk and a leather couch and chairs arranged for people to sit and talk. On the desktop was a framed shot of Marty posing with a good-looking dark-haired girl. Next to it was the Book of Mormon. DeJuan laid the sword on the desk, picked up the book and opened to a page, said: *The First Epistle of Paul and the Apostle to the Corinthians—Chapter 15.*

DeJuan read—read it in a voice trying to sound like the preacher of the First Baptist Church, where his grandmother had took him when he was about ten, his mother smoking rock pretty serious by then, disappearing for days at a time. "1. MOREOVER, brethren, I declare unto you the gospel which I preached unto you, which also ye have received, and wherin ye stand." Huh? Didn't understand why someone use words like *moreover* and *wherin*. Why not say *in addition* and *where*, make it easy on the reader? He closed the book, checked out the pictures on the walls. One called *Joseph Smith's First Vision* showed two angel-looking dudes with light behind them appearing to a young white dude. DeJuan wondering if this Joseph Smith was related to Marty. There was another picture showing a caravan of Mormons in covered wagons. A line under it said: *Crossing the Great Plains in 1847.*

He heard something, looked out the window across the backyard, saw a car pull in and park, a Jag. Good-looking woman—twin of the one in the picture with Marty—got out the car, went toward the house.

DeJuan stood at the door to the office with the sword pointed straight down, tip of the blade buried in the black wool carpeting, listening, heard her in the kitchen, sounded like the refrigerator door closing. Watched her cut through the living room and head down a hallway to the bedrooms.

Now he stood outside the bathroom door in Shelly's pink bedroom, listening to the water running in the shower. Should he go in now, drown Shell-bell in the bathtub? Hit her over the head, make it look like she fall in the shower? DeJuan thinking, he could do that, sure, but he was curious about her and Marty. Sleeping in their own bedrooms, his down the hall, no mistake about it, shit everywhere. He'd've thought Marty'd be neater. Man was a pig.

He checked out Shelly's dressing room, boxes of shoes stacked to the ceiling, name Manolo Blahnik on most of them and Jimmy Choo. Boxes of hats, too, and twenty feet of dresses and shit on hangers. He heard the shower turn off, went back in the bedroom.

He was sitting on the black-lacquered, four-post queen-size bed when Shelly opened the bathroom door, came out in a white robe, hair wrapped turban-style in a white towel, letting out a cloud of steam.

She fixed her gaze on DeJuan as if she was expecting him to be there and said, "Whatever he's paying you, I'll double it."

DeJuan wasn't expecting that. "Why he want to get rid of you, good-looking woman like yourself?"

"I get in the way," Shelly said.

DeJuan said, "Want me to reverse the contract, that what you're saying?"

"What's he paying you?"

"Twenty grand." DeJuan thinking, she don't know the going rate for assassinations currently, trying for the long dollar.

"He try to bargain with you?"

"Not that I recall," DeJuan said.

"You're lucky. Marty's worth millions, he makes the maids reimburse him for phone calls."

DeJuan said, "You don't look like you're doing too bad."

"I can pay you thirty."

"Seems fair, under the circumstances," DeJuan said. "Anything else I can do for you?"

Nine

Jack stood against the railing—Somerset Collection, second level—looking down at all the glitzy storefronts and the parade of shoppers, everyone carrying a coffee cup or bottle of water. When did that start? He remembered his sister telling him to stay hydrated. Huh? He didn't know what she was talking about but got it now. Everybody drinking water, carrying bottles with them so they wouldn't die of thirst on the way to the mall.

He saw a blond come out of a store called Williams Sonoma with a shopping bag in her hand and move past Gucci, stopping to look in the window, either at herself or a leather jacket on display. He watched her go into Barnes & Noble and took the escalator down to the first floor. He went in and couldn't believe how many people were in there buying books, Jesus. It was packed. He tried to remember the last book he'd read and thought it was *Catcher in the Rye* by J. D. Salinger, that much he seemed to recall, pausing now, trying to come up with the story line: A guy named Holden went to New York to find himself. Jack thinking the way he'd gone to Tucson. Only he couldn't remember Holden Caulfield committing armed robbery and spending thirty-eight months in prison.

He looked around; it was the biggest bookstore he'd ever seen. Dozens of people buying books and drinking coffee. He saw her in the section called New Releases. Recognized a couple names like John Grisham and Stephen King but had never heard of most of the others: Mary Higgins Clark, Patricia Cornwell, or Sue Grafton.

He moved closer and studied her face. She looked older. Who didn't? But she was still a knockout. Her hair different, cut shorter, and that's what threw him at first. She'd had shoulder-length blond hair the last time he'd seen her and he couldn't imagine her ever changing it. But that was sixteen years ago. He'd changed too. Thirty pounds heavier now, at least, and his hair was thinner on top at age thirty-eight.

Nothing to panic about yet: girls still checked him out when he walked into a room—even in a khaki janitor outfit—he discovered his first day out of prison at a grocery store in Tucson.

When he glanced over, she was gone. He scanned the checkout line, the coffee bar. Ran out of the store, looked down the mall concourse, first one way, then the other. Saw her, just a brief glimpse, walking into a store.

He felt strange going into Victoria's Secret, seeing all the negligees and female underthings. He saw her shuffling through a rack of pajamas and moved in close, holding up a skimpy negligee. "I think you'd look better in this."

She turned and looked at him, did a double take and said, "Jack . . . ?"

"It is you," he said. "I wasn't sure."

They moved toward each other and hugged. It was awkward.

He held her too long and she pulled away from him and seemed nervous.

They had lunch at P F Chang's, sitting across the table from each other in a booth after sixteen years. It felt odd and confining. Kate glanced at the menu, then at Jack. "What're you going to have?"

"Sweet-and-sour chicken. It's the only thing on the menu I've ever heard of."

He looked older, his face fuller and heavier, hair starting to go gray.

They ordered.

Jack looked at her and smiled and said, "It's good to see you. You haven't changed, it's amazing."

Kate looked down at the table. She was nervous, like it was their first date.

The waiter brought their drinks—tea for her and a Kirin for him—and left. Kate picked up the teapot and poured tea in her cup. She told him about Owen dying in a freak accident and about her son Luke.

Jack said, "How old is he?"

Kate said, "Sixteen." She sipped her tea.

"You didn't waste any time, did you?"

"You went out to get beer and cigarettes and never came back," Kate said. "What did you expect? I thought you were dead or in the hospital." She could feel herself getting angry again, reliving it.

"I called," Jack said.

He picked up the beer bottle and took a sip.

"What—two weeks later."

"You thought you were pregnant, I—"

"Uh-huh."

"Still pissed at me?"

The waiter came and served their lunch, put a plate of seared ahi tuna in front of her and sweet-and-sour chicken in front of him.

When the waiter left, she said, "John Lennon did the same thing to Yoko, although they got back together a year or so later."

Jack said, "How do you know we won't?"

He reached over and touched her hand, and she pulled it away.

Jack said, "What's the matter?"

Kate sipped her green tea, staring at him over the edge of the cup.

"Believe it or not," Jack said, "I always thought we'd hook up again. I read this article about couples who dated in high school and college, broke up and ended up together twenty, thirty years later. It's called fate or kismet."

"You're not going to tell me your sign, are you?" He sounded like he was picking up where he left off.

Jack met her gaze.

She said, "What do you want?"

He sipped his beer, speared a piece of chicken with his fork and looked at her.

"Don't tell me you happened to walk into Victoria's Secret and saw me standing there after sixteen years, and call it fate or kismet."

"I parked in front of your house and waited till you came down the driveway in your Land Rover."

"How'd you find my house?" She looked down at the plate of seared tuna and wasn't hungry now.

"The phone book," Jack said.

"Come on."

Jack grinned. "You're right," he said. "I saw the article about Owen in *USA Today* and I knew at that moment I had to come back here and see you. I wanted to do it right away, but I knew you'd need some time to sort things out."

"You think because it's been seven months," Kate said, "everything's okay now? I'm over him? That's all the time I get?" She was angry and couldn't stop herself.

"I didn't mean that," Jack said. "Take all the time you want." He took a bite of chicken.

"You sure?" She said it with the same angry tone.

"I just wanted to see if I could help you," Jack said.

"I don't need help," Kate said. "I'm okay."

"Yeah, you're tough, aren't you?"

She looked at him and he looked away. Moved the food on his plate around with his fork.

"You did well for yourself," Jack said. "Better than if we'd have stayed together."

"Still down on your luck, huh?"

"Is that the way you see me?"

"That's all I remember," she said, thinking about the night they walked out of the Pretzel Bell after dinner and saw an Ann Arbor cop car, lights flashing, double-parked next to the BMW he'd picked her up in. Kate asked him what was going on and he told her he just got the car but hadn't had time to register the license plate.

She said, "Well aren't you going to tell the cop?"

He said, no, they could arrest him on a misdemeanor charge. He'd wait till they got the paperwork straightened out and then claim the car.

It sounded believable the way he said it at the time, but in retrospect, it was total bullshit. It was a year or so later that she found out he stole cars and sold them to a theft ring. That's how he made his money. That, and selling weed.

She said at the time, "Were you going to tell me?"

He said, "What, that I steal cars? Are you kidding?"

Getting away from Jack was one of the big reasons she joined the Peace Corps. But he was also the person she called for help when she was in trouble in Guatemala. He didn't hesitate—flew down and took charge. He got a black-market US passport for Marina, and he knew a pilot who made regular runs from South Florida to Bogotá and arranged to have them picked up in Guatemala City and flown to Miami.

They got back together again after that, Kate feeling a sense of loyalty that lasted till he left town six months later.

She'd always been attracted to him and still was, staring at him across the table, thinking he looked like a movie star, a cross between George Clooney and Matt Dillon. But he was trouble.

Jack said, "I still have dreams about you."

"Stop it, will you?" she said, raising her voice.

A foursome of women at the next booth looked over at them.

"Take it easy," Jack said. He drank his beer.

"You show up after sixteen years and think you can pick it right back up, huh? It doesn't work that way."

"Tell me how it works," Jack said. "What're the rules?"

"You sound like your old self," Kate said. "The Jack Curran I remember."

He sat there staring at her but didn't say anything. Kate poured more tea in her cup from a ceramic pitcher with a wicker handle. She decided to change the subject. "Are you married?"

"You think I'd be here if I was married?" He sipped his beer. "After you, I never met the right person."

"Be patient. You will." She looked down at her untouched piece of tuna. "Want some of this? I'm not hungry."

He shook his head.

Kate sipped her tea and said, "What do you do?"

"You mean do I have a real job? Yeah. I sell real estate," Jack said. "Looking for an investment opportunity?"

He was angry, giving it back to her.

"I've got a manufactured home development—Eldorado Estates. The pro forma offers a guaranteed six percent per year, with an opportunity to realize nine or ten percent. You buy into the LLC and split the profits with investors and the holding company. With the stock market sputtering, real estate is a viable alternative."

He sounded like he knew what he was talking about.

"Ever heard of Sun Communities?"

Kate shook her head.

"Or Equity Lifestyle Properties? That's what we do."

Kate sipped her tea, eyes on him. Maybe she was wrong about him; maybe he'd cleaned up his act.

"I'd take a look at it if I were you," Jack said. "The upside is stratospheric."

Kate said, "I'll put you in touch with Marty Smith when he gets back in town." If it made sense to Marty, she might do it.

Jack said, "Who's Marty Smith?"

Kate said, "Owen's financial guy."

"When's he coming back? 'Cause this deal isn't going to be around for long."

"Next week," Kate said. "He has a place in Bermuda."

"Too bad," Jack said. "It closes Friday."

Kate said, "How much are we talking?"

"Minimum investment—fifty grand."

He sounded convincing, but hadn't he always? "Let me think about it," Kate said.

The bill came and Jack picked it up and studied it.

Kate said, "Do you want to split it?"

"I've got it," Jack said. "I think I can afford thirty-three bucks."

He left money on the table and they walked back into the mall.

Kate said, "It was good to see you. I'm glad things are going so well."

Jack said, "Can I take you out to dinner?"

"I don't think that would be a good idea," Kate said. "There's too much going on."

He kissed her on the cheek and said, "Think about it, will you?"

She left him standing there and headed down the mall concourse toward Saks.

He was thinking about what lunch cost. Thirty-three dollars for a plate of chink food, a beer, tea and a piece of raw fish she didn't even touch. He was getting low on cash now, down to about forty dollars, and he had to fill up his sister's car with gas that cost almost three bucks a gallon.

He heard a voice with a twangy southern accent say, "Dude, you never call, never write."

Jack turned and saw Teddy sitting on a bench outside the entrance to J. Crew: a tradesman in Levi's, construction boots and a flannel shirt with food stains on it. Teddy Hicks, an ice cream cone in his hand—looked like strawberry—checking out the teen shoppers. His sister'd said a redneck with a mullet stopped by the house looking for him, and he only knew one guy that fit that description.

Teddy said, "Still got a way with the ladies, don't you? Who's that little number you was having lunch with? I wouldn't mind some of that, I'll tell you." Teddy flicked his tongue out like a lizard with a mullet, licking the ice cream, keeping his eyes on Jack. "No possibility of parole, and surprise, you're out twenty-two months early. Just missed you in Tucson."

"That's too bad," Jack said. "We could've had dinner, talked about old times."

"What's too bad is how long we've been waiting for our money." Teddy wiped his mouth with the back of his hand.

"I don't have it." Jack moved past him now, heading down the concourse.

"What do you mean, you don't have it?"

Teddy was right behind him.

"I hid it in the motel room ceiling," Jack said. "Adobe Flats, it was called."

"And you're telling me you didn't go back and get it?"

Strawberry ice cream was running down the side of the cone into a napkin that was wrapped around the base.

Jack said, "It's gone."

"Maybe you got the streets wrong."

"Campbell and Hacienda," Jack said. "It's a strip mall now. Got a Starbucks, a Carl's Jr., and a few new restaurants that cater to upscale professionals like yourself."

"Huh?"

"Stop by next time you're out there."

They were walking by Johnston & Murphy, Jack checking out the expensive executive shoes on display, fancy ones with laces, in shades of brown and shiny black, and loafers with thin soles that looked like slippers. Teddy finished the cone, licked his fingers and dropped the napkin on the tile floor.

"I know you're a stand-up guy," Teddy said. "Didn't rat out your buds, didn't complain, did your time like a man. But it doesn't change nothing, you still owe us our money. Now you don't have it, we've got a problem."

"I just did thirty-eight months trying to stay alive and keep my butt from getting augered while you're out fucking around, having a good time, and you think I owe you, huh? What parallel fucking universe did you just step out of?"

Teddy grinned. "That's pretty good. You make that up yourself?"

Jack pushed through the door, Teddy following and now they were outside. Wind whipped across the parking lot, blowing Jack's hair back.

"You made a bad decision," Teddy said. "You lost our money, now you've got to pay it back."

Jack could feel the anger rising in him, coming up from his stomach, through his chest into his head, ready to blow.

"Don't get all mad," Teddy said. "Let's get back together and get back what you lost and a lot more."

"Not interested," Jack said.

"Sure you are. Just don't know it yet."

Teddy went back in the mall and got another ice cream cone, chocolate this time. He was sitting on his bench checking people out when Celeste walked up.

"Whoever she is, she's rich," Celeste said. "Lives in a mansion like movie stars do."

Teddy said, "Seen anyone around?"

"No," Celeste said.

"Get a name, at least?"

Celeste handed Teddy a stack of envelopes. He took them in his lap, dripping ice cream on the top one.

Teddy said, "What the hell's this?"

Celeste said, "What do you think it is?" She sat down next to him.

He looked confused.

Teddy said, "What're you giving it to me for?"

"Take a look."

He glanced at the envelope from Consumer's Energy, read the name Owen McCall, 950 Cranbrook Road, Bloomfield Hills, MI 48034. Owen McCall, the NASCAR guy? Had to be. Teddy was well acquainted with him. But Teddy'd swear the man had died. Remembered hearing it on the news, thinking that asshole got what he deserved. He looked up at Celeste who was standing next to him. "Who's the girl?"

Celeste said, "I'd say she's his wife." She gave him her smart-ass, know-it-all look.

Teddy said, "What's Jack doing with her?"

"That's the big mystery," Celeste said, "isn't it?"

"Well, he's on to something," Teddy said.

"What'd he say about the money?"

"Doesn't have it."

"What I tell you?"

Teddy didn't care for her tone but let it go. He slurped some ice cream, thinking, 'course Jack wasn't interested in them. He'd got his own plan.

Ten

They were sitting in Shelly's Jag in the church parking lot off Cranbrook near Lone Pine. Shelly turned sideways, leaning back against the door. She looked fine, DeJuan feeling a tingling in his manhood, thinking he'd like to get naughty with the bishop's wife, show her some moves she ain't seen before.

He imagined Shelly, cool, talking to the police, saying, "Marty had demons he couldn't control." Trying to explain why he'd taken his life. He bet she was a fine little actress.

It had been a couple weeks since Marty's funeral, DeJuan giving her time to get her act together. But now he wanted his money.

"First, my condolences," DeJuan said. "Sorry for your loss."

"What're you talking about?" Shelly said. Bitch in her tone.

"Your beloved life partner, Marty."

"You said you were going to make it look like an accident."

"No. You said that." He remembered exactly what he said, could recite the whole conversation ver-fuckin-batim.

She crossed her legs, DeJuan staring at her thighs in tight jeans, the jeans tucked into black boots.

"Let me ask you something," DeJuan said. "Did it work out or didn't it?"

"Why'd you write that dumb letter? You could've blown the whole thing."

Was she trying to get him to reduce his fee, or just fucking with him? He looked right at her and said, "Man like Marty take his life, he better have a reason, or the police going to get curious, start asking questions. They come over, interrogate you?"

"No," Shelly said.

"That's 'cause I took the time, wrote the dumb letter. It's all in the details."

She reached in her purse, took out an envelope, number ten–style, filled with money and handed it to him.

DeJuan said, "I don't have to count it, do I?"

"That's up to you," Shelly said. "It's the balance of the job, what we agreed to. Ten grand."

"The fuck you talking about?"

She broke into a grin now. "I got you."

"Yes, you did." He liked that. Bishop's widow fucking with him, showing a wicked sense of humor.

"You should've seen your face," Shelly said.

DeJuan looked at the money.

"It's all there," she said. "Fifteen thousand."

"Satisfaction guaranteed," DeJuan said, "or your money back. That's my motto."

"More people should adopt that attitude," Shelly said. "Stand behind their work like you do."

He slid the envelope in the inside pocket of his leather jacket. "Got any other odd jobs you need done?" He reached over and squeezed her leg, felt her ankle through the butter-soft leather boot.

"I'll keep you in mind," Shelly said.

DeJuan was feeling good the way things had worked out, wanted to go downtown to the MGM, play some roulette. Only problem, Teddy was coming over with news about Jack. Jack, who was supposed to be in Arizona doing time. Jack, who had their money—$257,000 they were going to split three ways. Now maybe hoping it was all his and thinking he deserved it after doing three years and change, his sentence cut short for some unknown reason.

He thought about Marty on the way back to his crib. Pictured him, man walking in the house shit-faced that night. Plan was to have Marty's favorite dish, spaghetti Bolognese, ready to heat up. Like Shelly, the loving wife, bought it for him before she left town. DeJuan picked up a carryout at Andiamo's.

He heard the refrigerator open and close, heard Marty put something in the microwave, and heard the *ding* when it was finished. Marty at the kitchen table eating spaghetti, washing it down with Grey Goose on the rocks—new Eye-talian combo.

DeJuan walked in the kitchen, Marty look at him, eyes little slits, said, "Wha you doing?"

Man was rocked, swaying in his chair.

DeJuan said, "Been a change in plans."

"Wha you mean?"

His head bobbed forward, chin on his chest. Ten sleeping pills crushed up in the spaghetti, mixing with the booze and the dude was starting to nod off.

What gave DeJuan the suicide idea was seeing the prescription container of sleeping pills in Marty's medicine cabinet. Man was already taking them. There was a precedent.

Marty was fading fast.

"Shelly outbid you for my services."

"Wha . . ."

"Shelly want to get rid of you more than you want to get rid of her."

Marty was moaning now. DeJuan got him up out of the chair, wrapped his arms around the dude's chest, slid around and tried to get under him, Marty collapsing on him now. DeJuan tried to lift with his legs, but this motherfucker was a load. He heaved, got him off the ground over his shoulder, took a couple of steps, crashed into the Sub-Zero, but didn't drop him. DeJuan, 175 pounds, toting this five-foot-seven Mormon butterball, had to be two hundred if he was a pound, carried him out to the garage.

He put Marty down on the hood of the Benz, breathing hard, heart pumping. He opened the driver's door, went back, got under Marty, picked him up, dropped him in behind the wheel, straightened him up, and slid the seat belt around his waist and buckled it. Marty's eyes popped open for an instant like he coming around and it freaked DeJuan, unexpected as it was.

"Going on a trip, my man," DeJuan said. "Relax, enjoy the ride." He reached over, put the key in and started the Benz. Marty, DeJuan figured, was halfway to the promised land, let carbon monoxide take him the rest of the way.

Back in the kitchen, DeJuan wondered about a suicide note. Man offs his self—he going to say why—tell his story. But why's a dude worth all that money going to do it? DeJuan thinking, he could be depressed. Yeah? Depressed about what?—money being the ultimate depression buster.

He decided it had to have something to do with being a Mormon. Did something he couldn't live with. Like what? He'd have to do some investigating. He sat at Marty's laptop, went to the Church of the Latter-Day Saints Web site, got an idea.

You were a Mormon, worst thing you could do was murder.

And right after that, running a close second, was fornication. De-Juan couldn't believe that one. Dude gets his self some trim, that's a sin? What was that about? DeJuan wondering how long he'd make it as a Mormon. Five, ten minutes before they excommunicate his black African-American ass.

He typed out a suicide note, printed it and read it. Sounded pretty good, thinking, he nailed it.

Brethren:
    I feel myself sliding into the abyss, so heinous are my sins.
I do not believe Jesus can forgive me for what I've done:
smoking marijuana and fornicating with young women.
I've betrayed my wife. I've betrayed my congregation.
And most of all, I've betrayed my Lord and Savior.
I can no longer live with myself.
May God forgive me.

DeJuan liked starting it with the word *brethren*. Like Marty writing it to all the Mormon brothers, the whole congregation. He also liked the words *abyss* and *heinous* and *sins of fornication*— man, like they right out the Book of Mormon. Only thing looked strange, he didn't have the man's signature. He found it in Marty's transfer folder, *Marty* in fancy script, saved in different sizes. Picked one and dropped it on the bottom of the letter. Right fucking there. Perfecto.

Teddy was waiting out front in the muscle car when he got back to his crib. Had a two-bedroom townhouse in Royal Oak. Walking distance to bars and restaurants. No gangbangers. No drive-bys. Nice easygoing 'hood.

Teddy came in with a six-pack—dude drank more beer than anyone he'd ever seen—and his girlfriend Celeste who didn't seem to go with him. Teddy with his Canadian haircut and BO and this nice piece of trim.

Teddy telling him about Jack and the rich lady—woman inherit her husband's NASCAR fortune and seeing opportunity for all concerned. Teddy said the man's name was Owen McCall. He finished his beer and popped another one, green longneck bottles of Rolling Rock.

DeJuan Googled Owen McCall and found out he'd built a NASCAR empire and had a fortune estimated at thirty million when he'd died in a bizarre hunting accident. Killed by the sixteen-year-old son. DeJuan decided that maybe there was something to what Teddy was telling him. He looked over at Celeste. She seemed bored, sitting on the couch staring out the window, not really paying attention to what they were talking about. Or was she? He wondered what she saw in Teddy, this fine-looking girl with the creamy white skin. He said, "Yo, Celeste, what do you think?"

She turned and looked at him. "I'd fish where the fish are."

Teddy said, "What the hell you been smoking?"

DeJuan thought about what she was saying. Get money where the money's at. Uh-huh. Her brain a couple car lengths ahead of Teddy's and pulling away fast. Fish where the fish are at—going after Jack's rich lady. One thing was clear: if it was going to happen, DeJuan was going to have to do it. Teddy left him the rich lady's address: 950 Cranbrook Road, Bloomfield Hills. That was some high-class living. Now, how was he going to go to Bloomfield Hills, do what he had to do and not stand out, not get noticed?

They got back in the Camaro and Teddy said, "What'd you think of him?"

"First black person I ever met in my life," Celeste said. "And I liked him." She was thinking about what her dad, Bob Byrnes, would've said if he'd seen her. He'd have said something like, "Don't tell me you were in a jig's house, setting on a jig's couch. That the way you was brought up?"

No. She'd been brought up to hate everyone who didn't have a hundred percent pure Aryan blood, which, as Celeste discovered, was a whole lot of people. It didn't make a lot of sense to her then and even less now.

She told Teddy her dad used to take the family to Haden Lake, Idaho, every summer to Richard Butler's Aryan Compound. Her dad said it was the international headquarters of the white race, and we Aryans are the biblical "chosen people."

Teddy said, "Chosen for what?"

"To lead the less fortunate."

"Lead 'em where?"

"It's a figure of speech," Celeste said.

"Oh," Teddy said.

Like he knew what a figure of speech was.

Teddy stopped for a red light at Nine Mile. She could hear the throaty rumble of the high-performance engine as he tweaked the accelerator with the toe of his boot.

"Me and my sister spent our time in the Aryan Youth Corps."

"What'd you do?"

"Learned how to burn crosses and demand excellence and reject all forms of pettiness and decadence—things like rap music, effeminate hair styles, sloppy clothes and vulgar verbiage. You wouldn't last too long with that mouth you got."

Teddy said, "Think I'd join a stupid fucking organization like that?"

"If I had to guess," Celeste said, "I'd say no."

"That why you got all them weird tats on your body?"

She was going to tell him the tats were her idea of personal artistic expression, but would he get that?

The light changed and they took off. Teddy finished his beer and asked for another one. She reached in the cooler at her feet and took a longneck Rolling Rock out of the ice, twisted off the cap and handed it to Teddy. He held the Z28 steady, passing through Ferndale.

He said, "Who's this Richard Butler character?"

He was a character, too. Like a demented uncle who always had a smile on his face. Celeste said, "He was the founder of the Aryan Nations. People called him Pastor Butler 'cause he was also head of a church called the Church of Jesus Christ Christian. I remember one time he pinched my cheeks and said with my beautiful blue eyes and white skin, I was a quintessential example of Aryan womanhood."

"Quina . . . what?"

Teddy's face had a look of pure stupidity on it.

"Quintessential. Like, the best."

"Oh."

"In his sermons, he'd talk about how white people everywhere had to develop a sense of racial identity, racial worth. No one has more to be proud of than we do, he'd say. We're the descendants of Magellan and Lindbergh, the kin of Plato, Napoleon and Sophocles, the folk of Dante, Wagner, Galileo and Newton."

"Who're you talking about?"

"Famous people," Celeste said, "you know, like philosophers and scientists and explorers from past history. Didn't you go to school?"

"Yeah, I went to school."

"Didn't you learn nothing?"

"I guess I've heard of some of them."

"My biggest problem with the Aryans," Celeste said, "nobody had a sense of humor. They were all so serious and uptight. Although my dad used to say, 'Know what the world's shortest book is?' And he'd go, '*Nigger Yachting Captains I Have Known*' and start laughing. He thought that was pretty damn funny."

Teddy looked confused.

"I wanted to tell him I had a book even shorter than that called *A Hundred Years of Aryan Humor*. It only had one page."

"How could a book only have one page?" Teddy said.

Did he get anything?

She also told him Aryans believed in the existence of a supra-human being called the cosmic being. "I'd go to my dad, 'What's all this cosmic being stuff have to do with us?' And he'd go, 'The Aryan race has been given a special mission by the cosmic being, who has endowed us with a character that's like the divine Being itself.'"

"You just lost me," Teddy said.

That wasn't tough, Celeste was thinking. "Let me put it another way. Aryans are warriors and warriors have a special destiny. By living like a warrior, we're undertaking the will of nature and the will of the cosmic being. Got any questions?"

"Yeah," Teddy said pointing to the cooler. "Got another cold one in there?"

Eleven

Delayna said, "I went to my doctor, who's a GP, for a physical. The nurse said do you want a gynecology exam, too, while you're here? I thought, why not? Get the full checkup."

Kate was leaning back with her head on the edge of a sink at the Bardha Salon, Delayna washing her hair. Kate was barely listening, thinking about Luke, worried about him. She had a strange feeling that something was going to happen. Just like she'd had the morning Owen and Luke walked out of the lodge to go hunting. She was anxious, agitated, couldn't relax.

Delayna said, "The doctor gave me the physical, then he brought this floor lamp over so he could shine it down there and check out my goody-goody."

Luke wouldn't eat dinner last night or breakfast this morning. He walked out the door without saying a word. He got in his car and Kate watched him pull out of the driveway. Even though he was failing every course, she was glad he was still in school—out of his room—in the company of his friends for part of the day.

Delayna said, "He put the lamp between my legs and turned it on and the bulb was burned out. God was he embarrassed. I'm lying there naked while he takes the old bulb out and puts a new one in. After the exam, I heard him tell the nurse he hadn't used the lamp in six months." Delayna laughed. "Can you believe it?"

Kate didn't say anything. She had to get out of there.

Delayna said, "Are you okay?" She'd styled Kate's hair for years, knew her well and could sense something was wrong.

Kate sat up and said, "I've got to go."

"I haven't cut your hair yet," Delayna said.

Kate said, "I'm not feeling well," stood up and pulled off the burgundy smock and put it on the chair.

Delayna was concerned, didn't know what to do. She said, "Did I say something?"

Kate was conscious of people looking at her, customers and hairdressers, as she crossed the floor of the salon, hair dripping wet, and went through the waiting room out to her car.

On the way home she doubted herself. She couldn't explain what she was feeling, just like she couldn't the last time. Her blouse was soaked now from her wet hair. She looked at herself in the rearview mirror. Was she cracking up, losing her mind?

She parked in the driveway and opened the kitchen door and saw the message light on the phone flashing. There were two calls. She pushed play. The first one was from Helen Parks at Luke's school, saying he didn't show up for class and they would appreciate a phone call or Luke would receive a detention. The second message was from a Detective Simoff with the Bloomfield Hills Police, saying that Luke had been arrested and he needed to speak to Mr. or Mrs. McCall ASAP.

She drove to the station and bailed Luke out and brought him home. He was a mess—still drunk from the vodka he'd had hours before. She took him upstairs and put him in bed and let him sleep it off. It was two o'clock in the afternoon. At five she woke him up and told him to take a shower and come down.

They sat in the small paneled den, Kate on the leather couch and Luke, a few feet away in a leather chair, staring at the antique Heriz rug, telling her he'd had half a dozen vodka and lemonades, run a stop sign on his way to Tower Records and hit a seventy-eight-year-old woman broadside. He said he tried to get away, but his car wouldn't start, the hood of his Volkswagen Jetta buckled, steam hissing out of the radiator.

"You hit a woman and hurt her and you were just going to leave?" Kate shook her head. This was hard to understand.

Luke didn't say anything, he just stared at the rug.

"Look at me," Kate said raising her voice.

He lifted his head, met her gaze. No expression.

"Say something."

He glanced down at the floor again.

Detective Simoff told her a police officer had arrived a couple of minutes after the accident. So did an EMS unit. The woman, Mrs. Decker, was taken to Royal Oak Beaumont Hospital. Luke, after he was breathalyzed and handcuffed, was taken to the police station, everybody wanting to know what a sixteen-year-old kid was doing on the road in broad daylight with a blood alcohol level that was almost twice the legal limit.

Kate did, too. She said, "What'd you do, wake up and decide to get smashed?"

"No."

"Well, you're on a hell of a roll. Do me a favor, will you? Tell me what you're going to do next, so I can be ready."

"I'm not going to do anything," Luke said.

He had his hand over his face like he was trying to hide.

She said, "You better not. You're in enough trouble as it is." She told him he had been charged with an MIP, minor in possession of alcohol. He'd be given a court date and would be on probation for a year. He'd have to do community service and attend alcohol awareness classes.

She told him his driver's license was restricted and he would have to submit to random alcohol testing. She told him he would have to report to a probation officer once a month and that he might have to spend time in the Oakland County Jail.

He looked stunned.

She got up and went over and put her arms around him.

"I'm sorry," Luke said.

He had tears in his eyes.

"I'll help you," Kate said. "We'll get through this. Just promise me you won't do anything else."

"I won't," Luke said in a voice that was barely audible.

He dried his eyes on his shirtsleeve.

She hoped not.

DeJuan was in the woods behind the house when he saw the Land Rover fly in, screech to a stop. Somebody in a hurry. Rich lady got out, ran in the side door. Not two minutes later she ran back out. Fired up the Rover, blew down the driveway.

He parked Scarface at Covington School, went across an athletic field, hopped a fence, walked through yards from there to McCall's, no one give him a second look. DeJuan in his dark blue DTE Energy uniform, carrying his meter reader.

His first instinct was to go stealth—under the radar. But when he went to check out the 'hood, saw a DTE truck and a sister, woman of color, walking through yards, reading meters, and a bulb went on in his head.

Now he was in the backyard of their French provincial manor home designed by some dude name Wallace Frost in 1926. Googled it. House had a slate roof. Leaded glass windows. Had a pool out back—still covered in late May. Tennis court. Gardens. It was some spread. Kind of crib DeJuan hoped to have someday.

He was on the side of the house in plain view when Mrs. Mc-Call drove in again, got out with the kid. Something going on. Could feel the tension between them. DeJuan wondering what the little man done to upset his moms. Thinking of a statistic he read. Something like: every ten seconds in America, some kid was fucking with his parents.

Rich lady glanced over at him on her way in the house. He waved, said, "How you all doing today?"

Kate went to see Luke's psychiatrist. She paced back and forth in front of Dr. Fabick's maroon leather couch, stopping over without an appointment, telling the receptionist she had to see him.

Fabick was wearing jeans, running shoes, and a white shirt and tie, sitting behind his desk, solemn eyes fixed on Kate, thumbs and fingertips pressed together, giving her his concerned psychiatrist look.

"Mrs. McCall, what Luke tells me in these sessions is confidential. It's how we build trust—"

Kate cut in. "He's in trouble. He needs help."

"Mrs. McCall, if you'd let me finish," Fabick said. "I also told Luke if he tries to harm himself that confidentiality would be compromised. Please sit down."

Kate sat in one of the chairs in front of his desk. "Tell me why he's drinking."

"Luke is trying to escape, withdraw. What he experienced was traumatic. His destructive behavior is a way of lashing out. He's angry. He's carrying this tremendous guilt, and doing what he did today is his way of punishing himself. He's reliving what happened over and over."

"How is he going to get better?"

"Therapy. I wouldn't discount the likelihood of long-term psychological effects. It could take years for Luke to resolve his feelings."

"Tell me something positive," Kate said. "Will you?"

"In our last session," Fabick said, "I was encouraged. I thought Luke was making progress. But it's not unusual in this kind of a situation for the patient to take a step forward and then take two steps back. That's exactly what I think has happened."

"What does that mean?" Kate wanted to grab his tie and pull him over the desk.

"He's regressing, getting worse."

"No kidding," Kate said. "How'd you figure that out?"

She got up and walked out of his office, wondering what the hell to do now.

Twelve

Kate studied her face in the makeup mirror. She followed the curve of her mouth, putting on lipstick, a dark red shade, pressed her lips together to make it even. She opened her mouth and checked her teeth, rubbing off a fleck of color with a Kleenex. Now she dusted her cheekbones with blush and stroked on a little under her eyes.

Jack had called that morning and invited her out to dinner. She told him she couldn't but then, in a moment of weakness, invited him over. She felt bad the way she treated him at lunch, giving him a hard time after sixteen years. Maybe he had cleaned up his act. When he told her about his real estate job, he was enthusiastic and sounded like he knew what he was talking about.

Now, five hours later, she regretted it and wanted to call it off. She tried the number Jack had given her, heard Jodie's voice on the answering machine and hung up. She was just going to have to get through it.

Kate thought about the night they met: at Jacoby's, after a Tigers game. They were standing next to each other at the crowded bar, Kate trying to get the bartender's attention. They started talking and hit it off—both on dates. Kate out with a guy named Bert Hulgrave who went to Notre Dame and wore a golf shirt with the collar turned up in back, which bothered her, and he ate hot-dogs with nothing on them—no mustard—which bothered her more.

Jack asked for her phone number. She gave it to him while she waited for a pint of Harp for her and a Miller Lite for Bert and was excited when Jack called that night at two in the morning, saying he couldn't wait to talk to her.

Kate told him guys usually held off for a few days—what was the rule, seventy-two hours?—so they didn't seem too interested or desperate.

He said he didn't care about bullshit like that and they talked till four thirty and met seven hours later at the hydroplane races on Belle Isle. He kissed her as soon as he saw her and said, "I've wanted to do that since I turned and looked at you in the bar last night."

Kate said, "Do you hold anything back?"

He said, "I try not to."

They watched Tom D'Eath pilot *Miss Budweiser* through the course on the Detroit River, had a beer and went back to Kate's and made out, both of them anxious to hold and touch each other, like they were meant to be together.

Kate was nineteen when she met Jack, going to be a sopho-more at Michigan. They dated the rest of the summer and when she went back to Ann Arbor, sharing an apartment with Stephie, her freshman roommate, Jack would spend four or five nights a week there. They were inseparable for two and a half years until Kate knew she had to get away from him and joined the Peace Corps.

Now he was back and she was concerned. She liked it but didn't like it.

Maureen came in the kitchen with her coat on. "God, it smells good in here. Don't worry, I'm not going to stay, I just want to meet him."

Kate looked up from the skillet of potatoes. "You're going to scare him away."

"I won't say anything to embarrass you," Maureen said. "I promise."

"You can't help yourself."

Maureen took off her coat and hung it on the back of a chair on the other side of the counter. Kate poured her a glass of white wine.

"What're you having?"

"Rack of lamb." She'd seared the rack in shallot butter and deglazed the pan with veal stock. Now she was making potatoes Anna, the skillet sizzling on the gas burner. "He's just coming over for dinner and I feel guilty about it."

"What're you going to do, wear a black dress for the rest of your life? We're not living in a Sicilian village. There's no time limit I'm aware of. You wait till you're ready. I think it's great."

"It's not a date," Kate said. "Nothing's going on."

"Whatever you say," Maureen said grinning.

Jack arrived and Luke came down from his bedroom and Kate introduced everyone. They ate in the breakfast room. Kate sat across the table from Luke and Maureen, half in the bag, sat across from Jack, firing questions at him while he ate his lamb and potatoes and sipped his cabernet.

Maureen said, "Ever been married?"

"No," Jack said. He picked up a lamb chop and took a bite.

Maureen said, "Ever been close?"

Jack said, "No." And shook his head.

Maureen said, "You have a girlfriend?"

"Not at the moment," Jack said.

Maureen said, "You're not gay, are you?"

Jack looked at Kate.

Kate said, "Maureen, stop interrogating the poor guy."

Maureen pointed at Jack with her fork. "What're you doing back in Michigan?"

"Visiting my sister," Jack said.

Maureen said, "What do you do?"

"Sell real estate," Jack said.

"Maureen does, too," Kate said. "Tell her about your deal."

"It's a manufactured home development in Tucson, Arizona," Jack said.

"I know a lot of people in the Tucson area," Maureen said. "Maybe I can send some investors your way. What's it called?"

"Eldorado Estates," Jack said. "I'll give you a copy of the prospectus."

"And you live in Tucson, I hear," Maureen said. "What part?"

"Rancho Mirage," Jack said.

"Where's that?" Kate said.

"Foothills of the Catalinas," Maureen said. "Very trendy." She sipped her wine. "I go to Canyon Ranch every year," she said, sounding like a snob. "I saw Michael Douglas one time and Richard Gere. I like it for about three days. They don't serve drinks—you can't get one—and there's no nightlife."

"That's the idea," Kate said. "You go there to get healthy."

"I bring a bottle of Skyy," Maureen said, "have a couple in my room before dinner and try to meet an eligible guy and bring him back for a nightcap."

Luke sat with them, eating in silence, Jack asking him questions whenever Maureen stopped talking, which wasn't often.

Jack said, "Luke, you a tennis player like your mom?"

"Uh-huh."

Kate said, "He has a big forehand and a two-handed backhand. Hits deep heavy topspin and has a hundred-and-ten-mile-an-hour serve." She looked across the table at Luke. "He's taking some time off, aren't you, honey?"

Luke didn't react. He seemed uncomfortable. He ate fast and asked if he could be excused. Took his plate to the sink and walked out of the kitchen.

Maureen got up, too, said she had an early appointment, told Jack it was nice meeting him and Kate walked her to the door.

Then they were alone.

Jack cleared the table and Kate did the dishes. She was at the sink, her back to him, rinsing out the wineglasses when he came up behind her, put his arms around her waist and kissed her neck.

She squirmed, wiggling out of his grasp, wet hands pushing him away. "Easy."

"I've wanted to do that since I saw you at the mall."

"Where've I heard that before?" She wondered how many times he'd used that line or a variation of it.

"I don't know what you're talking about," Jack said.

"That's what you said the morning after we met—at the boat races."

"How do you remember that?"

"I thought it was a good line," Kate said, "like it was out of a movie."

She showed him the house. They walked through the living room to the sun porch. The backyard lights were on, illuminating the pool and tennis court. It was dark out, wind blowing, kicking up leaves.

Jack said, "That Maureen's a trip."

"That's one way to put it."

"What's her story?"

"How much time do you have?"

She showed him the paneled den, her favorite room and the reason she wanted to buy the house.

"This place is unbelievable," Jack said.

"Not bad for a girl who grew up on Spam, huh?"

"Luke's a nice kid," Jack said. "I feel like I've met him before. He ever spend time in Tucson?"

"You're not going to start talking about fate and kismet again, are you?"

He moved closer to her and she stepped away. "I've got something else I want to show you." She took him to the billiard room, thinking it would be easier being with him if they had something to do.

Jack said, "Wow. Look at that."

There was a 1922 Brunswick Arcade pool table in the center of the room. It was made out of mahogany with six massive legs and weighed 2,760 pounds.

Kate said, "You want to play?"

Jack said, "It's been a while."

Kate said, "Are you hustling me?"

There was a cue rack on the wall. He went over and picked out a stick. He chalked the tip and grinned at her. "If I win, you let me buy you dinner tomorrow night."

She said, "What if I win?"

"You buy me dinner."

They played straight pool. Jack racked the balls and broke with a thunderous blast that put a couple in. He lined up a straight two-footer and banged it in the corner pocket. He kissed the second one in the middle pocket. She could see a swagger in his step now as he moved around the table. He sank six before he missed.

"You're not bad," Kate said.

Jack glanced at her and said, "What do you hear from Marina? Wasn't that the girl from Guatemala?"

"I get a Christmas card every year," Kate said. "She lives in Jersey with her husband, Benigno, who now owns the landscape company he used to work for."

Kate used the bridge and banked one into the corner pocket.

Jack said, "The American dream, huh?"

Kate was lining up her next shot. She glanced at Jack across the table. "You making fun of him?"

"No," Jack said. "She ever tell him about the cop?"

"I hope not." She drilled one into the side pocket.

"What was his name?"

"Emiliano Garza," Kate said. "Are you trying to distract me?"

"Still remember him, huh?"

Kate put her cue on the rail and leaned against the table. "I can still see his face staring at me. I used to wake up in the middle of the night, I'd swear I saw him standing at the end of my bed, grinning at me."

"You never gave me the full story," Jack said.

"I couldn't talk about it at the time," Kate said.

"How about now?"

She told him how she shot the two cops.

Jack didn't say anything. He just stared at her.

"The scariest part," Kate said, "was when we were on the bus, sitting there waiting to leave. Marina had the seat next to the window. She was grinning. We both were thinking we were getting away. Then a green Jeep pulled up next to the bus—*Policia* on the side. Captain Garza and two others got out.

"You should have seen the look on Marina's face. She was

scared to death. She turned to me and slid down in her seat. I reached into my bag and pulled out the Beretta and showed it to her. She said, 'What are you going to do?'

"I said, 'Whatever I have to.' I was thinking that they must have found the dead cops, or maybe the Jeep?"

Jack said, "How'd they know you were on the bus?"

She picked up the cue stick and put the butt end on the floor and leaned it against the long side of the table. "Unless you had a car," Kate said, "it was the only way out of town. I watched Captain Garza moving along the side of the bus, looking in the windows, smoking his cigar. He had an automatic in a black holster on his right hip. As he approached our window, we got up and offered our seats to an elderly Mayan couple Marina knew, the Olivares. Marina stood next to me in the crowded aisle, fighting for space as Garza's men got on the bus, one entering from the front and the other from the rear, yelling and pushing their way down the aisle.

"When they got within ten feet, I drew the Beretta and cocked the hammer. I turned my back as one of the cops approached. I could feel my heart pounding. I was ready to turn and shoot him, but he passed by me.

"They weren't looking for us. The cops grabbed a short thin Mayan who looked young, no more than twenty. They took him off the bus and tried to cuff his hands and he broke free and took off running across the dusty parking lot. People on the bus were cheering for him, hoping he'd get away.

"I watched Captain Garza draw the pistol from his holster, aim at the man, extending his arm and firing. The man staggered and fell forward in the dirt.

"I could see Garza standing by the Jeep as the bus pulled away. I released the hammer and dropped the Beretta back in my bag and put my arms around Marina. I remember the day; I'll remember it forever—San Pedro, Guatemala, August 11, 1990."

Jack came around the table and stood next to her.

"My god," he said. "I had no idea."

He put his arms around her and tried to kiss her.

Kate said, "Cool it, will you?" Hands on his chest, pushing him away.

"What's the matter?"

She pictured Owen watching her and said, "You should probably go."

"Yeah," he said. "What am I doing? It's got to be nine thirty, quarter to ten. I've got to go home, get to bed."

Luke watched part of *Spider-Man 2*. He was tired and he'd seen it four times. He pushed the power button on the remote and the screen went black. He bunched up his pillow and put his head down and closed his eyes. Leon was next to him, crowding him, so he moved over a couple inches. He heard the clock on the bedside table, ticking. Then he heard voices. He got out of bed and went to the window and looked down. Jack and his mom were on the driveway. Jack put his arms around her and Luke felt sick to his stomach. What was going on? His mom said they were old friends. It looked to Luke like more than that. He went back to bed, but he couldn't sleep.

Thirteen

The next morning, Jodie gave him a ride to the airport. Jack had told her he was leaving, catching an early flight back to Tucson to find a job. Nobody was hiring in Detroit. It was 6:30 a.m. when she dropped him off at the terminal. She parked at the curb, turned in her seat and locked her gaze on him.

"I guess I'll see you in four years."

That was how long it had been since she'd last seen him; Jodie being funny.

"Stay straight, Jackie, will you please? For me, if not for yourself."

Jack said, "My bad-boy days are over."

"You're a good person. You've got so much to offer. Get a job like the rest of us and make something of yourself."

Problem was, he wasn't like most people. He'd never be able to hold a job and play it straight. He thanked Jodie for everything, leaned over, kissed her on the cheek. He got out and opened the back door and pulled his knapsack out of the backseat. Jodie waved through the window and he waved back.

He went in the terminal, took the escalator to the second floor, read the signs, and went left looking for long-term parking. He walked behind the first row of cars. There was a cool breeze, wind whipping through the parking structure. He heard a jet, saw it through an opening in the parking deck and watched it take off.

A dark SUV approached and crept past him, looking for a parking space. He studied the nameplates on the cars, stopping at a Mercedes E500. He went around the car, checked to see if the doors were locked. They were. Checked the frame under the driver's door but didn't find what he was looking for. He moved down the row to a Cadillac Escalade, did the same thing again. No luck.

There was a green Lexus 430 in the next row. He walked around it and checked all the obvious hiding places and found a yellow magnetic box covered with road scum attached to the frame under the rear bumper. He pried it open and there was a spare key. He unlocked the door, threw his knapsack on the front passenger seat, and got in behind the wheel. The parking ticket was in a cup holder in the console.

He'd learned this trick in the early days of stealing cars. Keeping a spare key somewhere sounded like a good idea, but it was almost as dumb as going into a store for a pack of cigarettes and leaving your car running. Or parking in a bank lot and going in to use the ATM—it'll only take a minute—and leaving the keys in the ignition.

Best place to find the car you were looking for was to stake out a sporting event, movie theater, or airport. What he also did— and it took a little longer this way—was find a car he wanted at an upscale mall or market and follow the person home. He'd break in the next day, find the spare keys and boost the car. That way, it was nice and clean. Better than pulling the lock barrel out of the door with pliers or breaking a window. You didn't have to worry about car alarms, either.

Jack had worked for a guy named Torcellini, a Sicilian from Palermo who came over to Detroit when he was sixteen and still carried a switchblade in his zippered black boot. Torce, a fan of westerns, had a pencil-thin mustache and sideburns and wore a black Stetson and a duster. He thought he looked like Lee Van Cleef of spaghetti-western fame. "What do you think?" he'd say to Jack with a mean look on his face, the Stetson low over his eyes and Jack would say, "Yeah, I can see it."

Torce would give him a list of cars he needed, and Jack would find them and bring them in. He got $1,500 for a late-model high-end ride. Cash on the spot. Some weeks he made $9,000. Not bad for a twenty-two-year-old whose friends were trying to scrape together enough money to buy a six-pack.

Torce had chop shops around Detroit where they could strip a car down to its frame in six hours. If it had a blue book value of $20,000, they could strip it and sell the parts for $32,000, or more.

Or he'd boost a car, bring it to the shop, and they'd strip it clean and drop the shell on a street somewhere. The police would find it and tell the owner, who'd tell the insurance company, who'd sell it at auction to try to recoup some money. Torce's guys would buy the shell at auction, put the stripped parts back on it and sell it as a used car. It was beautiful.

They also shipped high-end Benzes, Bimmers, Caddies and Jags to buyers in Latin America and the Middle East. That's how Jack met Teddy and DeJuan. They all worked for Torce, until the operation got busted—Torce and fifty-six others arrested in a raid conducted by a joint task force of the Detroit Police and the FBI.

Jack had just stolen a Benz S600 from the Somerset Mall. He was outside Nordstrom. Watched the valet run to get a car and walked over to the curb when the Benz pulled in, an annoying guy on a cell phone, telling him to be careful, saying the car cost more than he'd make in four years.

Jack said, "Don't worry, I'll keep an eye on it for you," and he did.

When he got to the chop shop, an old brick warehouse on St. Antoine, it was surrounded by police cars, light bars flashing. He could see the Ren Cen, now the GM building, in the distance. Teddy pulled up behind him in a black Town Car. They decided it might be a good time to leave town, figuring someone would dime them for a plea, human nature being what it was—the urge to protect one's own ass overriding any sense of honor or loyalty.

Jack cruised out of the parking deck in the green Lexus, hands on the varnished wood steering wheel, engine so quiet, it didn't sound like it was running. He stopped at the booth, paid the parking fee with the fifty he'd borrowed from his sister, and drove to Kate's.

"Luke, I'm leaving," he heard his mom call up the stairs. "Are you sure you have a ride to school?"

Luke yelled, "Positive," from the upstairs hall.

It was 7:45. He didn't have a class on Friday till 8:30. He stood at his bedroom window and watched her pull out of the driveway. Luke stuffed clothes in a backpack, grabbed his iPod and went downstairs to the kitchen. The keys to his dad's Corvette weren't in the drawer where they usually were. His mom probably hid them somewhere. He checked her desk in the den, didn't see them. He went upstairs to her dressing room. His dad's clothes were gone, his side of the dressing area, cleaned out. Why'd she get rid of his clothes? Was she trying to forget him?

He found the car keys in her jewelry box. Slid them in the pocket of his jeans and went back down to the kitchen.

He heard a car and saw a green Lexus drive up and park. He saw Jack get out and come to the door, press his face against one of the glass panes. Knocking and then opening the door and coming in. What was he doing here?

Luke went through the dining room and circled around to the front of the house, hiding in the front hall closet, door cracked open half an inch. He heard Jack walk in from the kitchen, cowboy boots clicking on the slate floor. He stood at the bottom of the stairs and looked up. "Anybody home? Kate . . . ?"

Luke watched him go into the den, but couldn't see what he was doing.

Kate told him she had a dentist appointment at eight and knew Luke would be at school, so no one would be home. He sat behind Kate's antique desk, staring at her checkbook. He'd seen it the night before on the house tour. He was desperate for money and decided to write a check for a thousand dollars to hold him over.

Jack felt odd taking money from her, but then thought about Guatemala. How much did it cost him to get Kate and her friend back? Five grand—at least. She owed him. He made the check out to cash and traced Kate's signature from a letter he found in one of the drawers. It wasn't that difficult.

He stared at the check and for the first time in four years, Jack was feeling good about himself. Things were falling into place. He was as close to being rich as he'd ever been.

Leon came down the stairs now, stopped, sniffed the air and wandered over to the closet. Luke trying to get rid of him, "Leon, get out of here," saying it under his breath. "Go on." He pulled the door closed and Leon yelped and barked.

Jack saw the dog and called him. "Here, boy. What're you doing over there, huh?"

Luke cracked the door and Leon was sitting there, tail wagging, tongue hanging out, drooling, eyes fixed on Luke.

He heard Jack's boots on the slate floor again coming across the foyer toward them. "What're you doing?"

Luke could see him coming toward the closet.

"Something in there you want?"

Luke stepped back into the darkness, kneeling behind some boxes.

"Boy, want a treat?" Jack said. "Does the big man want a treat?"

He could see Jack heading for the kitchen, and Leon, to Luke's surprise, was following him.

Luke went through the living room to the sun porch, unlocked the door and went outside, moving along the back of the house to the kitchen. He looked in the window, saw Jack open the refrigerator, helping himself to leftover lamb chops, eating meat off the bone and throwing Leon scraps.

Ten minutes later Jack got in his car and left, Luke wondering what was going on, this old friend of his mother's coming in their house like that.

———

Jack cashed the check at the Chase branch at Cranbrook and Maple. He didn't have an account, but he flirted with the teller, a mousy little thing and she said she'd make an exception and he said, "Thanks, darling." Then he drove back to Kate's to wait for her.

Fourteen

Kate could feel a tingling in her jaw, the first indication that the Novocain was wearing off. She'd had a cavity in a back tooth filled, her dentist, Dr. Hanson, giving her two shots of Novocain, saying he had to drill pretty deep and didn't want to take any chances.

She drove in the garage and noticed the Corvette was gone and couldn't believe it. Thinking about what she said to Luke and how she said it. "Don't drive. Don't even think about it. You've got a restricted license. If the police stop you, they're going to put you in jail. And don't go anywhere unless you ask me first." What didn't he understand about that? She even hid the keys. He said he was going to straighten up and stay out of trouble. He wasn't going to use Owen's death as an excuse anymore.

Jack was sitting at the breakfast room table reading the paper, drinking a Coke, when she walked in the kitchen. It bothered her to see him in the house, reminding her of how he used to show up at her apartment in Ann Arbor. She'd come home from class, he'd be watching TV or taking a shower, like he owned the place.

Kate said, "Make yourself at home," an edge to her voice. "Can I get you anything?"

"I thought I'd surprise you."

"You did," Kate said. She didn't need this right now.

There were half-eaten lamb chops on a plate in front of him.

Jack said, "You don't mind, do you? The door was unlocked."

Kate said, "Have you seen Luke?"

The message light on the phone was flashing.

"No," Jack said.

"How long have you been here?"

"Half hour," Jack said. "You all right?"

She could see he was concerned. She moved to the counter, pressed the message button on the phone and heard Helen Parks's snippy voice say, "Mrs. McCall, Luke has failed to show up for school again. This is Mrs. Parks, please call as soon as you can."

Kate picked up the phone, called Luke's cell, heard his voice say, "This is Luke, leave a message."

Where was he?

Jack said, "There a problem?"

"I don't know."

She checked the den, the billiard room, the family room, walked through the living room to the sun porch, Jack behind her, crowding her. She went upstairs, looked in his bedroom. Leon was on the bed, but Luke wasn't there or anywhere in the house. Where would he go? All his friends were in school.

"Listen," Kate said to Jack, "I've got to go out for a while."

"What's going on?"

"I'll tell you later."

She could see Jack in the rearview mirror as she pulled out, Jack walking down the driveway toward the street, wondering, no doubt, what had happened. He'd asked if he could go with her and she said no. There was a Lexus sedan parked in front, Kate assuming the car was Jack's. It was the only one around. Last time he came over he was driving his sister's eight-year-old Chevy Cavalier. Where did he get a seventy-thousand-dollar Lexus? Did he buy it or borrow it—or steal it? Her distrust of him creeping back to the surface. She drove to Tower Records at the mall, one of Luke's favorite stores. She'd start there and then try the arcade.

DeJuan was checking her out—good-looking woman—as she walked through the record store moving fast, glancing around like she was looking for something. He'd followed her from the house. She lived half a mile from Marty, other side of Sixteen Mile Road, also called Big Beaver. He'd like to check her beaver out, imagined it waxed and trimmed, little arrow of fur pointing up at her knocks.

He liked the 'hood called the Village, with its nice wide streets and big houses set back a couple hundred feet from the road—lot of property between the cribs, so nobody snoopin' on nobody else's shit.

He was checking out a Mony Karlo CD—*For the Luv of Money*—DeJuan thinking, did this brother get it done? He most definitely got it done. DeJuan took his eyes off her for a minute and when he glanced back she was walking out the store— moving fast. He caught up to her at the escalator, riding down to the first floor. Waited while she went in an arcade. Came out, went to the parking structure, got in the Land Rover, while he got in his Malibu, tailing her back to her place, trying to stay close as she hit seventy on Sixteen Mile.

He watched her pull in the driveway and parked a couple houses away. Listening to an interview with Barack. Man was smooth as silk. Articulate, black US senator, scaring the shit out of white folks, saying he considering making a run for the presidency. DeJuan thinking, yeah, bring some rhythm and soul to the party.

Land Rover appeared five minutes later, blowing down the driveway. DeJuan firing up the Malibu, slipping it in gear, taking off. Twenty minutes later he passed a sign that said "Clarkston," traveling north on I-75, doing ninety-five, trying to keep up with her. Wondering where the bitch was headed. Thought it'd be an afternoon of errands and shit. Check out the mall while she shopped. Once she got somewhere, call Teddy; tell him to make his move. But it didn't happen like that, and thirty minutes later he was driving through Flint—asshole of the Midwest—wondering what the fuck was going on. To make things more interesting, he had just under half a tank of gas and there was no end in sight to this crazy-ass odyssey.

Then it hit him. He looked at himself in the rearview mirror and grinned. Sure, it had to be that. Bitch was going to the discount mall. Could buy ten of anything she wanted, but couldn't resist the idea of a deal. Like she taking advantage of somebody.

He remembered his moms, aunt and cousins driving from Detroit to someplace called West Branch, DeJuan and four ladies in an old Cadillac Deville, yakking, going on about girl shit, going up north for a day of shopping, listening to the Shirelles singing "Dedicated to the One I Love"—the memory coming back to him as he saw the West Branch sign and passed it.

Forty minutes after that, he was following her through Grayling, running on fumes when she pulled into a gas station. Big place had ten pumps, all of them taken except for the last one, place crowded with SUVs and RVs, big forty-foot-long motherfuckers.

He parked on the other side of the pump from her, filling his Malibu while she filled her Land Rover, catching glimpses of her, finally making eye contact, saying, "Yo, know where Traverse City at?"

"Follow 72," she said, extending her arm and pointing to the left. She seemed wound up, tense, like something on her mind.

He filled his tank and went inside the mini-mart and paid. Bought two chocolate doughnuts with sprinkles and a large coffee. When he came out, the Land Rover was gone. He scanned the lot—saw it pulling out of the station, going left. He dropped the doughnuts and coffee and ran to his car and got in. He had to wait for an RV to get the fuck out of his way. Floored it, jerked the steering wheel, tires squealing, blew out of the gas station parking lot, took a left, picking up speed, cruising now along the I-75 bypass, fast-food restaurants lining the road on both sides, reminding him how hungry he was. DeJuan picturing a platter of chicken wings smothered in hickory brown-sugar barbecue sauce, wash it all down with a 7&7 or a Cuba libre with a big slice of lime. Hadn't eaten anything all day, starving now at three thirty in the afternoon.

He thought for sure he'd lost her, thinking what a waste of time his day had been when he saw a silver Land Rover parked in a vacant lot next to a Mickey D's. He drove in the D's lot, went around the building, parked with a good angle on her, facing out.

What she doing, sitting there? Then the door opened and the dog jumped out. He watched it sniff around, do its business, while he sat there smelling meat cooking, starving, stomach groaning, making noises.

He took out his cell phone, called Teddy. "Yo, Theo, what's up?" It was a bad connection, a lot of static.

Teddy said, "I can barely hear you. Where the hell you at?"

"Ain't going to believe where I'm at."

On the way home from the mall, Kate had gotten an idea. The Corvette had OnStar. They could do a satellite check and tell her where it was. She called and talked to a patient customer rep with a nice voice; saying the Corvette was missing and asked if they could locate it.

The rep, whose name was Amy, told Kate the Vette was on Highway 72 just west of Kalkaska. Luke, it seemed, was heading back up to the lodge, which surprised her. It was the last place she would've expected him to go. She had an odd feeling, her stomach nervous, uneasy now. What was he planning to do? She called Dr. Fabick, the psychiatrist. The receptionist said he was on vacation in Europe. He'd be out of the office for ten days.

Kate said, "How can I reach him?"

The receptionist said she couldn't. He was on an airplane headed for Paris. She called the Leelanau Sheriff's Department and asked for Bill Wink. She said it was important and the deputy who answered the phone—she couldn't remember his name—said he'd get in touch with Bill and have him call her.

Kate drove home, packed a bag, put Leon in the car and took off. She was on I-75 passing Pine Knob when her cell phone rang. It was Wink. She told him the situation. He said he'd go out to the lodge and keep an eye on Luke till she got there. No problem. Bill and Owen had been friends. Fished together occasionally, and although Kate didn't know him all that well, she thought there was enough of a connection to ask for Bill personally.

She stopped for gas in Grayling, then let Leon sniff around, take care of business. It was now three thirty in the afternoon. She hadn't eaten since breakfast, but she wasn't hungry. Her stomach was churning. Cutting through town, she passed a convoy of military vehicles with camo paint schemes. National Guard troops wearing camo fatigues and helmets, on maneuvers heading back to Camp Grayling, glancing at her as she drove by in her silver Land Rover with twenty-inch rims.

Then she was on two-lane 72 driving behind an RV, and it reminded her of the time Owen pulled up in the driveway in a thirty-eight-foot Winnebago Adventurer, with its dizzying three-tone exterior, a look of excitement on his face.

He said, "Do you believe this?"

No, Kate wanted to say, but she couldn't talk, one of the few times in her life she'd been speechless.

"Let me give you the tour."

He opened the door and they went inside, Owen giving what sounded like a sales pitch: "The interior's a color called Caspian blue with washed maple cabinets—beautiful, isn't she?"

Kate wondering at the time why he referred to this RV behemoth in the feminine gender.

Owen said, "She was handcrafted by the Winnebago artisans in Forest Lake, Iowa, and has got all the comforts of home: flat-screen TV, home theater sound system, queen-size bed, and gourmet kitchen. What do you think?"

"Why don't you use it for the Cup season?" Kate said.

"You don't like it?"

"I'm not an RV person."

That was it. He understood and wasn't offended and never mentioned it again.

Kate slowed to twenty behind an eighteen-wheeler and a pickup towing dirt bikes. Why was Luke going back up, risking everything? She wouldn't let herself think about it before. Now she couldn't think about anything else. According to Dr. Fabick, he'd been severely depressed since the accident. She knew that, but didn't know how bad he was until the arrest. What did Fabick say? Luke was reliving the trauma over and over. But there had to be more to it. Why would he disobey her and take the car with all the trouble he was in? It seemed desperate. What was he planning to do? Was he going to kill himself? Now that was the only thing that made sense and Kate was frantic. She pictured Luke with her Smith & Wesson Airweight, putting the barrel against his head and she pressed down on the accelerator, gunned it around the semi, and then took chances, passing two and three vehicles at a time, forcing an oncoming pickup truck to slow down and let her in, horns honking at her questionable moves.

She made good time through Suttons Bay, passed the casino in Peshawbestown, the Leelanau Sands, going eighty up the western shore of Grand Traverse Bay, the water turquoise where it was shallow and turning dark blue where it got deep— nineteen miles to Northport and then ten minutes more to Cathead Bay.

Bill Wink's white patrol car was parked next to Owen's Corvette on the gravel drive outside the lodge. She let out a breath, relieved. She went in and heard explosions and lasers, watching them for a minute: Bill and Luke, with PlayStation controllers in their hands, faces animated, Bill looking like an overgrown kid in his brown uniform. He glanced at Kate, put the controller on the coffee table in front of him, grabbed his hat and stood up. He found the crease; fit the hat on his head.

"Luke, I've got to run," he said. "We'll finish it another time."

Bill Wink moved toward Kate now and when he got close, she said, "I'll walk you out."

They were on the gravel drive when he said, "Luke seems fine to me. He was playing *Halo* when I got here. It's a video game."

"That much I know," Kate said. "I really appreciate you coming out, keeping an eye on him for me."

"Anything else you need," Bill said, "give me a call, I'm serious." He grinned and took his hat off and got in the car, closed the door and put his window down.

Kate didn't know him that well and wondered if he was coming on to her.

"I have an idea," Bill said. "Think Luke would want to go out on patrol with me, see a real cop in action?"

It sounded like he was kidding but his tone was serious—a real cop in action. "I'm sure he'd like that, Bill."

He grinned. "Take her easy."

She watched him roll down the driveway, tires crunching on the gravel. The trees had their leaves and the sky was still bright at five o'clock, staying light longer as the season changed, heading toward summer, but it sure was cold. She felt a breeze blowing in from the lake and pulled her coat closed. Leon barked and chased a squirrel across the yard into the woods.

Luke was in the kitchen when she went back inside. He took a Coke out of the refrigerator and faced her. They stared at each other, Kate hoping he'd give her something—some reasonable explanation at the very least.

Kate said, "You promised me you weren't going to do anything else."

"I had to come back," Luke said.

"Why didn't you tell me?"

He pulled the tab on the can and took a drink.

Kate said, "What are you doing here?"

"I don't know," Luke said.

"You came back up here, but you don't know why?"

Luke looked down at the floor.

"You're not supposed to drive," Kate said. "You're not supposed to leave town."

"I don't care."

Kate decided not to say anything else. She was glad he was all right.

Luke said, "Why'd you call the sheriff? What'd you think I was going to do?"

"Nothing would surprise me the way things have been going." She was angry and wanted him to know it.

Luke's face tightened and he turned and walked out of the kitchen. She heard the back door close and moved through the lodge to the big picture window. She could see him heading down toward the lake. She went outside, walked to the end of the yard, stood on the bluff and watched him—regretting what she'd said—Luke on the beach skipping stones across the flat dark surface of Lake Michigan.

She couldn't believe how much their lives had changed in the past seven months. She was worried about Luke, but maybe this was a blessing in disguise. It was just the two of them now. She could spend time with him and try to help him.

DeJuan parked on the side of the highway, left Scarface on the gravel shoulder and walked—had to be a mile—through the woods. It was cold, too, freezing in his Fubu jersey and Sean John denims. Didn't have the right clothes on 'cause he didn't know he was going up north on vacation. His moms said his great-grandfather was Masai, lived in northern Tanzania in Africa. DeJuan looked it up. Masai were the dudes carry spears and herd cattle. Wore bright red cloaks. Young warrior called a *moran* had to go out, kill a lion with a spear. That's why DeJuan was freezing his ass off—'cause it don't get cold in northern Tanzania.

He could see the cabin through the trees now. Saw Mrs. Mc-Call talking to a sheriff's deputy in a brown uniform. It look like she knew him. They friends. DeJuan watched him get in the car and disappear down the driveway. Mrs. McCall went inside. But the dog was running around. Went in the woods and came up behind him, started barking. "Yo, pooch, be cool. Don't want no starving, skinny-ass black motherfucker."

He saw the kid come out of the cabin now, scan the front yard. "Leon . . . want a treat?"

Dog left DeJuan there, took off running.

DeJuan was so hungry he'd eat a dog biscuit right now. He moved through the woods to the side of the cabin. Could see Mrs. McCall and the kid—looked like they in the kitchen—having a heated conversation. He saw the kid walk out the room, then come out the back of the cabin. DeJuan followed him down to the water, look like the ocean, deep blue out to the horizon. Could see cottages way off—look like miles—in the distance on the other side of a long deserted stretch of beach. Nothing the other way, either.

At first DeJuan thought he going to have to call it off. But now he was thinking, wait a minute—this out-in-the-middle-of-nowhere location going to work out better.

Bill Wink was trying to think of a way to ask Kate out without being too obvious. Invite her to do something. Not make it sound like a date. Maybe include Luke, too. But, what?

He came to Woolsey Lake, took a right, passed a gold car parked on the side of the road. He didn't see anyone in it. He did a U-turn and drove up next to it—a 1980-something Chevy Malibu with a custom paint job and chrome alloys. He figured whoever was driving it ran out of gas or had car trouble. Lighthouse Point, the national park, was a mile or so down the road, and he guessed that's where it was heading. Person probably hitchhiked back to the Mobile station in Northport.

He backed up and stopped and punched the license number in his computer. The vehicle was registered to a DeJuan Green, who lived on Fourth Street in Royal Oak. He didn't check any further. His shift was over. He'd change, go into town and have a couple beers.

Fifteen

Luke listened to Wilco on his iPod, driving into town with his mother, turned the music up so he couldn't hear her, didn't have to talk to her. He liked "Hummingbird" on disc two; it was his favorite. He listened to it three times in a row, reminding him of "Mr. Blue Sky" by ELO. He saw a couple of deer as they drove on their private drive through the woods—almost a mile to the county road, and then passing cherry orchards on the way to Northport, trees blossoming with white flowers giving off a sweet smell.

They split up in town. His mom had to run some errands and he walked the street, stopped in a video arcade for a while, played a few games of *Mercenary Force* and then walked down to the lake. He could see the dark shape of a freighter creeping on the horizon, hull pointing south, heading for Chicago or Milwaukee.

He started to go back into town and saw Del's, an old log

building with a sign on the front that said "Hunting Outfitters since 1955." His dad used to take him there when he was younger.

Luke opened the door, went in, let it swing closed behind him and then it was quiet, not a sound. He stood looking at a wall of heads all staring at him—elk, caribou, whitetail, bighorn, pronghorn, antelope, boar, dik-dik, Kodiak blacktail—and more animals, their bodies stuffed and perched on the exposed log rafters: a fox, raccoon, badger. Across the room there was a seven-foot grizzly ready to attack, and next to it, a full-size polar bear with a king salmon in its claws.

From somewhere in the room, a voice said, "Dropped ever one of 'em with sticks and strings."

Now Del Keane appeared from some unseen place, a big man with a dense gray beard and gray hair combed straight back and tied into a braided ponytail that went halfway down his back, like a hippie version of Santa Claus. He wore suspenders over a flannel shirt.

Luke was staring at a deer head with a twelve-point rack.

"That fine gentleman," Del said, "was the Pope and Young world-record Kodiak black tail, November 1988. Put one through his wheelhouse, never knew what hit him. What's your name, boy?"

"Luke."

"You a hunter, Luke?"

"Not anymore."

"I'm Del Keane at your service, what can I do for you?"

"I don't know. Nothing, I guess." He was nervous, uncomfortable all of a sudden. He took a step toward the door and Del moved with him.

"You're Owen McCall's boy, ain't you?"

Del took a pipe out of his shirt pocket and lit it, blowing smoke that smelled like sweet cherrywood into the room.

"I better go," Luke said.

"Awful thing that happened," Del said. "Lost my own daddy when I was about your age."

He took the pipe out of his mouth, holding the bowl. He looked off across the room and then back at Luke. "Ever talk to him?"

Luke didn't know what to say.

"Your daddy," Del said. "Ever talk to him?"

"Mr. Keane, he's dead and buried." Luke moved closer to the door. He wanted to get away from this crazy old man.

"You've got to tell him what's on your mind."

Luke said, "I keep seeing him with that broadhead sticking out of his chest."

"Son, your daddy's not feeling any pain where he's at. Let me tell you something." He drew on the pipe and blew out a cloud of gray smoke. "What happened was an accident. Like I told you, go out to the woods, talk at him. Square things. I guarantee he's not blaming you. In fact, he's watching us right now, I'll bet. Up there with the likes of Art Young, Saxton Pope and my own daddy, Lester Keane.

"You tell him Del Keane says, hey. And get my room ready. I'll be joining him before too long."

"I've got to go," Luke said. He wanted to get out of there. He went through the door and let it slam behind him, walking fast and then running into town.

On the way back to the lodge, Kate looked over at Luke and said, "I saw you coming out of Del's. How's he doing?"

"He's weird," Luke said. "How old is he?"

"At least seventy, probably older." She went right, taking the highway out of Northport. There were cherry orchards on both sides of the road.

Luke said, "No wonder . . ."

Kate glanced at him. "What do you mean?"

"He was talking about dying."

"Something wrong with him?"

"He didn't say," Luke said.

"All I know is, he's a strange old guy," Kate said.

"And he doesn't shower much," Luke said, "I know that, too." He grinned big.

"Your dad used to say every six months, whether he needed it or not."

Luke grinned again. It had been a while since she'd seen him so relaxed, so animated, and it made her feel good, like he was his old self again. She wanted to hang on to this moment. Kate had always considered them close, good friends. He used to come home from school and tell her about something that happened in class—like the day they had a substitute teacher. Every time she turned her back to write on the board, everybody picked up their desk and moved it forward. Luke was laughing so hard he could barely tell it, describing the teacher's reactions as she wondered what was going on. He told her about chanting "Ohh-eee-ah! Ee *ohh*-ah!" from *The Wizard of Oz*. You could do it with your mouth closed, looking right at the teacher, and he'd freak 'cause he didn't know where it was coming from. He told her about Lauren, his first real girlfriend, admitting he liked her a lot and thought about her all the time and wondered if that was normal. They talked about music and movies and sports: tennis and the Detroit Tigers.

"Mr. Keane said his dad died when he was my age," Luke said. "At first I thought he was crazy, but what he said makes sense."

She glanced at him. "What did he say?"

They were passing Woolsey on the left, the world's smallest airport. Luke was turned toward her in his seat.

"I should talk to Dad. Go out in the woods and tell him what I think, what's on my mind."

Hearing it bothered her a little. This old coot with his back-woods psychology got through to Luke, made a positive impression with one conversation. Something a trained psychiatrist hadn't been able to do in almost seven months of sessions. Something she hadn't been able to do either. But if Del Keane's advice could help Luke, she was all for it.

When they pulled up in front of the lodge, Jack was there, leaning against the trunk of his car, a toothpick sticking out of his mouth. Luke looked over at her but didn't say anything. She couldn't read him, couldn't tell if Jack showing up bothered him or not. "I didn't invite him," Kate said. "If that's what you're thinking."

"It's okay, Mom," Luke said. He sounded normal, out of his funk for the first time in months. He got out of the Land Rover and went in the lodge.

"I decided I'd come up, take my chances," Jack said. "I got a motel room down the road in case you're worried."

Kate said, "How'd you know I was up here?"

"I called Maureen."

"That's right, she gave you a card, didn't she? She gives everyone her card. You want to come in and see the place?"

He followed her inside, standing in the main room that had to be fifty by fifty, varnished log walls, and a wood-plank floor partially covered by a large Oriental rug. There was a furniture grouping—couches and chairs and end tables and lamps—in front of a huge fieldstone fireplace you could walk into. There was a staircase that led up to the second level—and above that, a thirty-foot beamed cathedral ceiling supported by log trusses.

"The kitchen and breakfast room are over there," Kate said, pointing to the opposite side of the room.

He looked past the table and chairs into the kitchen. There was a stainless-steel industrial stove and Sub-Zero refrigerator-freezer. He liked it, big open floor plan.

Jack said, "How many bedrooms?"

"Four. All upstairs."

Kate took a check out of her purse and handed it to him. "I was going to give this to you earlier, but it slipped my mind. For your real estate deal."

Jack held it in his hand. Stared at it—fifty thousand.

"I couldn't remember the name of your company," Kate said.

"Eldorado Estates," Jack said.

"You can fill it in," Kate said. "I'm sure there will be some papers to sign, huh? You have them with you?"

Jack couldn't believe it. "Why'd you change your mind?"

"I didn't. You obviously think it's a good deal. So I'd like to take advantage of it and help you out."

Jack shook his head.

"What's the matter?"

"Nothing," Jack said. "I'm just surprised, that's all."

Surprised didn't begin to say it. He was floored. He was thinking of the things he could do with fifty thousand dollars—cash the check, be on his way. He saw himself on the beach in Cabo, living like a king for years in Mexico. But, on the flip side, he saw the money running out, and then what? Fifty grand sounded like a lot to him at the moment, but wasn't enough to even make it interesting.

Jack handed the check back to her. "You're too late. Deal closed yesterday at five o'clock."

"You sure?"

No, not completely, but he said, "Yeah, positive."

The way Jack looked at it, all he had to do was win her back and there'd be a whole lot more than fifty grand.

———

Teddy got a tree stand—gun hunter's special, plus climbing spurs and T-pads and seven-by-fifty Bushnell binoculars—at an outfitter in Northport. The owner was an old guy with a long gray beard, reminded Teddy of the bass player in ZZ Top. Man smelled like dead meat his dad used to hang in the cellar. Jesus, he was ripe. It was a strange place, filled with animal heads.

Old guy said, "You're a little early for deer season."

Teddy—thinking, you can't even buy a goddamn tree stand without somebody getting in your business—said, "Am I too early to see grosbeaks and warblers?"

The old guy perked up and said, "Ever see a Kirtland's warbler?"

"Kirtland's warbler?" Teddy said, pretending to be interested. "No, I don't believe I have."

"And you're not going to unless you go downstate between Grayling and Mio," he said, pointing at Teddy with the mouthpiece of his pipe.

Old graybeard was a real sexual intellectual, a fucking know-it-all. Teddy said, "I'll keep that in mind."

"Only eight hundred pairs still in existence," he said, wanting to tell Teddy every goddamn thing he knew about them.

That had all happened earlier. Now he was forty feet off the ground, setting in the tree lounge, drinking an MGD, watching Jack's rich lady's place that was about thirty yards away, just inside the tree line, and it was some place. Neither DeJuan nor Celeste knew from tree stands, so Teddy was elected.

Got up before dawn, drove over, walked a couple miles through the woods and found the tree.

DeJuan said, "Can't miss it. Biggest one near the house on the east side." He strapped on the spurs and T-pads, climbed the tree and set up the stand. He was drinking coffee, relaxing as the sun came up over the water.

He saw Jack's rich lady sleeping and saw her get out of bed, watched her through the binoculars—filling up the tub and then taking her clothes off and getting in, making faces as she got used to the water. Teddy zooming in and holding on different parts of her—looked like she was close enough to reach out and touch. She soaked for a time and then stood up and got out and dried off. Seeing her naked body warmed him up against the chill of morning. She was a looker. He'd drink that bathwater she was setting in.

Sixteen

The bar was packed shoulder-to-shoulder with men in work shirts and fertilizer caps, drinking beer and shots and smoking cigarettes. Kate and Jack sat at a table and ordered bottles of Bass Ale. They had their backs to the door and could feel the draft move across the floor when somebody came in. The band, four long-haired Indians, kicked it out from a stage at the far end of the room.

Luke was out for the evening, on patrol with Bill Wink— "seeing a real cop in action" was how Bill put it. Kate grinning, thinking about it. She took Jack to the Happy Hour Tavern for sautéed perch and now they were at Boone's Prime Time in Suttons Bay.

"I forgot why we came here," Jack said.

Kate said, "How many chances you get to see Crazy Horse live?" She tapped a cigarette out of her pack and lit it. "They take requests, I understand. What's your favorite speed-metal song?"

"I'm going to have to think about that," Jack said, "there are so many."

The band finished their set and said they were going to take a break. Jack got up, said he was going to the men's.

Kate was thinking about Jack's reaction when she gave him the fifty thousand. She'd agonized over it. She didn't trust him and figured that was a way to find out if he was still working a con. He could've taken the check, cashed it and disappeared, if money was what he was after. He shocked her by giving it back, and now felt bad she doubted him. It looked like he'd changed; he was a different person after all.

Kate felt someone staring at her, looked over and met the gaze of a rugged-looking guy standing at the bar. He winked at her and she looked away. Now he came over to the table and sat in Jack's seat. He had a longneck Rolling Rock in his hand.

"When they start letting injuns play instruments?" He drank his beer and said, "How you doing?"

Kate said, "I'm with someone."

"Yeah, I know and you could do a lot better if you ask me."

"I didn't," Kate said.

He had a square jaw and looked strong under the dark T-shirt and nylon jacket, like someone who worked construction his whole life. He had a mullet too.

He said, "How we going to get to know each other with that attitude?"

He was leering at her and it made her uncomfortable.

"What do you do," Kate said, "that makes you so confident?"

"I'm good."

"Yeah? What're you good at?"

"Anything I set my mind to."

He grinned, showing tobacco-stained teeth, and drained his beer bottle.

"Why don't you set your mind to going back where you came from, try that," Kate said.

He stood up but continued to stare at her.

"I've got a feeling we'll be seeing each other again."

"I wouldn't count on it," Kate said.

He moved to the bar, looking back at her, grinning and put his empty on the bartop. He was sleazy, scary-looking. He creeped her out—made her nervous.

She saw Jack appear now, coming back into the room and she was relieved. The guy with the mullet stepped in front of Jack as he walked by the bar. She could see them exchanging words. Mullet pushed Jack and Jack pushed him back. Then a young good-looking girl walked in and separated them. The girl put her arm around Mullet's waist and the three of them talked for a few minutes and Jack came back to the table.

Kate said, "What was that all about?"

"Some clown had too much to drink, was looking for trouble," Jack said, sitting down.

It didn't look that way to her, studying their body language, but Kate had no other explanation.

"Never seen him before in my life," Jack said, looking her in the eye. "You okay?"

"He sat down where you are now," Kate said, "tried to pick me up. Thinks highly of himself, very confident for a guy with a mullet."

"That's what shots and beers will do for a guy, give him a false sense of himself."

He sounded like an expert on the subject.

The car ahead of them was having trouble staying in a straight line, kind of swerving in the lane.

Bill Wink said, "Looks like we've got somebody's been over-served'."

They were cruising on a two-lane county road, flat, fallow fields on both sides. Luke was thinking about his dad when Bill flipped a switch on the dash and the light bar came on. Luke could see the multicolored reflection of the lights flashing through the windshield and off the white hood of the police car. More lights reflecting off the back of the car that was slowing down, pulling over, Luke listening to the dispatcher's steady, measured voice, broken up by static from the police radio.

Bill said, "First thing we do is run the plate, see if there are any outstanding warrants."

He punched the license number into the computer.

He said, "Know what kind of car that is?"

Luke said, "Z28 Camaro, '69 or '70." It was green with a white racing stripe that went over the hood and trunk lid. He knew cars. He'd grown up at the racetrack and could probably name every American car from 1960 on.

Bill had picked him up earlier and brought a Point Blank Pro Plus vest for Luke to wear, Bill saying it belonged to a lady deputy—the men's vests were too big—but that Luke had to wear one, departmental regulations. Luke wore it under his sweatshirt and was surprised how heavy and uncomfortable it was. Bill wore one too under his brown short-sleeve uniform shirt, showing off his arms.

"Ever been shot at?" Luke said.

"I was a rookie in Garden City. There'd been a shooting in the neighborhood. My job was to keep people out of the crime scene, make sure evidence wasn't contaminated. I was talking to this woman who walked down the street and I'd swear I saw these two dudes come out of nowhere, pick her up and put her in the back of an Escalade—kidnapped her. I'm going, what in hell's name is happening here?"

"What'd you do?"

"Followed them. They pulled into a shopping center; I pulled in behind them. I was doing a plate check just like this, see who I was dealing with. That's when the shooting started. One of 'em had a machine gun, opened fire on my patrol car. I called for backup but I was pretty much on my own. Found out later, they were former Iraqi soldiers, Republican Guards worked for Saddam Hussein, hired by a local A-rab."

"They hit you?"

"It's a miracle I'm sitting here," Bill Wink said.

"Did the vest save your life?"

"My patrol car looked like Swiss cheese," Bill said. "Guess how many rounds they fired."

Luke said, "Twenty."

"Twenty? Try a hundred and eleven. I was hit six times. Each round stopped by Point Blank Pro Plus body armor just like you're wearing."

Luke said, "Think somebody's going to shoot at us tonight?"

"No, I do not, but you never know. It's like wearing a seat belt, okay? It's better to be safe than sorry."

Bill glanced at the computer.

"Car's registered to Theodore Monroe Hicks, address in Clawson, downstate, and yes, it's a 1970 Chevrolet Camaro Z28. You know your stuff."

Bill picked up his hat, grabbed his flashlight off the console and opened the door. He looked back at Luke and said, "They give me any trouble, pick up that radio and call for backup. We're on County Road number 20, four miles from Empire. Can I count on you, partner?"

Luke said, "I think so." Wondering if Bill Wink was serious.

He could see the shapes of two heads in the Camaro as Bill approached the car.

Teddy sat in the front passenger seat, his eyes trying to adjust to the bright lights. Jesus, they were fucking blinding him. He opened the glove box, took out a big chrome-plated Sphinx nine, watching the cop get out of the patrol car. He saw the dark silhouette shape coming toward them.

It was a good thing Celeste was driving 'cause he was fucked up, trying to remember how many beers and shots of Jäger he'd had. He released the safety and racked a round into the chamber.

Celeste said, "Jesus, Teddy, you dipstick, put that away. I can handle this country boy."

He slid the gun under the seat.

She hit the button and the window went down. She had her hands on the steering wheel—ten and two, the way they taught you at driver's training—as the cop walked up and shined his flashlight in Celeste's face.

He said, "License and registration."

Now he swung the flashlight across the interior, holding on Teddy and then looking in the backseat. He was a sheriff's deputy. Teddy could tell by his Smoky the Bear hat.

Celeste said, "I don't think I was speeding, was I?"

She handed him her license and registration and insurance certificate.

He seemed to study the license.

Celeste said, "It's me. I had blond hair then."

"Do you know why I pulled you over?"

"No, sir," she said.

He was bending over, his head almost eye level.

"You were weaving all over the road," the cop said. "You been drinking?"

"No, sir. I'm not allowed to on account of my religious conviction. I must've taken my eyes off the road trying to find that national Christian radio broadcast Theodore and I listen to. It offers spiritual enlightenment—food for the soul. You should tune in sometime, officer. It's very inspirational."

"How's your driving record?"

"Clean as a whistle," Celeste said. "Never got a ticket in my life."

"All right, you have a nice evening. Keep your eyes on the road, let Mr. Hicks work the radio."

Teddy waited till the deputy was in his car before he said, "Never had a ticket, huh? Listen, he doesn't believe you, runs your license, sees you got more points than a boxful of pins, we're fucked. And what was that bullshit about Christian radio?"

"It's called quick thinking," Celeste said. She put the car in gear.

"Wait till he goes," Teddy said.

They watched the cop car pull out and pass them.

"You were laying it on a little thick."

"He believed me 'cause I was convincing." She looked in the rearview mirror, didn't see headlights, and hit the accelerator, picking up speed.

"He believed you 'cause he wanted a piece of ass. If I wasn't here he'd have asked for the order."

"It's over and done with. Why're you worrying about what might've happened?"

Teddy could really be annoying.

Bill and Luke were talking about their favorite movies, driving through the woods to the lodge, high beams illuminating the narrow road Owen McCall had cut through heavy timber so he could build his place by the lake. Jesus, he had a spread, bordering national parkland on one side. Probably the biggest privately owned piece of property in northern Michigan. Bill wondered if this kid sitting next to him had any clue how rich he was.

Luke said, "My top five are *Aliens, Terminator, Fargo, Rocky,* and *My Fair Lady.*"

"What'd you say?"

Luke said, "I was kidding about *My Fair Lady.*"

"Geez, I hope so. I was thinking you went gay on me."

"*Pulp Fiction* was my fifth favorite," Luke said.

"That's better."

"What about you?"

Bill was thinking *Full Metal Jacket, Rambo, Above the Law* with Seagal; he also liked *Rocky* and *The Rock,* the one set on Alcatraz. That had some good action scenes. They came through the woods and pulled into the yard. There was a car parked in the circular drive, a Lexus. He glanced at Luke. "You got company?"

"It's Jack," Luke said.

"Who's Jack?"

"An old friend of my mom's."

"He staying with you?"

"I don't know," Luke said.

Bill didn't like it. He thought he'd been getting somewhere with Kate. And now this old friend shows up.

Luke took off the vest and said, "Thanks, it was a blast." Got out and closed the door.

Bill couldn't remember if he said good-bye to Luke or not, his brain was so clouded at the moment. Jesus, she trusted him enough to call up and ask for him personally. And he saw the look on her face the other day when she showed up at the lodge. He'd had his share of relationships. Knew women and there was something there, he was sure of it. He was going to ask her out to dinner, take her to Windows on the Bay—have a gourmet meal and a good bottle of wine. Get to know each other.

Maybe the guy was just a friend, as Luke said, but Bill doubted it. Kate was too good-looking and rich. He'd have to give this one some serious thought.

Seventeen

Luke woke up to Leon licking his face. He pushed him away. "God, Leon." Wiped Leon's slobber on the bedsheet and looked at the clock. It was early, 7:15. Luke got up, went downstairs, opened the front door and let Leon out. He saw Jack's car still parked in the same place and was surprised. His mom said he was staying at a motel in Northport. He didn't mind Jack showing up if it made his mom happy but didn't like the idea of him staying over. They were on the couch watching TV when he got home, not even sitting close together.

He heard Leon bark, opened the door and let him in. He went upstairs and checked the other bedrooms—they were both empty. He went to his mom's room, tried the handle. It was locked. Now he was pissed. He couldn't believe she'd get together with somebody like this. He felt guilty 'cause his dad wasn't there, and it made him angry.

Luke walked back down the hall to his room, Leon trailing

him, took a shower and got dressed. When he went downstairs again his mom was in the kitchen making breakfast, a whisk in her hand, arm wrapped around a mixing bowl. He could smell bacon cooking. Leon was sitting on the kitchen floor, staring at the skillet on the stovetop, bacon grease popping.

"Morning," she said. "How was last night, did you have fun?"

He sat at the table his mom once told him came from Normandy, bleached wood with a drawer at one end. "Looks like you had more fun than I did."

She stopped moving the whisk and gave him a quizzical look. "What does that mean?"

"Where's Jack? He still up there sleeping?"

Kate said, "What're you talking about?"

"I can't believe you'd have him over. Don't you care about Dad anymore?" He was angry, couldn't hold back.

His mom looked stunned. "Of course I do. I don't know what you think happened, but you're wrong."

"Where is he, then?"

"I don't know," Kate said. "Maybe he's out taking a walk."

She put the bowl down and stared at him, then moved to the stovetop. He could see her flipping slices of bacon in the big cast-iron skillet. She made pancakes and piled them on a platter with the bacon and brought it to the table. Leon came over and sat next to Luke, looking up at the food.

She pushed the platter toward him. "Eat something."

He could feel the anger building in him, like it was under pressure, like he was about explode.

"What're you going to do today?"

He stared at the table, couldn't look at her.

His mom said, "Want to hang out? We could have lunch at the Bluebird."

He couldn't sit there any longer. Got up and walked past her out of the breakfast room.

His mom said, "Where're you going? Talk to me, will you?"

He moved through the lodge to the back door, put on his fleece jacket and a pair boots and went outside. It was cold. He could see his breath as he moved toward the woods.

Teddy smelled bacon cooking and it made him hungry. Could he ever go for a couple eggs sunny-side up, sausage and gravy and grits—with syrup over the top.

He could see Jack's car still parked in the yard. Spent the night but not with the lady. Maybe he was losing his charm. He watched her get out of bed and stretch her arms over her head and yawn. He watched her set on the toilet, do her business. He watched her look at herself in the mirror and brush her teeth. No bath this morning and Teddy had to admit he was disappointed.

He heard a door bang closed and saw the kid come out the back of the cabin, moving with purpose toward the tree line, then into the woods and not a minute later the kid was standing right below him. Teddy thinking this was the moment of truth. If the kid turned and looked up, their whole plan could come unglued in a split second. But he didn't and Teddy watched him head deeper into the woods and he took out his cell phone, dialed a number and said, "Let's do it."

Kate heard the front door open and close and Jack came in the kitchen, rubbing his hands like he was cold. "Sure smells good in here."

He took off his jacket and folded it over a chair and sat across from her.

She said, "Where you been?"

"Out in the woods," Jack said. "I saw a deer." He sounded excited.

161

"How about coffee and some breakfast?"

He said, "I like this laid-back up-north life. I could get used to this."

She got up and poured him a cup and made pancakes and put them on a plate with three slices of bacon and handed it to him. She was worried about what she was going to say to him and decided to just say it. "Listen, I've got a problem with Luke. Probably be a good idea if you gave us a little time alone."

He didn't react. It either bothered him or it didn't. She couldn't tell. He kept his eyes on her and said, "I understand."

Now, in retrospect, she realized she should've been smarter, more aware. Luke was hurting and vulnerable, and having Jack overnight was probably the dumbest thing she could've done under the circumstances. Nothing happened, in spite of Jack's persistent attempts to kiss her. He finally got the message and gave up and when the movie was over—they watched *One Flew over the Cuckoo's Nest*—it was late, and Kate said, "Do you really have a motel room down the road?"

Jack said, "Know where the Red Lion is?"

And Kate said, "That's on the other side of Suttons Bay, isn't it? You can stay here, if you want."

She took him up to the guest room and he put his arms around her and tried to kiss her again. She pushed him away. "Come on."

"I can't help myself," Jack said.

"Luke's right across the hall. That's all he'd need—open his door and see his mother making out with somebody."

Kate went to her room and locked the door, thinking that, in his current state of mind, Jack might sneak down and try to visit her in the middle of the night. What made it more difficult— she wanted him too—knew she was interested in him again. Maybe this time it would work. It was the third time their paths had crossed in twenty-some years, and wasn't the third time a charm?

When he finished his breakfast, she walked him outside and they stood looking at each other. "You all right?" she said.

"Fine. Why?"

"I don't know," Kate said. "You seem like you're somewhere else."

"Maybe I'm tired," Jack said.

"I can understand—all your effort trying to get me in bed. That can tire a guy out."

"Now, you know what you do to me and always have," Jack said. "I can't control myself around you."

Kate said, "I guess it's my fault, huh?"

He flashed his famous grin.

Kate said, "Where're you going?"

Jack said, "Back to Tucson."

"You sure?"

"That's what I'm thinking," Jack said. "But you never know."

With him you sure didn't. She put her arms around him and kissed him.

"Be careful," he said, "I'm in a weak physical state."

"You'll be all right," Kate said. "Call me, will you? Let me know what you're doing."

Jack stopped at the market in Omena to get something for lunch. He was paying for a sandwich and a Coke when a deputy sheriff came in and looked around. He saw Jack and stepped over to the counter. He had his hands on his hips, showing off his arms, staring at Jack, sizing him up. He wore the brim of his hat low over his eyes. Jack assuming this was his intimidation pose.

The cop said, "That your Lexus out front?"

Jack said, "Yeah."

In that stupid uniform, he reminded Jack of the two Tucson cops who'd arrested him at a picnic table outside Guero's Taco

Bar. He was taking a bite of a soft chicken taco when he saw two nine-millimeter Glocks aimed at his face.

Jack saying at the time, "You mind if I eat this? I'm starving."

They must've, 'cause they put him flat on the patio stones and cuffed his hands behind his back. He hadn't eaten in twelve hours. He thought about that taco for three and a half years, and it was the first place he went when he was paroled.

Jack met the deputy's gaze and said, "What can I do for you?" Jack thinking he was going to say, "You're under arrest for driving a stolen vehicle."

"You're a friend of Mrs. McCall's, aren't you?"

"I am," Jack said.

"You staying there?"

Jack couldn't figure out where he was going with this. "I was."

"Where you headed now?"

"Is there a point to all this," Jack said, "or you just making conversation?" He resented this yokel getting in his face.

The deputy stiffened up. "You've got a broken taillight," he said. "That enough of a point for you?"

Jack regretted what he said. Had always had trouble keeping his mouth shut in certain situations.

"Have your license and registration with you? I'm going to have to issue you a citation."

He took a pen out of his shirt pocket and opened his ticket book.

Jack said, "I got tagged last night in a restaurant parking lot in Suttons Bay. Dealership isn't open till Monday. Think you could cut me a little slack?"

"I'll give you forty-eight hours," the deputy said. "After that, I'm going to give you a ticket. We understand each other?"

Jack just stared at him.

"I didn't hear you," the deputy said with a grin.

"Yeah," Jack said. But, *no*, Jack was thinking, *we don't*. He didn't get why the deputy was being such a hard-ass. It didn't make any sense. But in his experience, it didn't have to—cops could fuck with you anytime they wanted.

Kate had to give Luke time to cool down, come to his senses. At eleven o'clock when he still wasn't back, she drove into town. Stopped at Tom's and bought cold cuts and Italian bread for lunch and a whole chicken for dinner. She'd fill the cavity with onions and lemons and thyme and roast it in the oven.

She expected to see Luke playing a video game on the big TV when she walked in the door. But it was quiet. She called his name. Nothing. Leon was stretched out on one of the leather chairs, eyes following her into the kitchen. He heard her putting groceries away and came in wagging his tail.

Kate squatted and held Leon's face in her hands and said, "Where's Luke? Have you seen him?"

Leon stared at her with sad eyes and an expression that said, I don't have a clue.

Kate went upstairs and checked Luke's room. No sign of him. She went back down and checked the garage. The Corvette was there. She opened the door to the storage room and saw Owen's bloodstained jacket hanging on a hook, and the memory of his death came flooding back, her adrenaline pumping now as she put a leash on Leon and went into the woods looking for Luke. They followed a trail for a while till it disappeared, Leon going crazy, sniffing and pulling her. They went up a slope to a ridgetop and down the other side. Kate yelling, "Luke," her voice sounding strange in the dense silence of the woods.

By four it was getting dark, difficult to see under the canopy, and she realized there was no way she was going to find him. She took Leon back to the lodge and fed him. Then she sat in a leather chair and warmed her hands by the fire, wondering what to do. She got up once and called Luke's cell phone and got his voice message. She looked at her watch—it was 4:45. He'd been gone for almost eight hours.

There was one more place she hadn't looked. She grabbed a flashlight from a kitchen drawer and walked out to the shed behind the lodge, opened the door, and went in. It smelled like aged wood. There was a worktable with tools on it and more tools hanging from a pegboard on the wall. It was a place where Luke liked to spend time. She hoped she'd see him sitting there, tired, ready to come in for dinner. But he wasn't there. He wasn't on the beach either, where Kate stood, facing directly into the wind. The sky overcast, lake water dark and heavy, wind turning up whitecaps that rolled in, pounding the shore. It was cold and the air was clean, smelling of pine trees.

Bill Wink had given her his cell number and she tried it now and got his voice mail and left a message.

Luke knew the woods, she told herself—knew how to survive. Owen had made sure of that. Even if he was hurt he could make a fire and be okay till morning. Still, she felt guilty. Should've done something earlier and now there was nothing she could do.

Kate stoked the fire and thought about being pregnant with Luke. He was ten days late when her water broke, and then labor—eighteen hours of contractions before he popped out and the pain was gone, and then complete elation, Owen by her side to help, but it was all Kate and Luke.

She thought about chasing him after his bath when he was four or five, running through the upstairs of their first house, saying, "I'm going to get your fanny," and Luke laughing and saying, "No, Mommy."

She thought about telling him the facts of life when he was eleven. He was going to have a sex education class at school the next day and she wanted to prepare him. They were in his bedroom. He was at his desk doing homework. Kate sat on the bed. She said, "Do you know how babies are born?"

He turned and looked at her and said, "They grow in your stomach."

Kate said, "Dads are part of it, too. God gives moms and dads the power to make babies."

Luke said, "You mean like a robot?"

He got up and came over and stood in front of her.

"The dad's penis goes into the mom," Kate said, "and that's how babies are conceived."

He gave her a puzzled, innocent look.

"Does he take it off and give it to you?"

Kate had to bite her lip to keep from smiling. "No, he lies down next to me."

"Why haven't I ever seen this?" His voice and expression full of surprise.

Kate said, "It's a private thing between a mom and a dad."

She could see Luke trying to grasp the concept, and when he did, fell on the floor and said, "I'm never growing up and I'm not going to school tomorrow."

She remembered telling Owen when he got home that night and laughed about it for weeks.

She thought about the time Luke climbed the maple tree in their backyard, spying on the dinner party she and Owen were having. Luke fell out of the tree and landed on the brick patio. He cracked his head open and Kate took him to Beaumont emergency, head wrapped in blue and white dish towels that were blotted with blood. She dozed off, thinking about spending the night in his hospital room, sleeping in a chair next to his bed, and woke up for real to the sound of someone knocking on the door.

Bill Wink's shift ended at midnight. He checked his messages and—he couldn't believe it—there was one from Kate McCall, but it sounded like she was in trouble. Bill decided not to call, just drive out there and see her. His heart was thumping he was so excited. He'd been thinking about her his entire shift. Bill saw himself with her, pictures in his head like snapshots: sitting at a table having a romantic dinner at Windows; cruising the bay in his Boston Whaler, snuggling on the couch in the big room at her place, watching a movie. Bill'd show her what a fun guy he was. He wished he could change, get out of the uniform, put on some Levi's and a comfortable shirt, but it would take too long. His place was in the opposite direction and it was already late.

There was no one on the road so he pressed it, doing seventy most of the way, and pulled up in front of the McCalls' fifteen minutes later. He got out and left his hat on the seat. He was off duty. He knocked on the door, waited, and Kate opened it, rubbing sleep from her eyes. She invited him in and offered him a beer. They sat at the kitchen table and she told him Luke had taken off that morning. He walked in the woods and never came back. To Bill it sounded strange any way he looked at it. How's a kid who knows the woods disappear? Bill thought the likely explanation was the kid ran away. Isn't that what Luke did when he came up north? Of course, Bill could be wrong. He'd try to get a couple experienced trackers and come back before sunup. He finished his beer and Kate walked him to the door. There was no point hanging around. He could see she wasn't in any mood to have a conversation.

Eighteen

She'd been awake since Bill left, pacing around in the dark, worried about Luke. She heard the police car drive in at five thirty and went out to greet them in a parka and jeans, no makeup, nerves frazzled, eyes heavy, breath smoking in the cold air of morning. It was still dark but she could see light breaking over the horizon on Lake Michigan.

Bill and two other men got out of his sheriff's deputy cruiser: Del Keane, unmistakable with his heavy gray beard and long hair and buckskins, and an Indian Bill introduced as Johnny Crow, a tribal cop from Peshawbestown. He was lean and dark with black hair that had a shine to it and a blues patch under his lower lip. Kate thought he looked like a roadie for a rock band, dressed as he was in Levi's and a dark green barn jacket with a dark blue collar. Johnny was quiet, low-key, which made him seem almost shy. He was in charge of security at the Leelanau Sands Casino, Bill said, and owed him a favor, Bill saying he'd helped a friend of

Johnny's out of a DUI. Bill said Johnny knew the woods and was the best tracker in the county and probably the state. Del was no slouch either, Bill said, but Johnny was part critter. "If Luke's out there, these boys will find him."

Bill was dressed in camo with an orange vest and a Red Wings cap. It was the first time she'd seen him out of uniform. He looked like an ordinary guy.

Kate thanked Del and Johnny for coming to help and offered them coffee and breakfast. They declined and said they were ready to get to it.

Kate said she wanted to go with them.

Bill said, "You better stay here, case he comes home."

Kate said, "If Luke's not home by now, he isn't coming home." She knew he could've been in a motel in Suttons Bay or on a bus back to Detroit, but her gut told her he was still out there somewhere.

They entered the woods, four of them, where Kate had watched Luke go the morning before, moving through heavy ground cover, breath condensing in the cold air. They'd gone maybe thirty yards when Johnny stopped. He saw something on the ground and hunkered down to take a closer look. Del hunkered next to him, turned to Bill, and said, "Found a boot print."

Kate and Bill went over for a closer look. Johnny pushed some leaves aside and she could see the pattern of the boot tread in the dirt.

Fifteen feet upslope, Johnny found another one, made by a different boot.

"There's two of them," Johnny said.

"They together?" Bill said.

Johnny said, "Could be, but I doubt it. Prints are too far apart."

Kate looked back where they'd entered the woods; she could see the lodge, a small section of roofline and a trail of smoke rising out of the fieldstone chimney. She scanned the trees and saw something that caught her attention, something that seemed out of place: a platform, it looked like—attached to a giant maple that had a full plume of green leaves. She moved toward it for a closer look.

Bill said, "Hey, where you going?"

Kate said, "Come here, will you?"

They walked over to the tree. It looked like a chair strapped to the trunk about forty feet up. "What's that?" she said to Bill.

"A tree stand," Bill said. "Hey, Del, what do you make of this?"

Del and Johnny came over now, Del squinting, looking into the rising sun, fixing his gaze on the upper part of the tree. "It's a tree stand," he said.

"I know that," Bill said. "Odd place to hunt, don't you think?"

Johnny said, "If that was their purpose."

Bill glanced at Kate. "You're sure it's not yours?"

"We don't own one," Kate said. "Owen was a bow hunter."

"Somebody setting up there watching the lodge," Del said. He spit a gob of tobacco juice, brown-colored spray landing in the heavy curls of his beard. "I sold one just like it to a feller the other day. That and climbing spurs and a pair of binoculars."

Kate said, "What did he look like?"

"Sturdy build," Del said, "dark hair, mid-thirties. He wasn't a tourist, I can tell you that."

That sounded like the guy in the bar. "Did he have a mullet?" Kate said.

"I believe he did," Del said.

Johnny took a long leather strap out of his backpack and wrapped it around the trunk of the maple and started to walk up the tree like a squirrel, and in no time at all he was sitting in the chair looking down at them.

He said, "Know anyone with the initials TMH? Fresh-carved in the bark."

"Like whoever it was had time on their hands," Del said. He launched another gob of tobacco juice, hit a leaf and it flipped over.

Bill said, "Why does that sound familiar?" He stared off like he was thinking.

Del said, "I give up."

Bill said, "I stopped a guy the other night, had those initials. Theodore Monroe Hicks."

Del said, "What the hell kind of a name is that?"

"A hick name," Bill said.

Del grinned. "That's pretty good." And spit.

The name sounded familiar. Sure, Kate remembered Teddy Hicks. He was the driver who broke Owen's collarbone and ended his racing career. Could it be the same guy?

Johnny came back down with a backpack. He opened it and took out a thermos, two empty beer cans, and a half-full bag of Kars salted peanuts.

"Whoever it is, I've got to believe he's coming back," Del said. "You don't just walk off, leave a $250 tree lounge."

Bill said to Johnny, "What'd you see?"

"Clear view of the lodge and the yard," Johnny said. "Could look right in the bedroom window, see the alarm clock on the table next to the bed."

Kate felt weird, uneasy, hearing that someone had been watching them, picturing the face of the sleazy guy from the other night and wondering if he was watching them right now. "I didn't think anyone even knew we were here," she said.

"Somebody did," Del said.

"Or somebody didn't," Johnny said. "Maybe they were checking the place out to rob it."

Bill glanced at Kate. "Where's your friend?"

"He went back to Detroit," Kate said.

"I saw him in Omena yesterday morning and I'd swear I saw him in Suttons Bay last night," Bill said. "Driving the green Lexus with the broken taillight."

He had the right car, but it didn't make sense, Kate was thinking. Jack had called about one o'clock, saying he'd driven straight back and was staying with his sister. Bill must've been mistaken.

Johnny was hunkered down again, studying tracks at the base of the tree. He said, "Mrs. McCall, what size boot does your boy wear?"

Kate said, "Ten and a half."

"I think someone was watching your lodge," Johnny said, "saw your boy come through the trees and followed him."

Kate felt a rush of panic. "Why would somebody do that?"

All three of them glanced at her like they knew something and looked away.

"That's what we've got to find out," Bill said.

They hiked for over an hour, the sun rising, filtering light through the trees that in places were so close together, it was difficult to move through them. They followed the tracks up a slope to a ridge and then down to a ravine. Johnny and Dell stopped and told them the tracks ended at the stream, which was cold and clear, about five feet wide, with a fast-moving current that rippled the water. Kate could see the orange flash of brook trout gliding by, and remembered being at this very spot with Owen, watching the excitement on his face as he landed four ten-inchers they took back and Kate dusted with flour and sautéed for dinner.

Bill said, "How you doing? Want to rest?"

"Don't worry about me," Kate said, "let's keep going."

Johnny took a chub out of his pack and ate it, the air smelling of smoked fish. Del spit a gob of brown juice, wiped his mouth on his sleeve and drank from a small silver flask, holding it up, saying, "Anybody care for a snort?"

No one did.

Kate smoked a cigarette. She was tired, nerves raw from worrying and lack of sleep.

They crossed the stream single file over a fallen tree, Bill walking behind her, holding her hips, trying to steady her balance. But it felt like more than that to Kate, like he was looking for an excuse to touch her. She turned and said, "Bill, I think it would be better if I did this on my own."

Bill said, "Sure, okay" and backed off.

Johnny picked up the trail on the other side. They hiked uphill for about twenty minutes and now stood on a ridgetop, Kate breathing hard, vowing to herself to quit smoking. The view looked like a landscape oil from a Traverse City gallery. There was a pristine farm spread out in the distance: a silo and a red barn and white clapboard house and outbuildings looking like pure rural Americana. Beyond the farm, she saw the deep green colors of the woods and beyond that, Lake Michigan shimmering blue in the distance.

Johnny scanned the woods below them with the binoculars. He said, "Something I want to take a look at."

They hiked down to a clearing where the woods ended and a cornfield began, Kate wondering if it was the field where the accident happened. There was a two-track road carved out of grass and dirt that bordered the farmer's land.

Johnny and Del followed the terrain down a hill to an area where the leaves had been kicked and scattered. They studied the ground, talking, interpreting what they saw.

Johnny said, "There was four of them all together."

Del said, "Somebody was running after somebody by the look of things. We found two more sets of prints. I'd say one belonged to a girl by the size of it."

Del and Johnny went over and talked to Bill in hushed tones, like they were trying to keep something from her.

Kate said, "Tell me what's going on, will you?"

All three of them looked over at her.

Bill said to Johnny, "Go ahead."

"Mrs. McCall," Johnny said, "I could be wrong, but I think this is where they grabbed your son." He pointed to the two-track road. "And that's how they took him out."

Kate said, "You don't know for sure. They could be hunters."

"Maybe," Johnny said. "But the boy's missing and someone was watching your place and these marks sure look like a struggle took place. Dragged your son across there to a vehicle they had and drove off."

"Come on," Kate said. "How can you be so sure?" It seemed impossible—none of it made sense. How'd they know Luke was going to be at the lodge when she didn't know herself? And how'd they know he was going to take a walk in the woods? Or where he'd end up? "What would anyone want with a sixteen-year-old kid?"

"Money," Dell said. "Oldest motivator there is."

She looked at Bill and could see he was nervous, unsure of himself. "Bill, what do you think?"

"You make a good point," Bill said to Kate. Now he glanced at Del. "If Luke was kidnapped, why hasn't there been a ransom de-mand?" He hesitated, like he didn't know what he was going to say next, and turned back to Kate. "But there's got to be some-thing to what these boys are telling you. If he's not back at the lodge and he's not out here, where's he at?"

She could see Bill was out of his element. He was used to pulling over tourists, writing tickets and keeping order at the cherry festival, not solving crimes.

"We're going to find him," Bill said with fake enthusiasm. "That's a promise."

Bill took out his cell phone, punched a number in the keypad and said, "Earl? Bill. I need you to do an all-points on Luke Mc-Call, age sixteen, five nine, brown hair—hell, you know what he looks like."

Nineteen

Kate got back to the lodge at ten thirty, after four and a half hours in the woods. Bill offered to stay with her, keep her company until she heard something. She said she wanted to be alone and that she'd call him if anyone tried to contact her. She still didn't believe Luke was kidnapped, in spite of the tree stand and all the tracks Johnny and Del found and their collective speculation. None of it made sense until she walked in the kitchen and saw the ransom note on the refrigerator, held there by a Detroit Tigers magnet.

The note was cutout pieces of newsprint centered on a white eight-and-a-half-by-eleven sheet of paper. It looked amateurish, like a grade school art project. It said:

WE HAVE LUKE. CALL THE POLICE AND
YOUR NEVER GOING TO SEE HIM AGAIN EVER

Kate splashed cold water on her face at the kitchen sink, trying to hang on to her emotions. She stared at her reflection in the window glass, wondering what to do. She dried her face and hands with a paper towel and picked up the phone and called Jack—got his voice mail and left a message. "Listen, something's happened. I need your help."

She walked in the main room and wondered where Leon was, thinking they'd done something to him. She called him, then saw his big head looking down at her through the slats in the railing on the second floor. He came down the stairs and she slid off the chair onto the Persian rug, hugging him, glad to see him, glad he was okay. Leon, the worst watchdog ever. If somebody knocked on the door—instead of getting up and barking, he'd yawn.

She looked out the window at the tree line and had a strange feeling that someone was watching her and ran upstairs to the bedroom and took her Beretta out of the gun box in her closet and checked the magazine. It was full—twelve nine-millimeter rounds ready to send some kidnappers into oblivion. She slid the gun in the waist of her jeans, felt the coolness of the metal against her stomach and moved across the room.

Owen kept binoculars on his nightstand next to the bed. She picked them up and looked out at the yard behind the lodge to the lake. The water was calm. She watched a couple gulls flying in low, searching for fish. She panned the beach to the tree line on the east side of the lodge. She crossed the room and looked out the side window, adjusting the focus, moving the binoculars slowly along the wall of trees, stopping, holding on a trunk, a branch, a section of ground cover. She zoomed in on the big maple, saw the tree stand—looking up at it forty yards away. She'd always thought the place was so secluded and private, but not anymore.

She moved down the hall to Luke's room. From the window she checked the yard in front of the lodge, then slowly panned the woods along the perimeter. The phone rang and it startled her. She ran downstairs and picked up the extension in the main room on the third ring.

"Hello," Kate said, thinking it would be Jack.

"You know we're not fucking around," the voice said, "don't you?"

"Where's Luke?"

"Right here. He cool. But he ain't going to be cool if you talk to the police."

It was a man's voice, distorted, like something was over the mouthpiece.

"You want to watch him grow up, capture the Kodak moments, it's going to cost you two million dollars—spare change for somebody in your tax bracket."

Kate said, "I want to talk to him."

"Get the money."

"How do I know you have him?"

"Got thirty-six hours before we start to cut him up and send him to you. What you want first—finger or a ear?"

He hung up.

Kate told herself not to panic, keep it together. They were saying that to scare her, make her believe they were serious. And it worked. She felt helpless, frantic. After everything Luke had been through, what would this do to him?

Of course, she'd get the money. But how was she going to get two million dollars in cash? Walk into a bank and make a withdrawal? She thought about talking to Dick May, ask his advice, but decided against it. She couldn't risk telling anyone but Jack.

She called the Traverse City Bank and Trust and asked for Ken Calvert, the manager. He'd handled the transaction when they bought the property in Cathead Bay.

He picked up the phone and said, "Kate, I'm sorry about Owen. My condolences."

He'd sent a note after the funeral and Kate thanked him for that and said she was in the process of buying a piece of land for two million, but the seller wanted cash. She looked out the kitchen window at the woods.

"Cash?" Calvert said. "You've got to be kidding. What's he going to do with it?"

She could hear him breathe through his nose.

"I don't know. Maybe he's planning to put it in shoeboxes under his bed," Kate said. "Draw comfort from the fact that it's there if he needs it."

Calvert said, "Hey, you know, that's why banks were invented, eh?"

She could hear his Canadian accent now.

"You don't have to convince me," Kate said. "I'm dealing with an elderly gentleman who doesn't trust technology."

"This wouldn't be Myron Cline, would it? I could see him doing something crazy like this."

Kate said, "I can't tell you." She glanced at the ransom note on the counter.

"That's a lot of money," Calvert said, stretching out the vowels: *a lot* coming out like *a loot*.

Kate remembered Calvert telling her he was from Sudbury, Ontario, when they'd met at his office to sign the papers for the Cathead property.

Kate had said, "Where exactly is Sudbury?"

Calvert said, "It's aboot a hundred kilometers from Tilbury."

He'd grinned, showing teeth that were the size of Chiclets. He was being funny, Kate realized—making a joke—a real Canadian zinger.

Calvert also said he'd played hockey for the Sudbury Wolves during the Bob Strumm–Wayne Maxner era and knew Todd

Bertuzzi. "Our most famous Sudburian," Calvert said, beaming with pride. "If you're ever in Sudbury, be sure to see the big nickel. It's a replica of the Canadian five-cent piece. Largest coin in the world—nine meters high and sixty-one centimeters thick."

Kate said, "I guess it doesn't fit in a pop machine, huh?"

Calvert grinned again.

"I'll have the money wired to you tomorrow," Kate said. Leon walked in the kitchen and bumped her and she patted his head.

"You can wire all you want, the problem is cash. We don't keep that much on hand," Calvert said. "I'll have to order it from the Federal Reserve in Chicago."

"So it's not illegal to withdraw two million?"

"No, it's not illegal. It's not safe, either. I'd have a sheriff's deputy escort me if it was my hard-earned dollars."

She heard him sneeze.

Kate said, "How long does it take?"

"I don't know—couple days. They'll put it on the regular de-livery, which, as you can imagine, is confidential information."

He sneezed again.

"Are you okay?"

"Got a cold," Calvert said.

"I've got thirty-six hours to close this deal." She glanced out at the lake.

"What's the big hurry?"

Kate said, "You'd have to ask the seller."

"I'll see what I can do," Calvert said, "but we're dealing with bureaucracy here. There're rules. Unless you're willing to pay ex-tra to have it expedited?"

Kate said, "I'll do whatever it takes."

"Whatever it takes? Whoa, I wouldn't say that till I heard the amount."

Kate said, "Ken, let me know and I'll make a decision, okay?" It annoyed her that Calvert, the frugal Canadian, was trying to decide for her.

He said he'd call her after he looked into it and got all the facts.

She had $400,000 in a cash management account at Martin Smith Securities. She could liquidate stocks to raise the rest— $1,600,000. Borrow it on margin if she had to. She called her broker, a former University of Michigan basketball player named Bill Lelich—Billy Lee—six foot six in black wing tips and his standard uniform: blue suit, white shirt and red tie, looking and sounding more like an evangelist or self-help guru than a broker. Owen had referred to him as the Rudy of the Big Ten, Billy Lee only seeing action for a couple of minutes in one game against Northwestern during his three-year college career.

Kate told him she was in Cathead Bay buying a piece of property and needed two million dollars and the money had to be wired to the Traverse City Bank and Trust the next day. Billy said, "That's all, pretty Mrs. McCall, my number-one client? That's all you need? Piece of cake." He'd have it there by ten the next morning. "Anything else? There must be something." Giving her his full-court confidence—like every request was a snap—if you dealt with Billy Lee.

Kate felt relieved the money was taken care of. Now she had to deal with Bill Wink, call him, because she knew it was just a matter of time before he'd show up again. He answered his cell phone on the second ring. Kate said, "I just heard from Luke; he's back in Bloomfield Hills. Freaked out and took a bus home. Can you believe it? Said being up here reminded him of his dad's death and it was too painful to handle."

Bill said, "I'm glad he's okay. But I've got to tell you I'm surprised. It didn't look too good this morning. Sorry if we scared you. Johnny and Del were pretty convinced about what they saw." He paused now, like he was trying to think of what to say next. "What're you going to do?"

"Go home," Kate said.

"Can I buy you dinner first?"

"Bill, that's nice of you to offer, but I better get back and keep an eye on Luke. Thanks for all your help."

That was it. He sounded like he bought it. Now she just had to be careful she didn't run into him.

Jack arrived four hours later. She heard a car, opened the front door, and there he was. She put her arms around him and hung on, feeling a sense of relief, like he was going to make everything better.

Jack said, "Hey, you all right?" He held her face in his hands.

"You always come through," Kate said, "don't you?"

"Tell me what's happening."

They went in the kitchen and she made drinks—Maker's and soda—and handed one to Jack. They sat on the same side of the breakfast room table, chairs turned, facing each other, Jack giving her his full attention. Kate showed him the ransom note and told him about the phone call from the kidnappers.

Jack said, "You didn't call the police, did you?"

Kate shook her head. She could feel tears well up, losing it now, telling herself she wasn't going to do that.

Jack got up and put his arms around her.

Kate said. "If they hurt Luke . . ." She let it hang—didn't tell Jack what she'd do, how she'd hire pros to hunt them down.

"Why're you talking like that? They're not going to hurt Luke. We're going to get through this," Jack said. "It's about money. They've invested too much time to fuck it up."

"How do you know how much time they've invested?"

Jack said, "I can understand how this can put you on edge. Listen, I'm here to help you."

"I'm sorry," she said, "why am I taking it out on you?"

He met her gaze and sipped his drink. "'Cause I'm the only one here."

She grinned. "I should be grateful, huh?"

"That would be in the right direction," Jack said.

"I'll see what I can do," Kate said. Then she told him about ordering the money. "It's coming by armored car from the Federal Reserve in Chicago."

"When's it get here?"

"The manager didn't know and wouldn't tell me if he did." Kate sipped her bourbon and said, "This remind you of anything?"

Jack said, "You're not talking about Guatemala, are you?"

"What else? You're the first person I think of when I'm in trouble."

"I don't know if that's good or not." He reached over and took her hand. "It's all going to work out."

"They said thirty-six hours or they'd cut off a finger or an ear."

"That's drama," Jack said. "To get your attention. If they've got a brain between them, they know you're going to want to see Luke before you pay them a dime. They hurt him, it'll screw everything up. They're trying to scare you—that's all."

"It's working," Kate said.

They had dinner—spaghetti carbonara and a bottle of Italian chardonnay called Cabreo that Kate said they'd brought back by the case from Tuscany. Kate picking at her food, barely eating, quiet, distant.

Jack said, "Where exactly is Tuscany at?"

Kate didn't answer, then looked up from her plate and said, "Huh?"

"You don't want to talk, it's okay."

"What'd you ask me?"

He repeated the question.

Kate said, "North of Rome, all the way up to Florence, which is the capital."

Jack was thinking if things worked out, he'd like to see the world. He'd only been as far west as Vegas, as far north as Toronto, as far east as New York City, and as far south as Guatemala City, a place he wouldn't recommend based on what he'd seen—his brief visit.

After dinner Kate picked up their dishes and took them into the kitchen.

Jack said, "Come and sit. I'll do those."

"I can't. I'm too wound up," Kate said.

"Let me help you."

She was at the sink with her back to him. He came up behind her and wrapped his arms around her. Kate turned and looked over her shoulder at him. "This is your idea of helping, huh?"

Jack grabbed her forearm and turned her toward him and kissed her and she kissed him back and held him. Then she took his hand and guided him out of the kitchen, to the stairs and led him up, never looking at him or saying a word.

And then they were standing next to her bed—moonlight coming through the windows—kissing and taking each other's clothes off and then they were naked in bed, the warm feel of their bodies pressed together. Jack studied her face in the dim light and thought she looked the same as she did in college. Could've been in her Ann Arbor apartment. The only thing missing was Marvin Gaye singing "If I Could Build My Whole World Around You" or "Distant Lover."

This is what he wanted to happen, but something wasn't right.

She wasn't herself, looking up at him without expression. He couldn't tell if she liked it or not. He kissed her and she reached down and took him in her hand and opened her legs and guided him in. He was conscious of his weight on her and the pleasure he felt, bodies moving together with vague familiarity. Like he knew her but didn't know her. And when they were finished, Jack said, "God, that felt good."

She didn't say anything, just slid out from under him and got up and walked across the room naked, Jack staring at her perfect ass. He said, "Hey, where're you going?" She was acting strange. And wasn't it her idea?

Her robe was hanging on the back of the bathroom door. Kate put it on and pulled it closed and looked at herself in the mirror. Knew why she did it. She was lonely and stressed out and liked Jack and needed someone to comfort her. Now she felt guilty. It didn't have anything to do with Owen. He would've encouraged her to move on. It was Luke. She felt like she was betraying him, going to bed with someone while he was being held hostage.

She went back in the bedroom. Jack was still under the covers with his head propped up on pillows, a grin on his face.

He said, "What're you doing? Get in here, we're just getting started."

Kate said, "I can't. I've got to go down and wait for them to call."

"It'll be over soon," Jack said. "Luke'll be home and you can get back to your normal life."

Kate said, "You think so, huh? I don't know what normal is."

Twenty

Did he dream it or did it really happen? He opened his eyes, focusing now on the handcuffs. His wrists stung where the metal cuffs had cut into his skin, drawing blood. The handcuffs were connected to a chain that snaked across the bed and continued across the scuffed floor to an eyebolt that was drilled into the hardwood.

He'd been there a day and a half and they hadn't said anything about what they intended to do with him, although it didn't take a genius to figure out what was going on.

He thought there were four of them: Camo, the girl, the black guy, and one more who wasn't around much—Luke thought of him as the mystery man. He'd seen the others but not him.

Luke could hear them through the thin walls of the cottage, talking like they were in the room with him. He could hear them doing other things, too, the bed shaking. He'd put the pillow over his ears so he didn't have to hear her making all the sounds. He'd never heard people having sex and it sounded awful.

Of all of them, Camo was the worst, coming in the room at different times, hitting him across the face or pushing him down. Luke nervous when he heard the man's voice—hick accent with a nasal twang—flinching when Camo walked behind him, not knowing when he'd get hit again, Camo laughing, getting a kick out of Luke's misery.

The girl wasn't much better. She brought him scraps of food, gnarled pieces of chicken they'd eaten but didn't finish—a drumstick, a couple wings with a few slivers of meat. For the first time in his life, he understood what it was like to be hungry. He could hear Camo saying, "Tell that little rich prick that's all he gets till his momma pays us."

She liked to taunt him, too.

"You a virgin, Luke? I'd like to help you out but . . ."

Then she'd pull her shirt up and show him her boobs and say, "They're beauties, ain't they? Want to touch them?"

He didn't know what to do.

She also liked to rub his leg and say, "How's that feel? That wake up the little trouser mouse? Him want to come out, have some fun?"

He couldn't help it, he'd get all excited.

She'd say, "Look at you popping the big tent, you little deviate. Teddy saw us right now, he'd come in cut that little thing off with a knife."

Then she'd get a grin on her face and walk out of the room.

Celeste and Teddy seemed like they were perfect together—a couple of freaks.

They were in their room, watching TV, a show called *Dog Eat Dog* that Teddy loved. After every outrageous stunt, Teddy'd say, "That looks easy. Shit, I could do that." He was sitting on a lawn chair in a black Drive-By Truckers T-shirt and Jockey briefs that had once been white but now were gray.

Celeste looked over at him and said, "What're we going to do with him?" Teddy wasn't what you'd call a great communicator.

He said, "Huh?"

"The kid," Celeste said. "What're we going to do with him?"

He said, "Don't have a lot of choice in the matter."

She wondered if he was being vague on purpose. "What does that mean?"

"You know."

It sounded like he was planning to do something bad. Celeste said, "I never agreed to nothing like that."

Teddy said, "He seen your face."

There was a bottle of beer on the floor. He reached down without looking, picked it up, and took a drink.

Celeste said, "What difference does it make, where we're going?"

Teddy slid his hand in his underwear and started scratching. He said, "Tell me that when your picture's on CNN and federal marshals are looking for you."

Celeste said, "That seems a tad exaggerated."

"Think so, huh?"

Celeste said, "How 'bout the mom?"

Teddy said, "How 'bout her?"

Celeste said, "She hasn't laid eyes on you."

Teddy said, "Want to bet? I talked at her in the bar. She seen you, too. Remember?"

That's right. She was sitting at the table. Celeste said, "What else you got planned?"

Teddy said, "Wait and find out."

Celeste said, "This is like going to a movie, you know it?" She took off her jeans and lifted her T-shirt over her head and sat on the edge of the bed naked.

Teddy glanced over at her. "Better, on account of we're in it."

Celeste said, "I've always wanted to be a movie star."

Teddy said, "Well, you look like one, setting there in the alto-gether."

There was a knock on the door. DeJuan swung it open and came in the room. "Nighty-night," he said, "and don't let the bedbugs bite."

Celeste saw him stare at her like a hungry dog. She picked up a pillow and held it up to her chest.

Teddy said, "What the hell you think you're doing? We got people undressed in here."

"You don't want visitors, lock your door."

"You check on the kid?"

DeJuan said, "Little man tucked in all cunchkey."

He turned, walked out and closed the door.

Teddy said, "That bother you, him walking in seeing your taters?"

Celeste said, "Not too much. My dad would be loading a shot-gun right now."

Teddy said, "Then it's a good thing he ain't here."

Celeste said, "I've been meaning to ask you—what kind a name is DeJuan? It doesn't sound like a jig name, sounds more like a character in a *Star Wars* movie. Hey, maybe he's really a space jig, come down from the cosmos to observe the ways of us white earth people."

Teddy said, "He didn't come from the cosmos. He come from the west side of Detroit. His given name's DeJuan Green. Think you can put your prejudice aside and work with him?" Teddy grinned. "That's not going to piss off the cosmic being or your warrior kinfolk, is it?"

Luke didn't have anyone to blame but himself. He shouldn't have come back up north. He shouldn't have yelled at his mom. He didn't know if she and Jack had slept together. It sure looked like it. But if his mom said it didn't happen, he believed her, contrary to what he'd said earlier. He felt like everything he'd done the past seven months was wrong—one mistake after another—like he was being controlled by someone else. He knew it made no sense, but that's what it felt like.

Luke was grateful for one thing. He talked to his dad and felt better about things, as Del Keane had said he would. He remembered looking up at the canopy, sunlight angling through the trees. It was mystical, like a scene from *Lord of the Rings*.

He said what was on his mind. Told his dad about seeing the first buck and how his hands shook and he couldn't breathe. He told his dad how dumb he felt and how sorry he was, and how he wished he could replay it, try it again.

It was strange. When he finished saying what he had to say, he felt relieved. Felt a sense of calm, like his mom's Land Rover had been lifted off him. He also remembered having a strange sense that someone was out there watching him. He turned a bunch of times, looking around, but didn't see anyone.

He walked to the edge of the woods, looked out at the cornfield where he left his dad, saw him alive for the last time. He thought about walking into the field and finding the exact spot, but what good what it do? What purpose would it serve? He'd reconciled his feelings and that was enough.

He could see the farm in the distance. He remembered the farmer, a big man with beard stubble, wearing a beat-up old blue parka and a grease-stained cap with a bent brim that said CAT DIESEL on the front. He hadn't said much or changed his expression when Luke told him what had happened, but the man came through. Luke's mom sent him a check for a thousand dollars thanking him for his help, and the farmer sent it back, saying he didn't deserve to get paid for doing the right thing. Which had a lot more impact when Luke heard his farm was going under; the man could barely make ends meet.

Luke walked back in the woods. He was going to the lodge to apologize to his mother—not only for what he'd said earlier but for the way he'd been acting since his dad died.

He saw something move on the ridge above him—a man in green camo—coming down the hill toward him. What was strange, he was dressed like a hunter, but he wasn't carrying a rifle or a bow. Something wasn't right.

Luke changed direction, started walking fast, moving away from him. He saw the second guy through the trees about thirty feet ahead. He was a black guy dressed in a gold tracksuit like Eminem wore. He looked out of place, lost.

Luke turned and ran for the cornfield about fifty yards away. He remembered being timed for the fifty-yard dash in gym class. The world record was 5.15 (Ben Johnson) and he'd run a 6.8. He looked over his shoulder and saw the two men running, closing in on him, and now a car appeared, a green-and-white 1970 Z28 Camaro driving up on the two-track road in front of him, cutting him off. It looked like same car Bill Wink pulled over the night before—unless there were two identical green Z28s with white racing stripes tooling around the Leelanau Peninsula.

He had to slow down to get around the car and that's when the black guy caught him, tackled him, took him down hard. Luke kicked the guy away from him, struggling to his feet, and that's when Camo ran up and hit him in the chest, knocking the wind out of him. Luke went down, trying to draw a breath.

Camo said to the black guy, "Nice of you to show up. Where the fuck you been? I've been tracking this little asshole going on two hours."

The black guy was rubbing a dirt stain on the knee of his track pants. He looked at Camo and said, "Want to know where we been? Been trying to find the road—that's where we been."

The girl said, "He's right, we couldn't find it."

Camo said, "You taking his side over me?"

"I'm not taking anybody's side," the girl said. "I'm telling you what happened."

"I said, take the two-track till it dead-ends. What's hard about that?"

"Got to be able to find the motherfucker to take it. We be like, is he fucking with us or what?"

The girl had a roll of duct tape in her hands. She said, "Think we could settle this later? Get the kid out of here before somebody comes looking for him?"

She had brown hair and pure white skin, a girl who was too good-looking to be involved in something like this. She handed the tape roll to Camo, pulled a long piece, and tore it off. She told Luke to get on his stomach—said it with authority, like she was used to telling people what to do. She taped his feet together, got another piece and taped his hands behind his back.

Camo and the black guy picked him up and put him in the trunk of the Camaro, wedged in between the spare and a toolbox. There wasn't a lot of room.

Camo said, "You just lie there, don't make a fucking peep." He slammed the trunk lid closed.

Luke bounced around as the Camaro moved along the uneven two-track road, tools rattling in the toolbox, the thick smell of exhaust making it difficult to breathe. He was on his side, facing in, arms behind him. He tried to find a more comfortable position, but he couldn't move. It was better when they turned on Kinnikinnik Road, the ride smoother on asphalt. He could hear the throaty rumble of the high-performance engine as the Camaro accelerated.

A few minutes later they stopped and he could hear voices but couldn't make out what they were saying. The trunk opened with a flood of light, Luke's eyes squinting and Camo, in his southern accent, said, "That's all you get. Just a peek." And dropped the lid closed. It sounded like Camo was showing him to someone. So there were four of them. Then he heard them arguing, then fighting. Loud voices. Then a few minutes later they were back in the car, moving again. He wondered if they'd contacted his mother and how much they were asking for him. Camo finally told him.

He said, "I hope your momma loves you, boy. Think you're worth two million dollars? You better hope so."

He'd finally fallen asleep as the sun was starting to rise and woke up a few hours later to the sound of the TV. He could hear it on in the next room, a Road Runner cartoon. He could hear the Road Runner say "Beep, Beep" and hear Camo's strange high-pitched laugh—not the kind of laugh you'd expect, the way he talked with that southern nasal twang he had.

Camo loved cartoons: Bugs Bunny, Daffy Duck, Elmer Fudd, Marvin the Martian, he watched them all. It was the third morning Luke had woken up to the man laughing, which seemed odd, 'cause he was such a mean person.

Now Luke worked on the eyebolt they'd screwed into the floor, trying to loosen it. If he could unscrew it, he could open the bedroom window and take off. He heard the black guy say they were at the Timber Lake Cottages. He'd never been here before but had seen billboards advertising them. They were in Northport, woods behind the cottages. All he had to do was get in the trees, they'd never find him.

He took his belt off and slid the skinny metal piece that was part of the buckle—he thought it was called the clasp—through the ring of the eyebolt, gripped it hard, using the buckle for leverage and tried to turn the screw till his hand hurt. They'd torqued it down hard. He tried it again, pressing the clasp and buckle together till his fingers were numb.

He heard Camo laugh again in the other room and it made him mad and he used his other hand now, gripping the clasp and pinching the buckle like it was a wrench, his hand in pain, and when he was just about to give up he felt the eyebolt turn.

Twenty-One

A couple days earlier DeJuan said to Jack, "Yo, welcome back to the famous Timber Lake Cottages. Been thinking. I see timber, don't see no lake. Theo, where the water at?"

Celeste and Teddy were getting out of the Camaro.

Teddy said, "How do I know?"

Like it was a real question. DeJuan believed, was dogs smarter than Teddy. Maybe not a street mutt, but for sure a Doberman or a purebred poodle. He was thinking of an experiment: switch Teddy's brain with a poodle's, see how much smarter he got. Get invited on Letterman and such, bring Teddy out on a leash. "My dawg, check him out."

He liked fucking with Teddy but really wanted to fuck his girl, fine creamy-skinned bitch with tats all over her pale white perfect body—ugly ones, graphic dark-blue shapes like she belonged to a cult. Had a big motherfucker on her back. Wasn't just a tat, was a scene—crazy, too. Bitch posing at the entrance to a cemetery, pumpkins lining an iron fence—huh? The tats hidden under her clothes. Never expect it, looking at her. He was peeking in their room through a crack in the door, saw her coming out of the bathroom naked, bitty little shaved muff like a mustache down there and a nice-sized pair of naturals with pink nipples. Lord God. That's all he could think of now. Couldn't get that vision out of his head. Girl had a profound effect on him.

DeJuan was on the porch of his cottage—kicking back in a green metal chair with rusted legs, cleaning his gun, his Sig. He said, "Where the kid at?"

Teddy nodded at the trunk.

"Just going to leave him?"

There were nine cottages that had seen better days—grouped together in threes, separated by stands of birch and cedar—spread out across a couple of acres. They'd rented the last three units: seven, eight and nine, only people staying there. Manager lived in Suttons Bay, said to call if they needed anything.

Jack ducked in his cottage while Teddy and Celeste lifted the kid out of the car. Jack saying he never wanted the mom or kid knowing he was involved. He was the hero—going to come back, keep momma cool till they got the money.

Teddy was walking the little dude to the cottage, stuck his foot out and tripped him. The kid, hands taped behind his back, went down. Sadistic motherfucker grinned, enjoying himself. Man had some strange ways about him.

He said, "Hey, rich kid, watch where you're going. You got to be more careful."

Teddy squatted and pulled the kid to his feet and walked him to the middle cottage where they cuffed his hands to a chain bolted to the floor. The chain long enough to stretch to a log bed against the far wall of the room and to the adjoining bathroom— his own crib.

Teddy came out of his cottage and said to DeJuan, "Hey, you leave the ransom note?"

DeJuan opened his eyes big, gave him a surprised look. Said, "Shit, I forgot."

Teddy said, "Godammit, do I got to do everything?"

DeJuan looked at him and said, "One thing you never have to worry about is this motherfucker doing his job. I'm reliable like FedEx, understand?"

If DeJuan hadn't told Teddy they needed a ransom note, it never would've come up. Hick moron took credit for it, thought it was his idea. DeJuan had modeled the note—the style, anyway—after the one in *Dirty Harry*, one the psycho sent to the police telling them he had the girl and they had twenty-four hours to deliver the money, the ransom. Words from the newspaper cut out and glued on a piece of paper.

Jack saw it and said, "What's that for? You don't need a ransom note, you make a phone call."

DeJuan had seen a lot of movies and believed this was how it was done. There were rules for certain things and you had to follow them. You kidnap someone, his family expect a note. That's how it worked.

When he made the phone call, he put his Fubu over the cell, voice coming out all garbled and such, couldn't tell if he was a southern Illinois sheep-banging bigot or a west Detroit black-power racist.

He got the idea of cutting the kid's finger or ear off reading about J. Paul Getty's grandson was kidnapped by Italian terrorists; J. Paul himself worth over a billion at the time. Kidnappers cut the grandson ear off, sent it to his moms. Mail come, there's a bloody ear in an envelope. That would get your attention, no doubt. He was thinking, no matter what you did it was all about details—mix in a little fact and fiction for dramatic effect.

Now they were waiting for Jack to do his thing.

Bill Wink was working a day shift. He drove out to McCall's and took a look around. He wanted to make sure the place was locked up and nobody was trying to rob it or vandalize it. He parked on the gravel drive, looked in the front windows. He walked around back, checked the doors and windows—everything locked up tight. He thought he heard a dog bark inside. Looked in the picture window in the big room, didn't see anyone, person or dog. Maybe he was hearing things—the wind, maybe.

That whole thing about Luke was strange. Taking a bus didn't wash, either. Taking a bus from where? He'd have to have gotten to Traverse City and how'd he do that? Something wasn't right. It didn't make sense. Unless Kate was making the whole thing up—hiding the fact that Luke really was kidnapped. He also considered the possibility that he was overreacting, his cop's mind looking for a crime where none existed.

He scanned the tree line, spotted the big maple with its high plume of leaves, the tree stand still attached about fifty feet up. He'd run the name Theodore Monroe Hicks on NCIC, found out he'd been arrested five times: robbery armed, grand theft auto twice, assault with intent and a DUI, his only conviction. This Theodore Hicks was a bad dude. Bill read a brief description of each of the charges. Under assault, it said he hit a man named Owen McCall with an impact wrench and broke his collarbone, Mr. McCall refusing to press charges. There, finally, was a connection. But, what did it mean? What was this Teddy Hicks up to now? He did an all-points on the Camaro Z28, but nothing had come up in the past twenty-four hours. Maybe Teddy had taken off, left the county, but Bill doubted it.

He walked down to the end of the yard, stood on the bluff looking out at the water and down the beach, deserted in both directions, not a soul for as far as he could see. He thought about Kate now, pictured himself having dinner with her, a romantic setting, looking out at the moonlit bay, drinking wine, talking and having fun.

Girls had told him he was nice-looking and he sure had a lot of interesting stories involving police work. He once saved a kitten from a burning building—girls loved that one. And he delivered a baby in the front seat of a pickup truck. That was another one that generated a lot of interest. Seeing that baby's head pop out of her—Jesus H. Christ—was something he'd never forget. The new mother was so grateful, she named the baby after him: Bill. Bill Cline. Telling these stories made girls think he was caring and sensitive and had gotten him laid more than a few times. He ended up marrying one of them, a farm girl with big knockers, named Artha.

When he met her he'd said, "I've never heard of Artha before. What kind of name is that?"

She said, "Martha without the *M*."

That became her nickname. He'd say, "How you doing, Martha without the *M*?" She'd giggle and her giant breasts would shake and heave.

The marriage ended after fifteen months, when Artha came home unexpectedly one day and found Bill in bed with a cute little court reporter named Tammi. Artha chased her through the trailer with a butcher knife and then outside and down the highway, Tammi naked, running with her clothes and purse under her arm.

The next day, when Bill was at work, Artha pulled the queen-size mattress off the bed, dragged it out in the yard and doused it with gasoline. She'd torched it along with all Bill's clothes—every goddamn thing except his spare uniform. He considered having her arrested but decided to let it slide. If that got the anger out of her system, maybe it was worth it.

———

Next time Kate came back up, he was going to make his move. He looked out at the water and down the beach. He didn't want to get ahead of himself, but he could see himself marrying Kate one day and living here. It was more than a feeling he had. He actually believed it was going to happen and it gave him confidence.

On his way to Leland, he told John Mitchell he'd stop and check on the cottages. He'd run into Mitchell the night before, having a beer at the Bluebird Bar, Mitchell saying he'd rented three units to this oddball group, said they was from Dee-troit. Said they was going to do some fishing but didn't have any equipment.

"That isn't a crime," Bill said. "What do you think they're doing out there?"

"That's a good question," Mitchell said. "I don't know. I'm just glad to have their money, that's all I can tell you."

"Want me to check 'em out, make sure the cottages are still standing?"

"If it ain't too much trouble," Mitchell said.

DeJuan was on his Mac G5 with the wireless Internet connection, checking out St. Tropez, his next destination. Looking at shots of the beautiful people on they yachts. Saw Jay Z and Beyoncé. P. Diddy dressed all in white, two hoes competing for his attention. DeJuan imaging himself in the music business, start his own label—Murder Dawg Records—like that. Have the capital to do it now.

It was day motherfucking three and he was ready to get out of Hicksville, cut Ted loose. Dude gave the whole white race a bad rap. Truth be told, he like to be back in his crib with LaRita, watching his flat-screen, smoking on some good. His patience on empty, a little left working on fumes. But then, reminded himself, he was close to collecting what was going to be his biggest payday ever—seven hundred large. And when everything shook loose, all the scenerios played out, it wasn't inconceivable he take home the whole thing, the mother lode, be set for life. And felt better.

He heard a car pull up, looked out, saw a white deputy sheriff's cruiser in the yard. He got up, grabbed his Sig, pushed the safety off and slipped it in his Sean Johns, covered by his warm-up. He closed the laptop and went outside.

He watched the deputy sheriff get out of the car. He wore a brown uniform with short sleeves, showing off his guns.

"Yo, how's it going, Officer? Perfect day, isn't it?" DeJuan said, looking up at the blue sky, not a cloud in it.

Deputy said, "That yours?" checking out his ride.

"1984 Chevrolet Malibu," DeJuan said.

Deputy said, "You have car trouble the other day?"

"Not that I recall," DeJuan said. Wondering what he was talking about.

Deputy said, "I saw it parked on Woolsey Lake Road."

DeJuan, picking up the thread, said, "Had to take a leak, you know, went in the woods."

"When you've got to go . . ." The deputy grinned. "We don't see cars like that around here," he said. "What's that say on the front?"

"Scarface." DeJuan had it customized in chrome script on the grille and also on the dash.

"After the movie?"

"No, the gangsta. After Capone." Man was the gangsta's gangsta. DeJuan didn't tell him about the hydraulics and such— twenty grand worth of electric pumps and cylinders powered by twelve batteries. He didn't tell him 'Face was a scraper, neither. Could do shit was unbelievable—go low, frame on the tarmac—go high, leap six feet off the ground. For real. He didn't tell him about ghostriding the whip or gas brake dipping, either, like the cracker deputy knew anything about getting hyphy.

"Where you from?" Deputy said.

"Beautiful downtown Dee-troit."

"I hear they fixed it up for the Super Bowl."

"Super Bowl long gone," DeJuan said. "Look like it old self again."

Deputy looked strong, in shape, flexing the muscles in his arms.

"What brings you up here?"

"Re-lax-a-tion," DeJuan said, stretching the word for emphasis. "Stress relief. Get out of the big city, breathe some clean country air."

"Good place to do it," Deputy said. "What kind of work you do?"

Celeste watched DeJuan and the deputy from the front window of the cottage. It was the guy from the other night; she recognized him. Good thing Teddy'd gone to get beer. No reason to call attention to themselves. She wondered what DeJuan was saying to him, the cop grinning like he said something funny.

He hung around, looking at DeJuan's lowrider, Celeste getting impatient, wishing he'd leave and hoping Teddy didn't come driving in. And just when she thought he'd never fucking leave, he got back in his car and went to the end of the property, made a U-turn and came back, going slow, looking around again and took off.

She went in to check on the kid. Opened the door, expected to see him, but he wasn't on the floor or the bed. The chain was gone. The window was open. Little fucker'd unscrewed the eyebolt.

She called Teddy's cell. He didn't answer. Where in the hell was he? She left him a message. "Remember the deputy from the other night? He was just here. We got another problem too. Get back here as fast as you can."

Teddy came flying in a few minutes later, locked the Z up in a cloud of dust, and ran in the cabin. She and DeJuan were in the kid's room. Teddy came in with a beer, looked around, said, "Where's he at?"

Celeste said, "He's gone."

Teddy said, "What do you mean, gone?"

"You see him in here?" Celeste said, wondering what he didn't understand. She pointed to the open window. "He escaped."

"I leave for fifteen minutes," Teddy said, "you let him get away."

Celeste said, "I told you bozos that screw in the floor was a bad idea."

Teddy said, "Like you know what the hell you're talking about, huh?" He was mad, spit flying out of his mouth. "Listen, if it had something to do with cooking or sewing, I might've asked your opinion. We don't find that little dick with ears, it's all over."

DeJuan said, "Everybody be cool. We find him."

But he didn't look like he believed it.

Twenty-Two

It was two forty-five in the afternoon when Ken Calvert called and said she was all set. The money had been delivered and Kate could stop by for her withdrawal. She went outside looking for Jack, who said he was going exploring. He'd been gone for a while, thirty minutes at least. What the hell was he doing? He knew she was going to get a call and they'd have to be ready.

She stood on the bluff, scanning the shoreline. She didn't see him. He wasn't out front either and the bank closed in a little over an hour. She'd have to leave, pick the money up herself. The only problem was the Land Rover. It was too obvious—Bill Wink, if he saw it, would recognize it in a second and then she'd have some explaining to do. She saw the key to Jack's car on the kitchen counter and decided to take the Lexus. She left Jack a note on the breakfast room table, got in behind the wheel and adjusted the seat. She'd go to the bank, they'd load her up and she'd come back. It sounded easy, but it didn't happen that way.

She drove to Traverse City and pulled in behind the bank building just as Ken Calvert told her to. She parked in front of the silver metal door that was the size of a garage door and watched it rise up and retract. She backed into a loading area that had a concrete floor and brick walls and a high ceiling, the metal door closing behind her.

Calvert was waiting with two uniformed guards. The money was on a hand truck, shrink-wrapped in bundles and looked like something you'd get at Costco—buy it in bulk and save.

She got out of the car and glanced at Calvert. He wore a white shirt and a Kelly green tie that reminded her of St. Patrick's Day, the only day you'd wear a tie that color. He had a clipboard in his pale hands that each had two gold rings, the rings seeming more excessive when she noticed the gold watch and gold ID bracelet on his wrists.

Calvert said, "I thought you were going to bring somebody with you."

Kate said, "It didn't work out."

"You've got two million there," Calvert said. "Let me call the sheriff, arrange for a police escort to your destination. We're more than a financial institution; we're your friend and neighbor. It would be irresponsible of me to allow you to withdraw such a large sum of cash without expressing my concern for your safety."

"I'll be fine," Kate said.

"I'm sure you will, but if anything happens, I want you to know Traverse City Bank and Trust is in no way liable," Calvert said.

"I understand," Kate said. And she did. He was just covering his Canadian ass.

He said, "There are a hundred hundred-dollar bills in each banded stack, equaling ten thousand—and a hundred banded stacks in each bundle. A hundred times ten thousand equals a million, if you follow me."

Kate said, "And two times a million equals two million, if I'm not mistaken."

He grinned, showing his Chiclet-size teeth that were so white they looked blue.

She signed for the money and the guards put it in the trunk. The metal door rose up, and as she drove out, she saw the Indian, Johnny Crow, behind the wheel of a black Chevy panel van, parked there. Bill Wink had said he was head of security at the casino. So she assumed he was waiting to pull in and drop off or pick up money. She made eye contact with him, met his gaze for a couple of seconds and drove past him.

Kate was on Bay Shore Road driving out of Traverse City, doing fifty-five, the lake calm and bright blue to her right. She glanced in the rearview mirror and saw a white deputy sheriff's cruiser behind her. At first she thought it was Bill Wink, but as the cop car got closer, she could see it wasn't. Maybe Calvert, disregarding her point of view, called the sheriff's department anyway, insisting on a police escort. Or maybe it was a coincidence, just a cop on patrol.

She saw the deputy sheriff pull out and drive up next to her like he was going to pass her—the cop looking over, checking her out—then slowing down and drifting back behind her. She heard bursts of siren and watched him in the rearview mirror and saw the flashers and looked for a place to pull over, but nothing looked good. She slowed and put her turn signal on and took a left on Dumas, a two-lane county road and pulled over. The sheriff's deputy followed her and stopped behind her. There were unplowed cornfields on both sides of the road and it smelled like manure.

He got out of his car, put his hat on, and as he approached, she noticed he had his hand on his gun. She pressed the button and her window went down.

He walked up and said, "Step out of the vehicle."

He stood behind her so she had to turn her head to see him. "What's this all about?"

"You are operating a stolen vehicle," he said. "Now step out."

"It isn't mine," Kate said. "I borrowed it from a friend." And as soon as she said it, realized how lame it sounded.

"I'm not going to ask you again," he said, raising his voice.

So Jack was still involved in his old trade after all. Kate considered the situation. She was driving a stolen car with two million in the trunk. How was she going to explain the car or the money?

She wasn't.

She couldn't.

She considered putting it in gear, let the hard-ass cop chase her down and try catch and her. At Owen's suggestion, she'd gone to an advanced driving school and felt confident behind the wheel, believed she could give this young rural police officer a run for his money. But she rejected the notion as being too risky. She didn't want to put anyone else's life in danger. She had a better idea. She slid the Beretta out of her purse and put it in her jacket pocket.

The cop opened the door now.

"You're under arrest," he said. He had his hand on his gun, but didn't draw it from the holster.

She stepped out on the blacktop road. Standing next to him, he looked like a Bill Wink clone—same height and build, same two-tone uniform. He pushed her against the front fender and bent her over the hood.

He said, "You have the right to remain silent. Anything you say can and will be used against you in a court of law."

He kicked her feet apart and ran his hands up her legs, and the inside of her thighs, getting a good feel.

She said, "What're you doing?"

"Seeing if you got any weapons."

"Is this how you get your kicks?"

"I'm the law, I can do whatever I want."

He said it like he believed it.

Kate knew it was now or never. He reached inside her jacket, ran his hands up her sides, touched her breasts, pawed her like a teenager feeling up his girlfriend for the first time. She turned now, and in one compact motion brought the Beretta out of her pocket and stuck the barrel in the center of his chest. His cockiness vanished in a split second. He looked surprised and afraid.

Kate said, "Think you can do anything you want, huh?"

"I didn't mean it," he said.

"You make a habit of doing things you don't mean?"

He said, "Listen, I've got a wife and two little ones at home." The hard guy tone gone now, replaced by concern.

Kate said, "You look worried and you should be. If you try anything else I'm going do your wife a favor and shoot you. Give me your gun."

He undid the strap on top of his holster and handed her his Glock—the shape unmistakable, the big *G* in script on the barrel—passing it to her with his thumb and index finger on the handle—showing her he wasn't going to try anything. She grabbed the gun and dropped it in the pocket of her suede coat.

She said, "We're going to walk over to your car now. You want to see the kids tonight? Don't do anything stupid like you've already done. I feel bad for your wife—married to someone gets his kicks like that—and your kids. What kind of pervert dad are you?"

She escorted him to his car and opened the door. "Give me your keys."

He reached in his pocket and handed them to her. Then he took his hat off and got in behind the wheel and she went around and got in the front passenger seat. He looked young without the hat—only a few years older than Luke. She aimed the Beretta at him and said, "Give me your handcuffs."

He took them out of a leather compartment on his duty belt and handed them to her.

"Where's the key?"

He gave that to her too, and she told him to cuff his hands through the steering wheel and he did and now he looked foolish, with his brush cut and pimples—like a high school athlete who'd gotten in trouble.

"Driving a stolen vehicle and using deadly force to resist arrest. I'd say you're in a whole lot of trouble," the deputy said. He grinned at her now. "They're going to catch you—you know that. Let me go, I'll put in a good word for you."

"I'd worry more about my own situation if I were you," Kate said. "I'd like to hear you explain how you lost your weapon and were taken hostage by a woman." She noticed his nametag for the first time. "How's that going to look on your record, impact your career, Deputy Lamborne?"

Kate opened the door and got out and moved to the Lexus and got in. There was no traffic, no one around. She took a series of arrow-straight county roads back to Cathead Bay—slowing down at one point, throwing Deputy Lamborne's Glock into a wooded area—and although it was a shortcut, it still took thirty minutes to get back to the lodge: time spent thinking about Luke, hoping he was okay and how she was going to deal with Jack.

He came out of the lodge grinning as soon as she pulled up.

"Why'd you leave without me?"

Luke ran till his lungs were about to explode. He was surprised, thought he was in shape, having played tennis since he was a little kid. It was the chain that weighed him down, made him tired. It didn't feel like anything at first and now felt heavier than a cinder block. He tried to position it so it didn't make noise, but it was impossible. It was the handcuffs too, metal digging into his wrists, drawing blood in two places.

Once he'd been able to loosen the eyebolt, it was easy. He waited, listening till he didn't hear them, and unscrewed it all the way. He coiled the chain into a circle and slipped it over his shoulder. He unlocked the window and lifted it open and slid out, dropped to the ground.

The sky was clear blue, sun up high as he moved through heavy woods, feet crunching on dry leaves. He slowed his pace, stopping, looking back, thinking that if they were coming after him, he'd hear them, wouldn't he? He didn't—just the rustle of the wind coming through the trees and an occasional formation of ducks quacking overhead.

It was getting hot. He felt beads of sweat run down his forehead and cheeks. He wiped his face on the sleeve of his flannel shirt. He was conscious of the gamey smell of his own body after not showering for three days, and the heavy sound of his own breathing.

He was afraid, but his fear went to another level when he heard Camo's booming voice behind him like a megaphone blaring through the trees.

"I'm going to find you—you little cocksucker—and I'm going to fuck you up."

Luke pictured Camo's face, with its square cartoon jaw and sadistic grin—and he picked up his pace. He had a sense of where he was, seeing the map of the Leelanau Peninsula in his head and reckoning the location of the cottages, about halfway between Omena and Northport, thinking he was heading east and he'd see the lake soon.

He stopped sometime later and heard them, and they sounded close. Luke ducked low and pressed himself against a stand of white birch, getting bark dust on his shirt. He saw Camo and the girl pass right by him, a few feet away—both carrying pistols.

Camo said, "I'm going to kill that little fucker."

The girl said, "Can you keep your voice down till we find him? He could be anywhere in here."

"Don't tell me what to do," Camo said.

The girl said, "Go ahead, then. You've probably already fucked it up anyway."

Luke held his breath, didn't make a sound even as an early-season mosquito drilled into his hand, sucking his blood. He wondered where the black guy was, wondered if he was sneaking up right now, about to surprise him.

Luke shifted his weight and the chain rattled.

Camo stopped and said, "What was that?"

The girl said, "What was what?"

"I heard something."

"No shit," the girl said. "We're in the woods. You're going to hear all kinds of things."

Camo started back toward the birch trees. Luke ducked down, disappearing in a tangle of alder and held his breath, watching Camo's feet coming toward him—black motorcycle boots and jeaned legs moving through heavy ground cover. Camo stopped a few feet from his head, standing there, not making a sound. Luke glanced up through the foliage and saw his face, eyes darting, scoping the scene. He held a big chrome-plated automatic in his hand, hanging at arm's length, Luke below him, right there, and he didn't look down. Not once.

The girl broke the silence. She said, "Anytime you're ready. He's just putting more distance between us."

Camo turned now and walked back toward her. Luke waited till they were out of sight, saw them disappear in the trees and then waited a few more minutes before he made his move, heading in the direction of the lake, figuring he could run down the beach, break into a cottage, and call the police.

He took off running and was surprised when he came to a

clearing—but it wasn't a clearing. It was a county road cutting across the peninsula a few miles west of the cottages. He was all turned around. He'd gone in the wrong direction.

DeJuan was listening to Keak do "White Ts, Blue Jeans, and Nikes," scanning the tree line, driving by in Scarface, doing twenty, exhaust of the Malibu popping some rumble. Thinking how fast a situation could change. Thirty minutes earlier he was going to be rich, counting the money. But he wasn't going to get nothing, they didn't find the kid, find him quick.

Looking out at the hood he needed a carwash, had pine needles and shit all over his custom gold metalflake paintwork, color called Aztec bullion, motherfucker had real gold in it—straight up.

DeJuan was driving slow, creepin', glancing at the wall of trees to his right. Saw something up ahead, dude appear coming out of the woods, running toward him, moving his arms like he trying to signal him. Was the kid, and as DeJuan drove up, you should've seen the look on the kid's face, he saw who it was.

Kid took off now, going back in the woods. DeJuan jammed on the brake, skidded to a stop. He grabbed the shotgun off the passenger seat, got out, went after him, running through the trees on this irregular ground, wishing he'd laced up his Nikes.

Caught the dude though, pushed his punk-ass down. Now De-Juan, breathing a little, racked the slide on the shotgun, a semiautomatic Remington Wingmaster twelve-gauge. Said, "Hear that? That's doom herself talking at you. She saying, fuck with me, fuck with me—don't fuck with me."

Little man got the message. Stood up looking scared, shotgun being a powerful communicator. DeJuan noticed the kid had mud on his pants, wondering now how he was going to protect his white leather seats. Had the hides dyed to match his Zegna suit.

Connolly motherfucking leather was some high-profile skins. Shit smell like money. Uh-huh.

The black guy made Luke sit on a blanket he got from his trunk, worried, he said, about Luke getting his ride all full of dirt. It was a strange car with these cheesy white seats and the word *Scarface* inlaid on the wood dash in chrome script.

"Like it? That teakwood," the black guy said, "come from Indonesia."

Like he was looking for Luke's approval.

He reached his hand out, rubbing it over the lacquered surface.

"Feel it, go on."

Luke stretched his arms out and touched the wood with his cuffed hands. It felt smooth and warm.

"Know what that motherfucker cost?"

Luke turned his head, looking at him.

The black guy grinned. "Twenty-five hundred dollars. Believe that? What they get for custom anymore."

Luke couldn't believe it. It was so tacky. Why would anyone pay that much to make their car look like that?

The black guy turned up the stereo.

"Twenty-four Bose speakers. What you think?"

He could feel the heavy *thump thump* of the base. They were listening to a rap song, the black guy talking to him, but Luke could only see his lips moving the music was so loud.

He turned it down and said, "Know Keak?"

Luke said, "What?" He could barely hear him.

"Keak Da Sneak, motherfucker, you deaf?"

Luke shook his head. Who was Keak Da Sneak?

"Born name Kunta Kinte. Mean 'warrior' in Swahili."

The black guy took a long uneven joint out of a compartment

in the console and lit it with a gold lighter. Luke watched him take a deep drag, hold it in till he looked like he was going to explode and let it out, blowing a stream of gray smoke into the windshield, engulfing him in a cloud of hydroponic herb. Luke coughed.

"Yeah, that's some good shit, ain't it?"

He extended his arm, handing the joint to Luke. "Want some?"

Luke looked at him through the smoke and shook his head.

"How you going to expand your consciousness, take your little punk-ass mind to another realm?"

He hit the joint again, held it in till his cheeks puffed up, till the smoke came out like it was under pressure. He turned the music up and started singing, rapping with the rapper, tapping his fingers on the steering wheel as he drove.

"Two outs, two strikes livin' in the ninth innin', smack over the gate, I hit the plate now I'm grinnin'."

He stopped when they pulled in the yard in front of the cottages, shut off the car and it was quiet, Luke's ears ringing like he'd been to a concert.

"My man, Ted going be thizzing over this. Fool has a temper, as you seen. Don't say nothing, see maybe I can chill him."

He was right, Camo was mad. Camo said, "I got mosquito bites all over my neck 'cause of you."

Good, Luke thought.

Camo came at him but stopped, faking like he was going to hit him.

Camo said, "Lookit him quiver like a little sissy."

Luke relaxed, let out a breath. Now Camo turned and hit him with a punch that stunned him and he went down. Camo kicked him in the ribs with his steel-tipped motorcycle boots. He looked like he was going to do it again when the black guy came in the room and stopped him.

"Yo, Ted, want to ease up on my man? Time to collect. Don't fuck with the merchandise. See, he like an expensive vase or something we trying to sell, want it perfect—no chips or scratches and such."

Camo said, "The hell you talking about?"

Twenty-Three

"Sorry," Jack said. "I lost track of time. I was running down the driveway after you, hoping you'd see me."

He was standing right there as she got out of the car.

He said, "Where is it?"

"I don't have it," Kate said. She closed the car door and moved toward the lodge.

"What do you mean? It wasn't there, or they wouldn't give it to you?"

Kate opened the front door and went inside, Jack right behind her.

He said, "Want to tell me what's going on?"

That's what she wanted to know. She took her coat off and hung it on the back of a chair in the breakfast room. She went in the kitchen and got a glass out of the cupboard, opened the freezer, put a handful of ice cubes in the glass, poured some bourbon, and took a sip. She wasn't going to offer him one.

Jack said, "You're kidding about the money, right?" Trying to sound calm. "You're jerking my chain, aren't you? It's in the trunk, isn't it?"

"Why're you so concerned about the money?"

"'Cause you need it to get Luke back," Jack said. "Why do you think?"

His eyes stayed on her, waiting for a response, but she didn't give him one. Now he turned, took a rocks glass out of the cupboard and poured bourbon in it and drank it straight, fixing his gaze back on her.

He said, "Where's my key?"

She took it out of her pocket and threw it to him. He caught it, put his glass down and walked out of the kitchen. She heard the front door open and heard it close when he came back in a few minutes later. He was tense, trying to hide it, but he couldn't.

"Okay, where is it?" Jack said. "Tell me what's going on?"

"I've got a better idea," Kate said. "Why don't you tell me?"

Jack said, "What the hell's gotten into you?"

"Giving the money back, the fifty thousand, makes sense now," Kate said. "With the ransom you'll make a lot more, won't you?" Kate had connected the dots and they led right to Jack. Who else? He knew the problems she was having with Luke. Knew Luke had taken off and they'd be at the lodge, the perfect place to pull it off—remote and isolated. Knew if he gave her the money back she'd think she could trust him, and it sounded like he was acquainted with the kidnappers—his comment about them "spending too much time to fuck it up," like he had inside information. But it was the stolen Lexus that brought it all together, proved Jack was still a crook and got her thinking.

"You're all stressed," Jack said. "You don't know what you're saying."

She looked right at him and said, "Where's Luke?"

"How do I know?"

He was lying, she could see it in his eyes. "You're the only one who could've pulled it off." She walked to the breakfast room table, bent down and took the Beretta out of the pocket of her jacket, racked a round in the chamber, and pointed it at him.

Jack said, "Put it down. This isn't Guatemala. You're not going to shoot your way out. These people are pros. They're good at what they do."

Kate aimed the Beretta at him. "How many are there?"

"Three. Listen to me," Jack said, "if you don't come up with the money . . ."

He didn't finish what he was going to say, but the implication was clear.

Kate said, "Where's Luke?"

"He's okay," Jack said. "That's all you need to know. Give them the money and you'll get him back. It's that easy."

"Them," Kate said. "Like you're not part of it, huh?"

"They were going to do it anyway," Jack said, "with or without me."

There he was—making excuses, as always.

"Let me ask you something," Kate said. "What's your share?"

"What difference does it make?" Jack said. "It's not going to change your life one way or the other."

"It already has," Kate said.

He swallowed the last of his drink.

"You've been at it all along, haven't you? Since the day you left me."

He poured more bourbon in the glass and looked at her.

"Never really stopped except for my time in stir," Jack said.

He was confessing now like there was truth serum in the

booze. He told her about his thirty-eight months in the Arizona Penitentiary.

Kate listened, not surprised by any of it.

"I'm the way I am," Jack said. "And I don't see myself changing. That much I've figured out."

"I came to that same conclusion about an hour ago when a sheriff's deputy pulled me over for driving a stolen car." She told him what happened.

He said, "Cop know who you are?"

"If he did, there'd be a fleet of white Crown Vics parked out front with their lights flashing."

She was in the breakfast room and he was in the kitchen, two feet of counter separating them, looking at each other.

Jack said, "Maybe they haven't found him yet."

"Haven't found him? He's right there on Dumas Road, a hundred feet from the main highway, handcuffed to the steering wheel," Kate said. "I'm the one they're going to be looking for." She thought about the consequences of what she'd done, but it seemed trivial in light of her current situation.

Jack said, "Where's the money at?"

"In a safe place."

"As long as you have it."

Kate said, "How's it going to happen? Are they going to call again?"

"You're supposed to give me the money," Jack said, like he was trying out the line. "I'll take it to them and bring Luke back here. That's what we agreed to. That's why I got involved—to make sure nothing happened to him."

"That's why you got involved, huh?" Kate shook her head. "To help a kid you don't even know. Why am I having trouble believing that?" She squeezed the grip of the Beretta.

"I'm being straight with you."

It sounded weak, like he didn't believe it either.

Kate said, "Do you really think I'm going to trust you with two million?"

"You don't have a choice in the matter," Jack said. "They want the money first."

"No way," Kate said. "First, I want to see my boy."

"I'll do what I can."

"You better do more than that," Kate said. "Tell them to bring Luke here, I'll give you the money. Tell them that's the way we're going to do it."

He said, "I just want you to know I'm sorry about all this."

"Is that right? I want you to know something too—this kid you've kidnapped and put up for ransom is yours." She let that sink in before she continued. "You hear what I'm telling you? He's your flesh and blood. You may recall I thought I was pregnant when you left town. Well, I was."

Jack grinned. "Come on?"

Kate said, "I figured you'd say something like that."

"If it was true you'd have told me before now."

"You think I'm making this up?"

Jack's face went pale all of a sudden, like he might be sick.

"You telling me your husband didn't know Luke wasn't his?"

"Sure he knew," Kate said.

"And he didn't care?"

"Owen knew it before he asked me to marry him and raised Luke like he was his own. Never said a negative word about it."

Jack looked out the kitchen window and then back at her.

"Why didn't you have more kids?"

"I couldn't," Kate said.

"Why not?"

"What difference does it make?"

"Look at it from my point of view," Jack said. "It's hard to believe."

"That's because you don't want to believe it," Kate said. "Then you'd have to admit responsibility and you've always had trouble with that."

"Whatever," Jack said.

Jack went outside and stood on the gravel drive, thinking about the bomb Kate just dropped on him. He never wanted a kid and didn't want one now. Why'd she tell him? So he'd make sure nothing happened to him? Nothing was going to anyway.

DeJuan suggested the kidnapping, although it had been stewing in the back of his brain too. Jack liked the idea 'cause it sounded easy and it solved a major problem. He could get Teddy and DeJuan off his back and make some money and cruise for a while. Kate was rich—it wasn't going to change her life one way or the other.

The plan: they'd split the take, return Luke to his mother and go their separate ways. Kate would never even know he was involved. They were going to grab Luke at the house the day he left: Teddy and Celeste would go in, get him after school, bring him to Teddy's place in Clawson, keep him in the basement till Kate got the money.

Jack's job was to keep Kate away from the house, then keep her calm, make sure she got the money and didn't call the police. He also had to tell them when and where to find Luke. Without him, it wouldn't have happened.

Luke taking off threw a wrench in the works for a couple days, but definitely made it easier in the long run. The remote location turned out to be an advantage too.

Now things were a little more complicated, but still workable. He'd get his share of the money and take off just like he planned. He didn't see that changing.

———

DeJuan was expecting the phone to ring and it did, but still surprised him. Heard 50 Cent doing "Candy Shop," his ring tone:

> *Give it to me baby, nice and slow*
> *Climb on top, ride like you in the rodeo*

DeJuan recognized Jack's number, said, "Yo—got the money, I
hope is why you calling. Going to be right over with it."

Jack said, "There's been a change in the plan."

"What's that mean?"

"We get the money when she gets Luke."

DeJuan said, "Don't sound like you got control of the situation. I hope there be no more surprises." He didn't like the sound
of this. They were telling her how it was going to be. She wasn't
telling them.

Kate watched him from the kitchen window. He took his cell
phone out and made a call, his face animated like he was arguing
with the person he was talking to. After a couple minutes he
closed the phone and put it in his pocket and just stood there,
looking out at the woods.

Twenty-Four

"They're here," Jack said, coming in the kitchen.

She heard them drive in the yard and looked out the kitchen window. There were two cars, an old Z28 Camaro and another one she could only identify as a customized mid-eighties Chevy. It had a custom paint job and rims and a landau top.

"Don't go out there with a gun," Jack said. "They might get the wrong idea. Give it to me or put it on the counter. Let's not have any trouble, okay?"

"No, it's not okay," Kate said. She walked past him and moved through the main room and out the front door.

She watched Luke being lifted from the trunk of the Camaro and it made her mad, made her want to raise the gun and shoot them. She was conscious of the black guy who held a shotgun across his body like he was getting ready to shoot skeet. He was on her left about thirty feet away. Jack was to her right, half that distance, and Mullet, Luke and the girl straight ahead on the gravel drive.

Luke's hands were cuffed behind his back like a criminal. They looked at each other, made eye contact and he tried to come toward her, but Mullet held him in place with a chain that was looped around the cuffs. She could see his face was bruised and he looked thin and weak standing there. "Luke, honey, are you okay?"

The girl aimed her pistol at Luke. She said, "He ain't going to be, you don't drop the automatic. I'll shoot the little asshole and wouldn't that be a shame after we've been so patient?"

They all looked familiar. Kate remembered Mullet, the creep from the bar, sitting across the table from her with his greasy hair and confident grin. She remembered him saying they'd probably see each other again because he knew they would, the kidnapping had been planned by then.

She remembered the girl too, thinking she and Mullet didn't go together. It seemed even more apparent now, as Kate studied her in her black pointed-toe pumps and bootleg jeans, sweater hanging below her tweed fitted jacket, the outfit displaying a mix of fabrics embellished with beads—like she just walked out of an Anthropologie catalog.

The black guy looked familiar too. She remembered the corn-row hair and the gold warm-up and the letter D hanging from a heavy chain around his neck—anodized bling. She'd seen him somewhere before, she was sure of it. But where? It was his gold metalflake Chevy that jogged her memory. She remembered it from the gas station in Grayling. He was filling up next to her. Asked her for directions, which seemed odd now, if he was following her. She remembered seeing him at the house, too. He was the DTE man dressed in a blue uniform, checking the meter in the backyard.

Mullet said, "Jack, you tell your girl what we talked about, what we decided?"

Kate said, "No, Jack, I don't believe you did." She thought Jack would take charge of the situation, but he stood there looking like he wasn't sure what to do or who he was siding with.

Jack said to Kate, "There's only one way out of this, you've got to give me your gun."

Jack stepped toward her and she raised the Beretta and aimed it at him.

He put his hands up and said, "Take it easy."

The black guy said, "Yo, Jack, where the money at?"

"I don't know," Jack said. "She hid it somewhere."

The black guy said, "He got one job to do, can't even do that."

Mullet said to Jack, "You better tell her what to do, or I will." Mullet grinned at Kate, the grin mocking her—and in a flashback she saw the face of the skinny cop in Guatemala—looking at her the same way, underestimating her.

Kate held the Beretta at arm's length down her right side. She'd shoot the black guy with the twelve-gauge first. Then go for the girl. She'd never get Mullet, though, with Luke standing in front of him. She said, "Let him go."

"We let him go, you put the gun down," the black guy said. "We cool? You give us something, we give you something—everybody happy."

"What're you asking her for?" the girl said. "You tell her."

"Back nuba, simba," the black guy said. "We negotiating."

"Why don't I just shoot her," the girl said, "put an end to all this?" She extended her arm, aiming her gun at Kate.

"You hear this thug gangsta bitch?" he said to Mullet.

"You got the twelve-gauge," the girl said, "you do it, then. Why we putting up with this?"

The black guy said, "Everybody be cool. We gonna make the

transaction. Ain't nobody gonna shoot nobody. We like family now."

Kate said, "If you shoot me, how you going to find the money?"

"I was wondering the same thing," the black guy said to Kate. "Let's quit flambosting, chill this motherfucker. Give peace a chance."

Mullet pressed the barrel of his gun, a big chrome-plated automatic, against Luke's temple. He looked at Kate and said, "You got ten seconds—one . . . two . . ."

"Don't worry," the black guy said, "doubt he can count that high."

"Mom," Luke said, "just do what they want, will you?"

Mullet stopped counting.

Everyone turned and looked at him.

Kate dropped the Beretta.

The girl said, "Kick that little weenie gun over here."

"Little man like Talleyrand," the black guy said.

"What you talking about?" Mullet said, "Running your mouth, you never stop."

"Talleyrand, Charles Maurice, motherfucker—French diplomat, homie a Napoléon."

Teddy said, "Who?"

The black guy shook his head. "Man doesn't know who Napoléon is."

Kate knew, of all of them, he was the one to keep an eye on. Don't be fooled by the street rap, the hip-hop cool, the fractured syntax—he was the smartest one by far, including Jack, who, instead of taking charge, waited to be told what to do like he was the hired help. What happened to him?

Mullet unlocked the handcuffs now and Luke ran to her and put his arms around her and held on tight and she could feel him tremble in her embrace.

The black guy grinned at her and said, "Now we making progress. Got the little man back, take me to the mon-ey."

When Bill Wink heard the eyewitness account, he couldn't help but think it was Kate. Joe Lamborne said she looked rich and then described her in perfect detail: a real knockout, five seven, a hundred and fifteen, blond hair, nice rack, looked about thirty-five.

If it wasn't Kate McCall, she had a twin. The car she was driving sounded familiar too. Wasn't her friend cruising around in a green Lexus? Sure, the one with the busted taillight. Bill remembered it parked in front of the market in Omena.

He didn't say anything to Joe, who'd been suspended without pay, pending an investigation—or to his sergeant. The way he viewed it, Kate was in trouble and this was the perfect opportunity to help her and be a hero.

Of course, his first question was, why was she driving a stolen car? Bill's mind wrestled with that one until he got a call from Johnny Crow, Johnny saying he saw the rich lady—you know, the one from the woods—she was picking up money, a lot of money, from the bank in Traverse.

Bill called the bank manager, Mr. Ken Calvert, who'd said Mrs. McCall had withdrawn a substantial amount of cash but bank-customer confidentiality prevented him from giving Bill any more information—even in his law enforcement capacity. Although Calvert said he could tell the deputy that he understood it was being used to consummate a real estate deal.

As far as Bill was concerned, it all pointed back to the kidnapping theory. He believed Luke was being held hostage somewhere, and Kate, he believed, was in trouble—needed his help, but was too afraid to contact him. He was pumped thinking about it, standing in front of the mirror in his bathroom getting dressed, looking at himself, his face with the confident grin. He was wearing his uniform pants and a white T-shirt. He turned sideways and flexed his right arm, the biceps rolling up, making a muscle. He looked strong. He was strong. He could bench-press 325 pounds. Do it five times.

He slipped on a Point Blank Pro Plus vest. It was their top-of-the-line body armor, designed to stop a .357 Magnum 158-grain round, a 240-grain .44 Magnum, and even a 148-grain .762 Nato round fired by an M16. Only thing it couldn't handle was a 30.06. If one of the kidnappers had a big bore rifle he was out of luck, but he seriously doubted that would be the case.

He put his uniform shirt on over the vest, buttoned it and tucked it in his pants. He strapped his black leather Safariland duty belt around his waist. Fully loaded it weighed fourteen pounds and had everything he needed: his ASP tactical baton, two sets of handcuffs, two extra magazines for his Glock, flashlight, key keeper and pepper spay. The pepper spray had an aerosol projector for long-range deployments, which meant he could blind a perp from fifteen feet or more. He unhooked his holster and drew his Glock 21, pointed it at the mirror image of himself.

He'd cleaned the gun the night before, dipped a patch in solvent and passed a jag through the bore to loosen the fouling. The barrel was still dirty, so he did it again. Then he'd dipped a phosphor brush in solvent and scrubbed the forcing cones, ejectors and slides where a lot of powder residue had built up, working it until everything was nice and clean. He'd popped in the magazine, pulled back the slide and loaded a hollow point in the throat.

He looked at himself in the mirror again, nodded his approval and walked out of his trailer where the mud-splattered cruiser was parked. He made a mental note to get it washed. He was a Leelanau County sheriff's deputy, and as such, he had to portray a positive image.

He opened the trunk, took out his Hi-Standard Flite King twelve-gauge and loaded it with five Hevi-Shot Nitro Magnum shells. He closed the trunk, got in the car, put the shotgun on the floor—barrel pointing down. He forgot his hat and went inside to get it.

His stomach was nervous when he got back in the car. The full import of what he was about to do weighing on him now. Should he call for backup? He couldn't say with absolute certainty that something was actually going to happen. It was all a hunch and if he was wrong, he'd look like a fool. But if he was right, then what?

Twenty-Five

Teddy said, "I never seen so much money in one place in all my days. I'm going to buy me a Ford F250 4×4 with the extended cab and a set of twenty-inch rims. That is one sweet truck."

He reminded Kate of a kid on Christmas.

Celeste knelt across from Teddy. She put her pistol on the rug, picking up crisp, just-off-the-press packets of money. The white bands that went around the bills had "$10,000" stamped on them.

"What're you going to get yourself?" Teddy said.

"Anything I please," Celeste said.

"That's the way," Teddy said. He was eating potato chips out of the bag, drinking a can of Bud. He said, "Hey, know what the best beer in the world is?"

Celeste didn't acknowledge him, her attention fixed on the money.

"Free beer," Teddy said.

"What if you don't like it—it isn't your brand?" Celeste said.

"Who cares?" Teddy said. "If it's free, it's good."

Kate watched them from the breakfast room while she set the table. *Like the two million in front of you*, she was thinking. She didn't care about the money, just wanted them to leave.

Teddy was on his knees on the floor, picking up handfuls of it. He glanced at Kate and said, "Well, I sure am grateful to you for this. It's been a pleasure doing business with you. Now, where's my supper at?"

"It's cooking," Kate said.

"Well, hurry it up," Teddy said. "I'm so hungry, I could eat the ass out of a wild boar."

Celeste got up and sat on one of the leather couches, feeding Leon a pretzel. She said, "Does him yike that? Does him tink it's nummy? Does him?"

She sat on the edge of a cushion now, patted her thighs, looked at Leon, and said, "Uppy. Come on, uppy."

Leon looked at her like she was crazy and then thought what the hell and lifted his front paws up. She grabbed them and said, "Thay, thay, thay . . ."

Then Celeste let go of Leon's paws and slid off the couch on her knees, hugging the dog who went down and rolled over on his back, pink tongue hanging out the side of his mouth. Celeste scratched his chest and rubbed his neck. "Him's tha big man, yeth him ith, yeth him ith."

Leon rolled over and got back on his feet and Celeste gave him another pretzel. She said, "Him's a cooter, ithn't him?" She took his head in her hands and rubbed it. "Yeth him ith. Yeth him ith."

Teddy took a swig of beer and said, "Why're you talking in that stupid fucking voice? God, that's annoying."

Celeste said, "You're annoying. You don't like it, don't listen."

Jack was on the other side of the room by himself, sitting in a leather chair, cuffed to a belly chain. He looked helpless. Kate met his gaze, thinking, you brought this on yourself, don't look at me for sympathy.

She went back in the kitchen and flipped the burgers that were sizzling, grease popping in a fourteen-inch skillet. She'd made six patties from a two-pound mixture of round and chuck. Teddy'd said he was hungry and told her to get her ass in the kitchen and make them supper. Her real motivation was to feed Luke, who said he hadn't eaten much in three days.

Kate heated up a couple cans of Bush's beans and made potato salad with red skins and celery and red onion mixed with oil and mayo. She was thinking about the scene in the yard as she watched the meat fry—the situation tense till Luke diffused it: Mom, just do what they want, will you?

After they released Luke she led them to the pump house, a log structure that looked like a mini version of the lodge and had a well inside. The pump house was in plain sight, nestled between the yard and the woods. She opened the door and there was the money stacked on the floor. She'd parked in the woods and un-loaded it.

DeJuan said to Jack, "What's the matter with you? Money right here, Jack still looking for clues."

Jack said, "You got it, don't you? What's the problem?"

They'd turned on him after that, like it was their plan all along. DeJuan brought the chain from his car and cuffed Jack on the spot.

DeJuan said, "Check it out—Hiatt-Thompson belly chain, answer to all your security needs. Meets US National Institute of Justice tests for workmanship, strength and tamper resistance."

He glanced at Teddy and said, "Best of all, it's made right here in the good ole US of A."

Kate was thinking a belly chain could've come in handy with

the neighborhood men who'd hit on her—lock them down and send them home to their wives.

Jack said, "What is this?"

DeJuan said, "This payback, motherfucker." He pulled on the chain. "How that feel? Feel like you back in the joint, I can see it."

Teddy said, "We've been waiting a long time for this."

"Jack," DeJuan said, "he not loyal to no one but his self."

Kate could relate.

She heard DeJuan's voice now, turned and saw him come in the room, still carrying the shotgun. Teddy was on the floor hoisting handfuls of money like a pauper idiot.

"Yo, be cool," DeJuan said. "Don't be bruising the greens."

Teddy said, "Huh?"

DeJuan said, "Give a brother some love."

He threw a banded packet and DeJuan caught it with his right hand. He brought the stack of bills up to his nose, inhaling like it was something he'd just taken off the barbecue.

"Nothing like the smell of fresh green," DeJuan said.

Luke was in bad shape—face beat up, wrists bleeding from the handcuffs. Kate rubbed Neosporin on the cuts and gave him Motrin for the pain. His clothes were mud-covered. He was standing at the kitchen counter stuffing food in his mouth: cheese and crackers, hunter's sausage, slices of bread and butter. She'd never seen him so hungry. She held his little face in her hands and said, "What'd they do to you?"

"Teddy likes to hit people."

Kate could feel herself getting angry. "Well, he's not going to hit you anymore."

"It's my fault," Luke said. "I shouldn't have come up here."

"They were going to do it anyway."

"I thought Jack was your friend."

"I did too," Kate said.

Luke had tears in his eyes and she hugged him and said, "It's going to be okay now."

"No, it isn't," he said.

"They'll be gone soon and we'll go home," Kate said.

He glanced down at the floor and back up, meeting her gaze. He looked like he was about to say something, but hesitated.

Kate said, "What?"

"I heard them talking," Luke said. "We know what they look like. They said they're going to . . . kill us."

"That doesn't make sense," Kate said. "They got what they wanted. There'd be no reason to." Then she thought about the killers in *In Cold Blood*. They didn't have a reason, either.

"No reason to do what?" DeJuan said, coming in the kitchen.

"You want something?" Kate said, her voice tense.

"Checking up on northern Michigan cooks. There a meal somewhere in our future?"

Kate said, "We're all set. Everybody sit down."

"Well halle-fucking-lujah," DeJuan said.

She couldn't stop thinking about what Luke said. There was no way, she told herself. They were going to eat and leave. Jack would never have agreed to that. But, as she analyzed the situation, Jack didn't appear to have much sway at the moment. Kate brought the burgers to the table on a platter with slices of red onion and tomatoes and dill pickles. She went back in the kitchen and got the bowls of potato salad and beans and put them on the table next to the burgers. She said to Teddy, "Okay, here you go."

Teddy and DeJuan and Celeste sat down and filled their plates and ate like it was the last supper. Kate thought it was odd that these people who'd just collected two million dollars were so concerned about their stomachs.

DeJuan held his burger in his hands and said, "You and the little man sit down, join us,"

"I'm not hungry," Kate said.

"Don't matter," DeJuan said. "Want your company."

She knew their names now: Teddy, Celeste and DeJuan—Teddy had introduced everyone earlier like they were neighbors getting together for the first time. Luke sat on the end next to DeJuan, with his back to the room. Kate sat next to Celeste, across from Teddy, who was shoveling potato salad in his mouth and had grease from the burger dripping off the end of his chin.

"What about Jack?" Kate said.

"What about him?" Teddy said.

Kate said, "Can I give him something to eat?" She wanted a chance to talk to him, find out what he thought, what he knew.

"Hell no," Teddy said. "He gets to set there, smell it and get hungry."

Kate could feel her patience wearing thin.

Teddy had mayo in the corners of his mouth, talking while he chewed his potato salad. "I was thinking I might get me a Harley—"

Celeste said, "Think you could stop talking with your mouth open, use your napkin? You got the manners of an animal, I swear."

DeJuan said, "Man spent his formative years hanging with sheep. What you expect?"

Kate felt the tension building. She couldn't hold it in any longer and said, "You've got your money. Why don't you take it and get the hell out of here?"

"Whoa," Teddy said, and grinned. "What the hell's got into you?" He winked at Celeste and she smiled. "I don't think she likes us."

"I don't think about you one way or the other," Kate said. She made eye contact with Luke, could see he was worried.

"Oh, you don't, huh?" Teddy said. "What's the matter? We not good enough for you?"

"She wants us to leave," Celeste said. "Then what's she going to do, call the police?" Celeste looked across the table at her. "You going to tell them what we look like?"

" 'Course she is," Teddy said. "She's going to tell them everything about us."

Celeste said, "My-oh-my, what should we do with 'em?"

Teddy looked at her and flashed a lunatic grin. "You know what we're going to do."

Kate could see he got pleasure out of this—making them squirm. She glanced at Luke and then at Teddy. "You're not going to do anything," she said, trying to convince herself. She was afraid now, but smiled at Luke, trying to ease the tension.

Celeste said, "I'd be worried if I were them."

"Don't listen to that," Jack said. "They're just trying to scare you."

Teddy glanced over at Jack and said, "The fuck do you know?" Now he looked across the table at Kate and said, "He tell you what happen in Arizona?"

Jack said, "That's old news."

Teddy ignored him and said, "We hit A.J.'s—this rich-folk gourmet market in the foothills of the Catalinas. Planned it for Sunday evening, get their take from the weekend. Do it with a lot of people around, we don't attract attention. Me and him," indicating DeJuan, "filled up carts like real shoppers."

He shoveled a forkful of beans in his mouth and kept talking.

"The office was upstairs, so Jack and I go up and open the door and catch the manager fooling around with this young cute thing, had her blouse off, man pawing her sweater puppies. They both looked at us and manager says, 'Can I help you?'

And Jack says, 'Yeah, you can take your hands off her and show us the safe.' The manager says, 'Is this some kind of a joke?' Jack pulls his Colt Python and says, 'Does this look like a joke to you?'

"Jack went in the other room and cleaned out the safe and I duct-taped the manager and the girl together and watched the door. After about ten minutes, I went to check on him, and he wasn't there. Disappeared with $257,000. Left me standing there holding my dick. Pardon my French."

Teddy glanced across the room at Jack. "That sound about right to you?"

What Teddy left out—the most important part—was the police showing up. Jack had cleaned out the safe, filled two A.J.'s grocery bags, the kind with paper handles. Glanced out the window behind the store. There was a driveway for delivery trucks to pull up and beyond it a brick wall that bordered the employee parking lot. He watched two Tucson police cars cruise in at high speed, lights flashing, and hit their brakes.

He crossed the room, went into the manager's office. The manager and his half-clothed assistant were still on the couch, duct-taped together. He didn't see Teddy at the door and he left the office and walked into the hallway. He heard the din: sounds and voices coming up the stairs from the market floor. He followed the hallway to the end, pushed open a steel door that had a sign that read: DO NOT OPEN ALARM WILL SOUND.

It didn't.

And now he was running across the green metal roof of the strip mall over Starbucks, Target, Blockbuster, Subway, Home Depot. He hid behind a giant air-conditioning unit, catching his breath. He looked back, saw a cop in a tan uniform appear on the roof a hundred yards away, holding his gun with two hands, swinging his arms in a short jerking motion like cops on TV.

Jack opened a roof hatch, slid his hands through the handles of the paper bags and climbed down a steel-rung ladder into the Home Depot stockroom. He saw boxes arranged on huge floor-to-ceiling shelves. He could see a guy driving a Hi-Lo across the room and walked in the opposite direction, went out a swinging door into the showroom with his two A.J.'s grocery bags full of money and kept going.

Jack walked four blocks to the Adobe Flats motel, checked in and poured the money on the queen-size bed and counted it. There was $166,000 (although A.J's would later say it was $257,000 and that was the amount quoted in newspaper articles).

He took a wad of bills and folded it and put it in his pocket and put the rest back in the bags. He stood on the bed and reached up and pushed a ceiling tile in. The room had a drop ceiling. He put the money up in the space and replaced the tile.

He heard sirens outside and got off the bed and went to the window and pulled the curtains apart and saw two police cars speed by on Campbell, lights flashing. If they got split up, they were supposed to meet at the Rodeo Bar on Speedway. But first he had to have something to eat. He was starving, hadn't had a thing since morning and it was going on six in the evening. He walked out of the motel and crossed the motor court and went two blocks to a taco stand with picnic tables he'd seen earlier, called Guero's. He wanted an ice-cold Dos Equis for his parched throat and a plate of chicken burritos and beans and rice for his empty stomach but got a couple of Glock nines in his face instead.

Jack never found out who dimed him but suspected the old dude who checked him in the motel. He was watching TV when Jack came in the office, a western-dandy type with a waxed moustache, wearing a lot of turquoise and silver jewelry.

DeJuan said, "Motherfucker got greedy, decide to take it all for his self."

Teddy grinned, showing a mouthful of beans. He said, "Now you know why he's over there and we're over here."

They didn't have a clue and Jack wasn't going to explain it. He felt like a fool for letting these clowns get the jump on him. Never saw it coming. But he had to admit, DeJuan was a lot smarter than he seemed.

What bothered Jack as much as losing his share of the money was finding out he had a kid. Never thought he'd be a dad, marriage not being something he ever wanted any part of. And yet, he found himself studying Luke, checking him out to see if there was any resemblance. Looked at his features: his nose and eyes and ears and forehead and cheekbones. Jack thought he favored Kate more than him. Had her fair complexion and thick full hair and thin build. But it was Luke's hands that caught his attention. They were his hands—only a smaller version. Luke being his kid wasn't going to change anything. It was way too late for that now.

Jack thought about his life and wondered: If he could do it over, would he do it different? And the answer was—no. He pictured himself belly-chained like he was, going back to prison—a two-time loser—doing ten years this time and it scared the hell out of him. He had to figure a way out of this somehow.

He watched the group at the table like some dysfunctional sitcom family. Kate got up without saying anything and moved into the main room.

Teddy said, "Where you think you're going?"

"Upstairs," Kate said. "I've got to get Luke some clean clothes."

"The hell you are," Teddy said.

Kate ignored him. She went to the stairs and started up.

"Hey," Teddy said, "you hear what I told you?"

DeJuan got up. "I'm on it." He came around the table and went after her.

She was in Luke's room, taking a pair of jeans out of his dresser, when DeJuan came in, standing in the doorway, the shotgun in his hands like it was glued to him. He sat at Luke's desk, watching her.

Kate glanced at him. "I'm not going to hurt you."

DeJuan smiled. "You not? What a relief."

"You don't need the shotgun."

"Which probably mean I do."

She opened the closet and took a red and blue flannel shirt off a hanger, draping it over the jeans.

DeJuan said, "What up? What you really doing?"

Kate said, "What's it look like?"

"Getting feisty, huh? Givin' DeJuan attitude. What it look like—look like you tryin' to sneak out, get away. That what you doing?"

"Why don't you go back down?" Kate said. "I'll meet you in a few minutes. I've got to get something in my room, go to the ladies."

She walked past him now, out of the room, carrying Luke's clothes. He followed her down the hall to her room. He got on the king-size bed, leaned back against the headboard, pillows propped under him, laid the shotgun on the comforter.

She went to her dresser, opened a drawer, and took out a brown cable-knit sweater she bought at Nordstrom, remembering the price—$180 marked down three times to $22. She opened her underwear drawer—not knowing what he could see—and gripped the Smith and Wesson .357 Airweight, bringing it out of the drawer, hiding it in the pile of clothes between her sweater and Luke's shirt.

DeJuan said, "Now this the kind of bed I like—extra firm."

She closed the drawer and glanced over her shoulder, saw him grin at her and grab his crotch.

"Yo, girlfriend, I got something else over here extra firm." He patted the bed next to him. "Got something special for you—never seen nothing like this."

She started moving across the room toward the door.

He slid off the bed, leaving the shotgun where it was and caught her before she got to the door. Stood in front of her, acting like he thought she was interested.

She gripped the handle of the Airweight under the clothes and said, "Let's see what you're so proud of." Wanting to pull the trigger, get it over with, but knowing she couldn't. It was too risky with Luke downstairs.

DeJuan dropped his pants to his ankles standing there posing—his thing hanging out—a sly grin on his face.

Kate said, "That's all you got?" She stepped past him and he tried to grab her, tripped over his pants and fell on the floor. She ran along the upstairs hall and went down the stairs. Celeste met her at the bottom, pointing the Ruger at her chest.

"What do you think you're doing?" she said and slapped her across the face with an open hand.

Kate had her finger on the trigger. Jack was still in the same chair like he was paralyzed. She didn't see Luke, and that was what kept her from making a move. Don't be dumb, she told herself.

"Put it on the floor," Celeste said. "Let's see what you've got there."

Kate bent down and placed the clothes on the rug.

Celeste shuffled through the pile and the Airweight fell out. Celeste picked it up and aimed it at Kate as DeJuan appeared at the top of the stairs and said, "Yo, we got company."

Teddy came in the room now, pulling Luke by his shirt collar, and said, "Cop just pulled in. Sheriff's deputy."

Celeste said, "How many?"

"Looks like just one," Teddy said. He glanced at Celeste. "Stay here and watch 'em."

"You stay here," she said. "I'm gonna take care of this one. It's my turn."

Twenty-Six

Celeste watched him get out of the car with the shotgun. He was wearing his two-tone uniform and a brown baseball cap with a gold star on the front. He took his hat off and rubbed his brush cut. He looked around and went to the front windows and looked in.

Now he walked along the west side of the cabin. Staring at the tire tracks in the grass, following them, then stopping, looking through a side window into the main room. He held a shotgun in his hands, looking alert, and came to the far edge of the cabin almost in the backyard.

Celeste came around the corner and met him. She said, "What's up, Officer? Remember me?"

He aimed the shotgun at her. She could tell he was nervous. He looked left toward the woods, turned and looked behind him.

He said, "Mrs. McCall here?"

"She's inside," Celeste said. "Want me to get her?"

"You look familiar," the deputy said.

Celeste said, "Would you mind pointing that scattergun somewhere else? It makes me nervous."

He aimed the shotgun barrel at the ground.

"What's the problem, Officer?" She had the Ruger tucked in the waistband of her jeans, could feel it pressing against one of her butt cheeks. "You expecting trouble?"

The deputy stared at her.

Celeste said, "Carrying a shotgun and wearing a vest?" She could see the impression of it puffing out his shirt.

"Don't leave home without it," the deputy said.

"That's clever," she said. "Ever considered a career in advertising?"

"Yeah," he said, "that's why I became a cop."

He grinned, showing he was a fun guy.

She saw DeJuan appear, coming around the south side of the cabin, moving toward the deputy, leveling his twelve-gauge.

"You aren't by chance an Aryan, are you?"

DeJuan was getting closer—thirty feet away now.

"My parents were committed, but I never bought it myself," the deputy said. "Why do you ask?"

"I had a feeling," she said. "I don't know." But she did. It was the muscles and the brush cut and the blue eyes. He looked like one of Richard Butler's Ayran Warriors. "How do you feel about blacks?"

DeJuan was closing in—twenty feet now.

"I don't dislike anyone 'less they give me a reason," he said.

"How about city jigs with shotguns, who want to do you great bodily harm?"

"I'd take issue with that," he said.

" 'Cause there's one behind you right now."

The deputy turned like she knew he would and brought the

shotgun up, but he was too late. DeJuan fired. Boom. The first blast hit him in the chest, blowing the shotgun out of his hands, sending him backpedaling.

DeJuan racked the twelve-gauge, moving toward him. The second blast hit him in the head and he went down, body twitching. Celeste pulled the Ruger from her waistband and shot him twice and he lay still.

Celeste said, "Think he told dispatch where he was going?"

DeJuan said, "Why you asking me?"

Teddy appeared now, walking up behind her, and looked at the deputy. "O death, O death, won't you spare me over for another year," he said in a singsong voice. "I guess not." He glanced at her. "I'm death, I come to take the soul. Leave the body and leave it cold."

Celeste said, "What the hell's that?"

"Them's words from a song my uncle used to sing when somebody passed away."

"This motherfucker didn't pass away," DeJuan said. "He blown away."

"Where they at?" Celeste said.

"Locked up tighter than a jaybird's ass," Teddy said.

"How about Jack?"

"Dumbass setting there in his bracelets," Teddy said, "tryin' to figure out what the hell happened."

Teddy picked up the deputy's shotgun, which was now pocked with buckshot, the pump lever hanging from the barrel. "That's a damn shame—ruined a perfectly good Hi-Standard Flite King twelve-guage."

"We through with the small talk now? Got to get the deputy out of here," DeJuan said.

Celeste said, "What if he told the station where he was going?"

"What if he did?" Teddy said.

"They don't hear from him," Celeste said, "they send rein-forcements out here to have a look."

"I think we'll be gone by then," Teddy said.

"What if we're not?"

Twenty-Seven

Kate heard the first shotgun blast and then another one, followed by two pistol shots and she knew somebody was probably dead and hoped it wasn't Bill Wink.

If she had any doubts about what Luke had said earlier, she didn't now. If these lunatics had no qualms about killing a police officer, they weren't going to debate too long about Luke and her.

They were locked in the storage room. It measured twelve feet by fifteen feet, with a high ceiling that had exposed log beams like the rest of the lodge. There was a window up in the peak behind the rafters, letting in afternoon sunlight.

One side of the room had shelves stocked with canned goods and kitchen supplies. The other side had hooks in the wall where coats and jackets hung. Under the hooks were shelves for shoes and boots.

She stared at Owen's bloodstained camo jacket hanging there and his hunting boots that were covered with dry brittle mud.

Some of it had come off and looked like gray dust on the wood shelf. She pictured Owen that last morning, Owen with his low-key manner, surprised by her fearful intuition. Yeah, she'd thought something was going to happen but had no idea what. She thought about how his death set into motion a whole series of events that led to their current situation. There was no way anyone could've predicted it—it was too bizarre.

Owen's compound bow was in its case, hanging from a strap behind the camo jacket. Teddy'd either missed it or hadn't considered it a threat when he checked the room and locked them in. He'd gone through Owen's field pack and found his buck knife. He took it out of the sheath and held up the eight-inch blade.

He said, "Will you lookit this pigsticker? Bet you could gut a whitetail, huh?" He grinned at Kate. "Or anything else you please."

He slid the knife back in the sheath and glanced at Luke. "Hey, what'd it feel like to kill your old man?"

Luke stared at him, gave him a hard look, but didn't say anything.

Teddy said, "Do it on purpose, did you? Tired of him messing with you?"

She saw Luke's body tense, knowing Teddy's cheap shot had hit a nerve.

"You want to take a swing at me, don't you?" Teddy said, still grinning. "Have at it, you got the guts."

Luke took a step toward Teddy and Kate wrapped her arms around him, holding him back from doing anything stupid.

Teddy said, "Well, okay, I'll check back with you later."

He walked out of the room and closed the door and she heard the key rattle against metal as he locked it.

Kate let go of Luke and said, "Don't listen to that lunatic. He wants you to give him a reason to hurt you." She went over and lifted the bow case off the hook and put it on the floor and opened it, staring at Owen's Browning Mirage with its built-in quiver of razor-tipped arrows.

Luke said, "What're you doing?"

Kate said, "Giving us a chance. You were right, they're not going to leave any witnesses."

She closed the bow case and handed it to him, but he wouldn't take it.

He said, "I can't."

Kate said, "Do you understand what's going on here? This might be the only way."

He seemed to consider what she was saying and reached out and took the case and slung it over his shoulder.

Kate glanced up at the window. "You've got to get out of here and go to Autry's, tell Elvin to call the sheriff's department." The Autrys were their closest neighbors—about a mile and a half away.

"I'm not going to leave you," Luke said.

"You're not going to have to—I'll be right behind you. But you've got to go first and not worry about me."

She watched him climb up the shelves to the top. He stood up and swung his leg over the center beam—a log that had to be two feet in diameter—and balanced himself on it, the log between his legs like he was riding it, the strap of the bow case slung over his shoulder across his chest. He shimmied to the other side of the narrow room and climbed up into the rafters and made his way to the window.

Kate said, "Be careful."

He said, "I'm not leaving till you come up here."

Jack looked out the window and watched DeJuan and Teddy lift the deputy, put him in the backseat of the patrol car. DeJuan drove off in it and Celeste followed him in the Camaro. He watched Teddy go around behind the lodge, standing on the lawn, smoking a cigarette, staring out at the lake.

This was the opportunity he was waiting for. Jack got up and moved into the kitchen, looking for a carving knife. He remembered being in the yard one day talking to a biker named Lunchbox who lived in C Block. Box had a gut and looked like an extra in *Hell's Angels Forever*.

He'd said, "With the right tool, you can open a pair of handcuffs in a matter of seconds. The locking system in every handcuff made in the last hundred years is the same pawl-and-ratchet mechanism. You want to defeat it, you got two ways to go: you can jimmy-jar it or you can pick it. Me, I'd pick it. Get myself a paper clip, bend it in the shape of an *L*. Then move it in a circular motion to disengage the pawl from the ratchet. Or even easier—get yourself a knife with a slim blade, drive it into the keyhole and move it aggressively in a circular motion till you hear the pawl and ratchet break."

That's what Jack did.

He started working on the left cuff with his right hand. Put the tip of the blade in the keyhole, pushing and turning the knife till the pawl and ratchet broke and the cuff popped open.

God bless Lunchbox.

He freed his other hand and unhooked the belly chain.

Before DeJuan left, Jack saw him lock the money in a heavy oak armoire with a skeleton key and put it in his pocket.

Teddy said, "What're you doing?"

DeJuan said, "Protecting my capital."

Teddy said, "Huh?"

Celeste said, "Why don't you let me hang on to the key?"

DeJuan said, "What's the matter, girlfriend—don't trust me?"

"Would you?"

DeJuan grinned at her, took the key out his pocket and tossed it to her.

For Jack, it came down to money or freedom, and freedom looked pretty good right now. He'd made his decision. There was nothing he could do for Kate and Luke. He had a slim chance of getting away himself and he'd take it and be grateful. The good Lord showing him the way, giving him another opportunity, as Chaplain Uli might've said.

He opened the door to the garage and saw the Corvette in the first space, Kate's Land Rover parked next to it, and the Lexus next to that. He found the keys to the Land Rover in Kate's purse in the kitchen, got in the SUV, and started it up. He looked at himself in the rearview mirror. Couldn't believe this turn of events. Considered it an omen, a sign. He pressed the remote on the sun visor, and the garage door went up. He put it in gear and accelerated, pulling out across the gravel drive.

The deal was: DeJuan and Celeste would get rid of the deputy and his car; Teddy'd stay back, do the mom and kid. He'd never shot anyone before, but knew it had to be done and knew he could do it. He didn't want to spend the rest of his life looking over his shoulder. And with the money he had, it looked like it was going to be a pretty goddamn good life.

Teddy decided to practice in his mind what he was going to do, kept going over it again and again: picturing himself unlocking the door—not saying a word—and just shooting them, two bullets each, in the chest or head, unless he missed or they were still twitching. He had to have a cigarette first. Stood out back, staring out at that beautiful water. When he finished his butt, he'd go in there, get it done.

Luke turned the handle on the window, pulled and it swung open into the room. He stuck his head out and looked down and saw Camo right below him, smoking a cigarette. He could see a gun in the waist of his Levi's. Luke ducked his head back in and sat there, trying not to make noise. His mom looked up and he signaled to her with his index finger over his mouth, telling her not to say anything. He motioned that somebody was out there. From an angle inside the rafters, he watched Camo walk about ten feet, take a final drag on his cigarette, and throw it toward the tree line and move toward the back door of the lodge.

Luke said, "He's gone."

He waved to his mom and went through the window and stood on the sill and reached up for the roof.

Kate was about to climb up and follow Luke when she noticed the trap. It was in the corner leaning against the wall, a Sleepy Creek number 6 coil-spring bear trap. Owen bought it but never used it, thinking after the fact that it was cheating. You hunt a bear, you don't trap it. Where's the sport in that?

She went over and picked it up, surprised how heavy it was. The trap was three feet long and must've weighed fifty pounds. She positioned it on the floor near the door, used her feet and the weight of her body to push down on the springs, and the cast-iron jaws opened, exposing jagged metal teeth. She remembered Owen saying a trap was risky 'cause you could forget where you put it and step on it yourself and God help you if you did. The force would break your leg and probably send you into shock. It might even kill you.

Twenty-Eight

Johnny Crow saw it from a ridgetop some distance away. He didn't have binoculars with him, so it was impossible to judge it precisely. He would have guessed five hundred yards. Maybe even six hundred. It was on the other side of a long stretch of pastureland partially concealed in a wooded area that was on national parkland. It was the afternoon sun, the reflection, glinting off it that caught his attention.

He was still a little tense from the standoff between tribal police and this armed group who'd barricaded themselves in the Tribal Center. The FBI and the Bureau of Indian Affairs even showed up, turning a difference of opinion into a circus.

The protesters claimed the tribal chairman was trying to control the reservation by limiting the number of eligible votes. Johnny said, let them have their say and move on. His idea: bring both sides together, sit across a table and try to reconcile the issues.

He'd come out here to get away from the insanity and clear his head, unwind a little. He could feel the stress and pressure of the day begin to disappear as he walked down the ridge and crossed the pasture, amazed as always by the restorative power of nature. Two cows looked up at him as he passed by and said, "Evening, ladies."

When he got closer he could see the reflection was a light-colored automobile—white or silver—the sun hitting it like a mirror.

From seventy yards he recognized it as a county sheriff's cruiser, could distinguish the light bar on the roof. What was it doing out here? There was a flattened cattle gate where it had driven in along dirt tracks that served as a road.

From ten yards, he could see blood on the window and door and door handle. He walked up right next to it and looked through the glass on the driver's side and saw a body sprawled across the backseat on his stomach, head down, facing the opposite side. It was a sheriff's deputy.

He walked around the car and opened the rear door and went down on one knee and looked at the deputy's face—what was left of it—and thought it was Bill Wink. That opinion based more on the man's muscular build than his facial features, which were nearly obliterated. There were blood and bone fragments and brain tissue on the floor. Johnny'd never seen a man shot this way and it made him queasy. He stood up and stepped away and took a couple deep breaths, getting himself under control. He came back, hunkered down and touched the deputy's skin. It was still warm. He was thinking it hadn't been long—maybe an hour or so.

First thing Johnny thought: It had something to do with the woman. Bill had called and told him some story about her finding the kid. Far as Johnny was concerned, it didn't wash. He knew what he saw that day in the woods. Knew what Del saw—their interpretations being similar, if not exact. Then the woman was at the bank withdrawing a lot of money, which was also strange, particularly since Bill said she'd left town, gone back downstate. Now he took out his cell phone and called the sheriff's department, told a Sergeant Romeo who he was and what he found and gave him the coordinates.

He thought about Bill on the way to his truck. Remembered the day they met. Johnny was chasing a drunk who'd cut across reservation land and he radioed the sheriff and told them to be on the lookout for a red Porsche—license number delta-alpha-tango-one-five-nine.

The Porsche, driven by a college student, finally pulled over, and a sheriff's deputy pulled up with its lights flashing and that deputy was Bill Wink. Johnny wanted to beat the hell out of the kid, teach him some manners.

Bill said, "You know who this kid is?"

Johnny shook his head.

"His father owns about twenty-five car dealerships. You lay a hand on him, they'll put you away."

Sure, Johnny understood—that's the way life worked. You had money, you could do pretty much what you wanted.

Bill and Johnny bumped into one another occasionally after that, Bill joking about the beads and feathers Johnny had hanging from the rearview mirror of his truck.

Johnny said, "What do you expect? I'm an Indian, ain't I?"

"I thought you were called Native Americans now. Isn't that the politically correct term?"

"I prefer Indian, if you don't mind."

"No kidding," Bill said.

"No kidding."

"Tell me, what's the hardest thing about being a tribal cop?"

Johnny didn't have to think long. He said, "Dealing with non-Indians. They don't have a lot of respect for us. Don't believe we're the law on the reservation, or that local cops have no juris-diction. Just like we got no authority off it."

Bill said, "People're fucking stupid, aren't they?"

"Isn't that the truth."

Johnny grinned and Bill grinned back at him.

Twenty-Nine

Kate thought she heard a car drive off, tires rolling over the gravel. Ten minutes later she heard the garage door open and another car drive out. She was sure they'd left, taken the money and taken off and she had a sudden feeling of relief. It was finally over.

She looked down at the bear trap on the floor. It was a couple feet from the door, its metal teeth and gaping jaws open. Then she heard the key in the lock and saw the door open. Teddy came in the room grinning and looked up at her in the rafters, knowing he was too late to stop Luke. She could be mistaken, but if two cars were gone, he had to be here by himself. She didn't know what was going on, what they were doing.

Teddy aimed the big chrome-plate automatic at her and said, "Move another inch, it'll be your last."

She was thinking the same thing about him, hoping he'd take another couple of steps.

"Get that kid back in here and come down."

She said, "You dumbass hick—why don't you come up here and get me?"

He grinned at her and said, "If that's the way you want it, puss."

She climbed out the window and was standing on the sill when she heard the trap spring closed, the loud metallic snap of the metal jaws hitting with force. She reached up and felt the steep pitch of the roof and swung her body up and turned on her back, the heels of her hiking boots digging into the shingles, trying to hold her position. She heard a car and looked over the roofline and saw the Z28 drive in and then disappear as it pulled up in front.

Luke was on the ground running for the treeline. He turned and looked back at her. She heard gunshots and two bullets ripped through the roof next to her and then two more. She lifted her heels and slid down to the flat roof over the porch, landing on her feet. There was wood stacked five feet high in a metal rack that was built into the side of the lodge. She'd lower herself onto it and climb down. That's what she was trying to do when DeJuan appeared, aiming the shotgun at her.

DeJuan was preoccupied on the ride back from taking the deputy, fiending on Celeste, staring at her driving the Camaro. Picturing her naked body with the tats. He'd had white trim, black trim, Asian trim, French Canadian trim, but this Celeste, man, she got to him. Why she turn him on so?

At one point, she glanced over, caught him with his eyeballs popping out. Said, "Take a picture, it lasts longer."

Busted him like she could read his mind.

He heard gunshots when they drove in—four of them— wondered what was going on. He and Celeste looking at each other—going for their own guns now. They got out. He went right around one side of the lodge and she went the other way, no discussion, knew what to do and did it.

DeJuan moved slow, coming along the east wall of the cabin, looked in the window, saw the kitchen. Looked toward the water, saw the kid standing at the edge of the woods, then disappear. He couldn't believe it—leave for ten minutes, come back, somebody shooting, kid escape again. Little motherfucker like Houdini. Where the fuck Theo at?

DeJuan was going after him but stopped when he saw Kate on the roof. Had a better idea. He yelled in the woods. "Yo, little man, better not leave your moms. Something happen to her, you be all alone in the world."

Bitch on the roof said, "Luke, don't listen to him. Run."

DeJuan racked the twelve-gauge. "Better listen to this—not say another word, Mr. Remington going to talk at you. Don't want to hear what he got to say. Now come on down here."

He watched her get on her stomach and lower herself, feet finding the wood pile, putting her weight on it, standing and balancing, climbing down the rails of the metal rack that held the wood in place.

DeJuan had seen a lot of movies, seen people react in a lot of real-life situations. Was convinced he knew something about human nature and he'd bet his share of the money—look like seven hundred large—rich kid wasn't going nowhere, still in the trees, watching him. Afraid for his moms—and DeJuan was going to play on that fear.

"You leave her," DeJuan said, "you going to blame yourself. Like when you shot your pops. Don't be doing it again." Laying it on the little guy, fucking with his head.

DeJuan's new three-step plan: get the kid back, take 'em in the lodge, pop his little Houdini ass, then do his moms. That was step one. Step two, repeat the process with Teddy and Celeste. Step three, get the fuck out of there—retire.

———

Luke watched Teddy come out of the lodge and he was mad—that was pretty obvious, running to his mom, hitting her and going crazy. Punched her in the face and knocked her down.

Luke wanted to run out there and hit Camo and keep hitting him.

DeJuan said, "Yo, Ted, what you doing?"

Teddy said, "Paying her back."

DeJuan said, "Be cool on the violence."

Teddy grabbed a fistful of her hair and put the barrel of his gun up to her face. "Think I ain't gonna see a three-foot-long bear trap on the floor? How dumb you think I am?"

His mom didn't say anything, although Luke bet she wanted to.

Teddy pulled her across the yard by her hair—closer to the tree line.

He said, "You see her, boy? You see your mother standing here quivering like a scared animal? You gonna let her die?"

Teddy pressed the barrel of his pistol against the side of her face. He was grinning, enjoying himself and now Luke was mad.

DeJuan scanning the tree line, said, "It all in your hands now, little man. Come on, show your moms some love."

He held the back of her hair in his fist, pulling on it and pressing the barrel end of his automatic against her cheekbone. He was trying to hurt her and he did. Kate could feel his body pressing against her from behind. She didn't know if Luke was still there or not and said, "Luke, don't listen to him, run."

Teddy let go of her hair and swung her around so she was facing him and said, "Better shut the fuck up."

He hit her in the face with his fist and she went down, dazed from the blow, her vision hazy, trying to focus on DeJuan. He was moving to the tree line, holding the shotgun level across his body, finger on the trigger, aiming at the trees. Teddy bent down and picked her up by the hair.

"Luke, you see him," Kate said. "He's coming after you."

Teddy hit her again and she stumbled but didn't go down.

He said, "You don't learn, do you?"

Luke saw the black guy heading toward him with the shotgun, just inside the trees. He moved straight back, out of his path and hid behind a giant maple.

"I'm gonna count to ten," Teddy said. "You're not back here, I'll shoot her dead, so help me God. You hear me, boy?"

Luke put the bow case on the ground and opened it and lifted out his dad's Browning Mirage. Slid an arrow out of the quiver and nocked it. He wasn't going to let Camo hit his mother again.

Camo said, "One . . ."

He was standing behind his mom—to her left.

"Two . . ."

They were twenty yards away. Luke had a clear shot. He was at the edge of the tree line. He looked right, saw the black guy through the trees, coming back toward him.

"Three . . ."

Luke's chest tightened as he tried to raise the bow. He couldn't breathe. Didn't have the strength to draw the string. He could feel it happening again.

"Four . . ."

Teddy pulled the hammer back on the chrome-plate automatic and pressed the barrel against his mom's cheek, pushing it into her face.

"Five . . ."

Luke could feel his hands shake and could feel sweat drip down his face.

"Six . . ."

DeJuan was thirty feet away now, leveling the shotgun.

"Seven . . ."

He tried to pull the bowstring. It wouldn't budge.

"Eight . . ."

He heard his dad like he was standing next to him: "You can do it. Lock your arms, use your shoulders. Shoot the son of a bitch."

It was as if he'd been in a trance, hypnotized, the sound of his dad's voice snapping him out of it. He felt strong, raised the bow and put Teddy square in the red circle of the laser sight.

Boom. He heard the shotgun roar and saw a limb blown off a foot away from him.

"Nine . . ."

He pulled back the string and locked it—in full draw now.

"Ten . . ."

It was like it happened in slow motion. He stopped digging the gun into her face and let go of her hair, the pain she felt was suddenly gone. Teddy staggered back. She heard the heavy sound of his pistol hitting the hard ground. She glanced over her shoulder and saw the broadhead in his chest—blood blotting his shirt—Teddy staggering like he was drunk, reaching for the arrow, hands grabbing the white bloodstained fletching, trying to pull it out. He looked like he was going to say something—blood bubbling out of his mouth—but didn't or couldn't. There was fear in his eyes, knowing he was going to die and knowing there was nothing he could do about it. His hands let go of the arrow and he fell over on his back. His eyes were open, looking up at her, but he was gone.

Now she heard the heavy *boom boom* of DeJuan's shotgun. DeJuan coming out of the woods now, racking and firing into the tree line, blowing off limbs. She picked up Teddy's chrome-plated automatic and moved toward him.

He turned and looked at her and grinned, pointing the shotgun. "Better drop it," DeJuan said. "Mine's bigger."

"There's just one problem," Kate said. "You're empty." He'd fired five times—she counted, knew the magazine capacity. Her dad had one just like it—a Remington Wingmaster twelve-gauge.

"You wrong, you dead."

He racked it and pulled the trigger and she heard it click. He looked surprised, dropped the shotgun and said, "Whoa. Hang on now. We can work this out. I'm gonna take the money and let y'all be."

"You're not taking anything," Kate said.

"Think you got the nerve to shoot another human being?" DeJuan said. "Take a life, nice God-fearing suburban momma like yourself?"

Luke appeared now, coming out of the woods. She glanced over at him, took her eye off DeJuan for a second, and when she looked back, he was pulling a gun from under his gold warm-up. She raised the chrome-plate, aimed at his chest, fired and blew him off his feet. She walked over and checked to make sure he was dead. He was, eyes open, a look of surprise frozen on his face.

Luke ran to her now and she put her arms around him and they stood there like that for a long time, not saying a word.

Thirty

Johnny left his truck on national parkland, deciding to approach McCall's place from that direction, figuring it was less than a mile. There was no easy way to get there unless you took their private road and he wasn't about to do that, announce his arrival to whomever happened to be there, armed and dangerous.

He had his great-granddad's lever-action 1890 model Winchester. A hundred and eighteen years old and still as accurate as any rifle he'd ever fired. Carried it in the truck, wrapped in a blanket behind the seats. He thought it was more appropriate than a bow for what he might encounter. He took the rifle out and loaded it with .30–30 cartridges. The sky was starting to cloud up and Johnny smelled rain. It was six thirty, getting dark, when he entered the woods. He had about eight-tenths of a mile to go and figured it would take him fifteen, twenty minutes. He just hoped he'd get there in time.

———

When they went back in the lodge Kate expected to see Jack sitting there in his chains. She had DeJuan's SigSauer in her hand as a precaution but assumed Celeste had taken the money and was long gone. She was wrong. The two shrink-wrapped bundles of money were stacked on the floor in the breakfast room. Now Celeste came up behind them and put the barrel of her gun against the back of Kate's head.

Celeste said, "I know what you're thinking—if you move real fast you can turn and get me before I get you—the way people do in movies. Let me tell you, it ain't going to happen."

Kate held the SigSauer at arm's length, in her left hand. Luke was a couple feet to her right.

Celeste said, "Anybody seen Jack? Must've slipped out the back. Got a new plan, Stan. What was the name of that song?"

Kate said, "You got the money—what else do you want?"

Celeste said to Luke, "You go over there, lay on the floor where I can keep an eye on you."

Luke looked at her and she said, "It's okay. Everything's going to be fine."

"Why're you lying to him?" Celeste said.

Kate said, "There's no reason to do this." She glanced down and saw Celeste's shoe behind her and to the left.

Celeste said, "That's where we disagree. Funny thing is, I feel like I owe you for getting rid of Teddy and DeJuan. I was going to do it myself, just didn't know when or how."

Kate said, "Take the money, have a good life. Far as I'm concerned, you were never here."

"I'd probably say something like that too if I was in your situation. But we both know it's bullshit, don't we?"

It was quiet for a few seconds. Kate could hear the ticking of the grandfather clock in the front hall.

Johnny heard a shotgun blast in the distance. He levered a cartridge in the chamber of the Winchester and started to run. He remembered this stretch of woods from the day they went looking for the boy. He'd already crossed the stream, running uphill, over a ridgetop and then down through stands of birch and pine when heard the shotgun go off again—four more times, then a pistol shot. It was quiet after that and Johnny was sure he was too late. He picked it up, ran as fast as could now, and through a clearing in the trees, he saw the roofline of McCall's cabin.

"On second thought," Celeste said, "I guess I could tie you up, call the sheriff's department in a day or so, tell them where you're at. Drop the gun, I'll think about it."

Kate knew she was lying. She looked over and saw someone in the breakfast room window. At first she thought it was Jack but now recognized the Indian, Johnny Crow, aiming a rifle.

Kate heard the *click* as Celeste cocked the hammer on her pistol, and she swung the SigSauer back and squeezed the trigger and shot Celeste in the foot—put one through her black Franco Sarto pump, the sound deafening, like an explosion. Celeste screamed, the shock and pain throwing her off balance and Johnny did the rest, fired through the side window and blew her off her feet.

Kate looked back and saw Celeste sprawled on the floor, blood pooling under her. Luke was curled up in a ball, hands covering his ears. She helped him to his feet. His face was white and he looked like he was going to be sick. She took him in the kitchen, and he threw up in the sink. She poured cold water on a towel and wiped his face and hugged him and said, "It's over. They're never going to hurt you again."

Johnny came in the back door of the lodge, their eyes met, but neither of them said anything. There was nothing to say. Johnny got down on a knee and touched Celeste's neck with his finger, checking for a pulse. He shook his head.

Kate said, "I'll be right back."

She took Luke upstairs and helped him take off his muddy clothes. She tucked him in bed and kissed his forehead and whispered, "It's going to be okay now." Luke closed his eyes and she pulled the covers up to his chin, Leon snuggling next to him, his pink tongue hanging out, tail moving back and forth as always.

Jack walked in the front door of the cabin, saw the money stacked in the breakfast room, saw Celeste dead on the rug. He'd seen Teddy and DeJuan out in the yard and was thinking things couldn't have worked out better. Then he saw the Indian. Where'd he come from? Jack looked at him. "Who're you?"

Guy didn't say anything, just stood there.

"Where's Mrs. McCall? I'm a friend of hers."

He didn't answer.

Jack saw DeJuan's Sig on an end table next to one of the couches. He wandered into the main room, trying not to make it too obvious. He glanced back at the Indian. "How about Luke, is he okay?"

No answer.

Jack picked up the Sig, thinking, you dumbass. He turned and the Indian had a rifle pointed at him, stock against his shoulder, ready to fire.

The Indian said, "Put it down or you're dead."

Jack believed him, Jack thinking, who is this guy? He was so close.

———

Kate saw Jack drop the gun on the floor and it was almost like she expected to see him, expected him to be there. She was on the second-floor landing. She walked down the stairs and glanced at Johnny and said, "You should have shot him."

"He said he was a friend of yours," Johnny said.

"He's not a friend," Kate said. "I don't know what he is." She looked at Jack. "Back for the money, huh? You couldn't leave two million and just walk away, could you? Decided to wait till it all played out so you wouldn't have to get your hands dirty."

Jack came across the room toward her.

"That's not it," he said. "A few miles down the highway I started thinking about you and felt guilty. I came back to make sure nothing happened to you."

She couldn't listen to any more of his bullshit. "Don't say anything else, okay?"

"You tell Luke about me?" Jack said. "Tell him who his real dad is?"

No, she hadn't and wondered if she ever would. "The way I see it," Kate said, "you've got two choices. You can keep talking till the sheriff gets here, or you can get in your car and take your chances. Just give me my key."

He took it out of his pocket and threw it to her.

Kate and Johnny stood on the slate porch and watched the Lexus pull out of the garage and head across the gravel drive, picking up speed.

Johnny said, "He's not going to get too far in that car. They're looking for it."

"I hope he doesn't," Kate said.

"Why'd you let him go?" Johnny said.

Kate had asked herself the same question and decided she was paying him back for getting her out of Guatemala. That's how she justified it, anyway. Now they were even. She glanced at Johnny and said, "It's a long story."

"I'll bet it is," he said.

It started to rain.

They went inside. Kate offered Johnny a beer and they sat at the breakfast room table, drinking their beers, waiting for the sheriff to get there.

Johnny told her about Bill Wink and she felt terrible. Then he surprised her and brought up Joe Lamborne, the deputy who liked to feel up his prisoners.

Johnny said, "That was you, wasn't it?"

He smiled.

She was thinking that was the first time she'd seen him relax, let his guard down. He had a nice smile. "I don't know what you're talking about," Kate said and grinned.

Johnny said, "I know him. And I'll bet he deserved what he got."

"Under the circumstances," Kate said, "I think he got off easy."

Johnny said, "How's your boy?"

"I don't know."

"He'll be all right," Johnny said. "Kids are tough."

Kate hoped he was right.

She heard sirens in the distance and got up from the table and went to the front door and watched the police cars drive in—four of them—and two EMS vans, lights flashing.

She thought about Luke. They'd get in the car in the morning, drive home and start over—just the two of them.